LONE RANGER

What Reviewers Say About VK Powell's Work

Side Effects

"[A] touching contemporary tale of two wounded souls hoping to find lasting love and redemption together. …Powell ably plots a plausible and suspenseful story, leading readers to fall in love with the characters she's created."—*Publishers Weekly*

To Protect and Serve

"If you like cop novels, or even television cop shows with women as full partners with male officers…this is the book for you. It's got drama, excitement, conflict, and even some fairly hot lesbian sex. The writer is a retired cop, so she really writes from a place of authenticity. As a result, you have a realistic quality to the writing that puts me in mind of early Joseph Wambaugh."—Teresa DeCrescenzo, *Lesbian News*

"*To Protect and Serve* drew me in from the very first page with characters that captivated in their complexity. Powell writes with authority using the lingo and capturing the thoughts of the law enforcers who make the ultimate sacrifice in the fight against crime. What's more impressive is the command this debut author has of portraying a full gamut of emotion, from angst to elation, through dialogue and narrative. The images are vivid, the action is believable, and the police procedurals are authentic…VK Powell had me invested in the story of these women, heart, mind, body and soul. Along with danger and tension, Powell's well-developed erotic scenes sizzle and sate."—*Story Circle Book Reviews*

Suspect Passions

"From the first chapter of *Suspect Passions* Powell builds erotic scenes which sear the page. She definitely takes her readers for a walk on the wild side! Her characters, however, are also women we care about. They are bright, witty, and strong. The combination of great sex and great characters make *Suspect Passions* a must read."—*Just About Write*

Fever

"VK Powell has given her fans an exciting read. The plot of *Fever* is filled with twists, turns, and 'seat of your pants' danger...*Fever* gives readers both great characters and erotic scenes along with insight into life in the African bush."—*Just About Write*

Justifiable Risk

"This story takes some unusual twists and at one point, I was convinced that I knew 'who did it' only to find out that I was wrong. VK Powell knows crime drama, she kept me guessing until the end, and I was not disappointed at the outcome. And that's not to slight VK Powell's knack for romance. ...Readers who appreciate mysteries with a touch of drama and intense erotic moments will enjoy *Justifiable Risk*."—*Queer Magazine*

Exit Wounds

"Powell's prose is no-nonsense and all business. It gets in and gets the job done, a few well-placed phrases sparkling in your memory and some trenchant observations about life in general and a cop's life in particular sticking to your psyche long after they've gone. After five books, Powell knows what her audience wants, and she delivers those goods with solid assurance. But be careful you don't get hooked. You only get six hits, then the supply's gone, and you'll be jonesin' for the next installment. It never pays to be at the mercy of a cop."—*Out in Print*

"Fascinating and complicated characters materialize, morph, and sometimes disappear testing the passionate yet nascent love of the book's focal pair. I was so totally glued to and amazed by the intricate layers that continued to materialize like an active volcano…dangerous and deadly until the last mystery is revealed. This book goes into my super special category. Please don't miss it."—*Rainbow Book Reviews*

About Face

"Powell excels at depicting complex, emotionally vulnerable characters who connect in a believable fashion and enjoy some genuinely hot erotic moments."—*Publishers Weekly*

By the Author

LONE RANGER

by

VK Powell

2016

ISBN 13: 978-1-62639-767-5

This Trade Paperback Original Is Published By
Bold Strokes Books, Inc.
P.O. Box 249
Valley Falls, NY 12185

First Edition: November 2016

Credits
Editor: Shelley Thrasher
Production Design: Susan Ramundo
Cover Design By Sheri (graphicartist2020@hotmail.com)

Acknowledgments

I've been blessed to pursue two careers that brought me great satisfaction. The first allowed me to help people and promote advancement for women in a profession that often overlooked them. In the second, I parlay that career into stories of survival, the struggle to balance love and livelihood, and the fight between good and evil. To Len Barot and all the wonderful folks at Bold Strokes Books—thank you for giving me the chance to tell my stories.

My deepest gratitude and admiration to Dr. Shelley Thrasher for your guidance, suggestions, and kindness. You always take time to talk me off the ledges in my mind, even when you're up to your neck in projects. Working with you is a learning experience and a pleasure. I'm so proud of our collaborations and of your success as a Bold Strokes author.

For BSB sister author, D. Jackson Leigh, and friends, Jenny Harmon and Mary Margret Daughtridge—thank you for taking time out of your busy lives to provide priceless feedback. This book is so much better for your efforts. I am truly grateful.

To all the readers who support and encourage my writing, thank you for buying my work, visiting my website (www.vkpowellauthor.com), sending e-mails, and showing up for signings. You make my "job" so much fun!

CHAPTER ONE

Four days after she'd caught Sheri cheating, Emma Ferguson drove through the Virginia countryside, vehicle packed with her belongings, windows down, breathing what she hoped would be the air of a fresh start. The wind that lashed her hair into knots ushered in the earthen scent of fallen leaves and the faint smell of a wood fire while chilling the tears on her cheeks. Why couldn't Sheri have been honest? Her infidelity stirred Emma's vulnerabilities—her struggle for excellence and her lack of sexual passion. Would she ever find the right fit, a woman whose ambitions matched her own and who sparked that ever-elusive desire? If so, would she recognize and accept her? In light of her most recent failure, she doubted it.

"Snap out of it, Emma." She swiped her eyes with the back of her hand, imagining what her parents would say about her lapse into self-pity. "You've risen from the ruins of relationships before, and you'll do it again. At least you've got a job to pay the bills for a few weeks." But she wanted more, something with a steady income so she wasn't living hand-to-mouth.

She glanced at the notes clipped to her calendar and recalled the conversation with her new employer a week ago.

"This is Fannie Mae Buffkin of Stuart, Virginia. I'm calling for Emma Ferguson the reporter."
"Yes, Mrs. Buffkin, how can I help?"

"I'd like you to write a story on my family. My father founded the Thompson Furniture Company in Stuart. If you're interested, I'd love to talk with you further."

"Could you give me a few more details? I need to know I can sell the story to someone, to make it worth my time."

"I'm willing to pay for your time, travel, and accommodations if you'll come up and hear me out. I'd rather discuss the particulars in person, Ms. Ferguson. The story might evolve into something entirely different. I'm not being evasive, just honest. And I find the best way to see if we're a good fit is to meet face-to-face."

Maybe she could do a travel piece in the area and knock out two stories in one trip. "Well, you certainly know how to pique a reporter's interest. I accept your invitation to talk, but I make no promises until I've heard more. Agreed?"

"Of course. I'll send an advance immediately, to be kept whether or not you do the story. Please come as soon as possible. Time is of the essence."

"Why the urgency?"

"An out-of-state construction company wants to purchase the site of our first factory and raze it…in four weeks' time. I'd like you to see the place before that happens."

Emma's curiosity jangled and she couldn't wait to hear the whole story. "Why did you call me instead of a local reporter?"

There was a long pause. "You're freelance and don't owe allegiance to a newspaper or magazine. And I think you'd appreciate my situation. That's all I'll say for now, but I hope you'll take the job. You can name your price."

Fannie Buffkin could've led with her last statement. Maybe Emma could get several stories out of this job, if the old lady wasn't crazy and actually had the money to back up her offer. Something in Mrs. Buffkin's Southern drawl sounded urgent, almost pleading. Maybe this story would be a springboard to the future Emma had always imagined—a distinguished career as an investigative reporter like her father.

When Emma turned onto the blacktop at the entrance to Fairy Stone State Park, she pulled off the side of the road and checked her appearance in the rearview mirror. The wind and damp air had whipped her naturally curly red hair into a Medusa-like mess. She raked her fingers through several knots before settling for a simple pat-down. No real progress could be made without a hairdryer and brush. She reapplied lipstick and dabbed concealer under her eyes, puffy from crying. Damn Sheri. She'd had hopes for their relationship, but hoping seldom led to real-life results, at least not in her world.

"Good enough, Emma. You're at a park in Virginia, not a five-star Marriott in DC."

The Fairy Stone State Park office sported a freshly stained wood frame with rust-colored shingles and shutters that blended with the autumn surroundings. Bad memories of childhood summers spent in the wilderness her parents called summer camp returned, and she choked down a wave of sadness. She inhaled the cool night air and heard sounds she couldn't identify coming from the nearby forest. Why had she chosen this natural habitat over civilized surroundings—Sheri would've loved it? Roughing it was so not Emma's thing. Canceling the reservation would've cost more than the original booking, and even though Fannie Buffkin was paying the tab, she hated wasting money. She regretted her choice, but she was stuck. She squared her shoulders and walked toward the office door.

"Base to Ranger One," Emma heard as she entered, the scent of cloves and cinnamon an unexpected welcome. The plump, gray-haired attendant pushed the base radio aside, peered over the top of rimless glasses, and smiled as Emma entered. Her nametag read *Ann*.

Pale-yellow curtains capped windows on either side of the office and pooled on the floor. Overstuffed leather recliners that showed signs of wear flanked a wood stove behind the counter, and a small kitchenette rounded out the homey feel.

Ann pushed up the sleeves of a pink polka-dotted white shirt and hooked her thumbs in the sides of lavender coveralls. This woman was a character any writer would be lucky to find. Already drawn into her colorful tableau, Emma looked forward to learning more.

Ann's gaze roamed up and down Emma's body and came to rest confidently on her eyes. "Evening, ma'am. Welcome to Fairy Stone Park. Have you been here before?"

"No, I haven't. Emma Ferguson. I have a reservation."

Ann shuffled through the short stack of yellow papers on the counter and slid one from the bottom. Looking from the registration form back at Emma, her eyes sparkled. "Here we go, but this reservation is for two people."

"I'm sorry." Emma tried to control the redhead's blushing curse that always announced anything embarrassing or personal. She lost, and heat consumed her face. "Yeah, that's not happening. Is it a problem?"

"Not at all. You're staying with us for five days, Mrs. Ferguson?"

"Possibly longer, but I'll keep you posted in case you need the cabin. And it's Ms. Ferguson or Emma."

"I'm Ann, pleasure's mine," she stated, offering her hand across the counter and exchanging a firm shake. "Vacation or working visit?"

"Mostly work, but I hope to relax a bit as well." Emma liked this woman, especially her vibrant clothes, welcoming smile, and demeanor that said what you see is what you get. Maybe one day she'd allow herself that freedom.

"What do you do, if you don't mind me asking?" Ann held up her hand. "On second thought, let me guess. I'd say you do something creative, maybe an artist, sculptor or…" Ann twisted her mouth to one side and squinted.

"I'm a freelance reporter." Her answer lacked enthusiasm, and she wondered when her profession had become just a job.

"That was going to be my next guess, a writer of some sort. Well, I'm afraid you won't find much to write about around these parts, but good luck."

Emma pegged Ann as a nosy neighbor—curious, watchful, and a great resource for a writer. "Have you lived here long?"

"All my life in Stuart, off and on. I had a brief stint in the national guard when I was young but always came back home."

Emma signed the registration, provided her vehicle license plate number, and slid cash across the counter to Ann. "I might want to ask some questions about Stuart—its history, people and such—if you're willing and not too busy."

"I would absolutely love to help, and I'm never too busy for a little tongue-wagging." She tucked the money into a cash drawer and pulled the base radio closer. "Let me see if I can get some help around this place, and we'll get you settled."

"Thank you, Ann."

"Base to Ranger One." Ann shrugged. "Rangers…where are they when you need one? Most think they're God's gift to the great outdoors." Flashing Emma a wide grin, Ann said, "Probably out checking on possum flatulence in the park."

Emma started to smother her laughter but enjoyed it instead. She hadn't laughed in days and felt the tightness in her chest release. While they waited for the ranger to respond, she pictured a male version of Ann—a squatty gray-haired fellow, ample stomach scarcely covered by his ranger's shirt, pants hanging on a butt-less behind, puffing and scrambling back to his vehicle to answer the duty call.

"Base, this is Ranger One. Go ahead, Ann." The orotund female voice shattered Emma's mental image, and she tilted her head to one side, eager to hear more. Her journalistic curiosity took over, and she imagined a tough butch who could start fire with two sticks, track lost campers, and name every variety of wildlife in the forest. How clichéd.

Ann grinned, a toothy smile that sparked in her gray eyes. "Ranger One, you got a key to cabin seven? Maintenance picked mine up earlier and hasn't returned it yet."

Another long silence followed, during which Emma imagined a very efficient, painstaking inspection for the right key.

"I've got one. What do you need?"

"Would you meet this lady over there and let her in? You can leave the key with her. She's staying several days."

The length of her stay was probably more information than the ranger needed. Maybe Ann liked the sound of her own voice, talking on the radio, or maybe it was the nosy-neighbor syndrome.

"Ten-four Base, Ranger One out."

"Thanks, Carter." Turning to Emma with a nod of accomplishment, Ann continued with a kind but unnecessary relay. "Ranger West will meet you at your cabin with the key. You'll like Carter. We're family. She's my niece, and we run this place like it's our own home. Take the driveway beside the office and follow the signs to number seven. Enjoy your stay, and if you need anything, don't hesitate to ask. I've always got a pot of coffee and an array of spirits on hand if you feel the urge, but don't spread the part about the spirits, against park policy."

"Thanks for your help, Ann."

As the last of the evening sun settled between tall pines, Emma approached the cabin that would be home for a while. She breathed deeply, as if sucking in the magnificent view. The cottage was perched on an incline overlooking a clear, still lake surrounded by deciduous and evergreen trees. The setting was postcard pretty.

Two empty wooden rockers on the sprawling porch foretold the days and nights she and Sheri would never spend in this place. Had Sheri wanted to be found in bed with another woman? Had the betrayal been her easy way out? If Sheri had known the truth—that Emma had never felt real passion for her—she would've left much sooner. Maybe Emma had been the dishonest one, the cheater. Her stomach tightened and she clutched the steering wheel.

She sighed, mentally brushing away the past, and got out of her car. She dragged her luggage and laptop case over the uneven ground to the edge of the porch. Up close, the exterior of the cabin was rustic, with intermittent logs and faded chinking. She rubbed a finger between two logs, and the mixture of mud and straw crumbled. Would she be safe from vermin and wild creatures? Could she adjust to this environment with strange noises in an old log cabin with no insulation in the woods? She shivered. She'd botched Camping 101 as a child, a refresher as a teenager, and the immersion course as a baby dyke and had no desire to revisit her failure. What had she been thinking?

A gust of wind plucked harvest-colored leaves from the trees and cast them to the forest floor, as Emma hugged her light jacket around her and started toward the lake's edge. The short heels of her leather-soled shoes sank into the soft ground, and she struggled with each step like she was walking in quicksand, apropos of her life.

The final rays of daylight danced near the mountain peak when Emma heard rustling behind her and turned toward the cabin. A park ranger stood at the top of the incline. The dimming light cast a soft glow across high cheekbones and dark eyes that reminded Emma of her beloved grandmother's Native American heritage. The woman was outlined in green pants and a beige shirt, an equipment belt visually breaking the two. Her right elbow rested on top of a gun at her side, and she raked her left hand through dark hair. Emma felt like a cliché from a Harlequin romance, stunned into silence by the appearance of a dashing stranger. She continued to stare until the silence became awkward.

"Ms. Ferguson, I'm Carter West. Sorry for the wait."

Emma shook the pleasantly unsettling image from her mind and struggled up the hill and into a huge spiderweb that stuck to her face, hands, and clothes. "Ahhhh!" She flailed her arms and swatted at the clingy snare. From the corner of her eye, she saw Carter West bite her lip to suppress a grin, with the smug assurance of those comfortable in their surroundings. Emma wiped her face again with the sleeve of her jacket and continued up the slope.

As she climbed toward the crest of the hill, the rocks shifted under her feet. She was on solid ground, and the next instant, she was falling. Carter grabbed her around the waist, and the air whooshed from her lungs as Carter hefted her onto level ground. Carter's cocoa-brown eyes turned dark with tiny flecks of green, and her pupils constricted. Her lips parted, and the breath that swept across

Emma's face was hot and slightly minty. The muscles in Carter's upper arms, where Emma's hands rested, were taut, infusing Emma with a sense of safety.

Emma felt weightless for the interminable seconds until her feet touched down again. Carter's full lips moved and then curled into a broad grin before Emma realized Carter had asked a question.

"Huh? Oh, sorry."

"Not the outdoors type?"

"No. Not at all."

"Imagine how the poor spider felt." This time Carter didn't suppress her laughter, and it echoed through the trees, deep and heartfelt.

"Do all the rangers have such an odd sense of humor?" Emma hated being a screw-up, especially when someone else was watching. She brushed at her clothes more out of nervousness than any real need. "And I'd stay well back if I were you. I'm a bit clumsy, and I wouldn't want to take you over the side with me next time." She was mildly annoyed, but the sound of Carter's genuine joy proved contagious, and she chuckled in spite of herself. Twice in the past hour she'd really laughed and meant it. Maybe the fresh air was getting to her in a good way.

"Duly noted," Carter said. "Let's get you settled and a fire going before the chill deepens." She smiled again, and Emma's annoyance completely vanished as she followed Carter to the cabin and up the steps. "Do you need help with your bags?"

Emma wanted to say all her worldly belongings were in the trunk of her car and it would probably take hours to unload them, just to keep Carter close. Was she afraid of being alone in the woods, or was it something else?

"Ms. Ferguson?"

"Sorry. More like boxes instead of bags, but everything I need tonight is over there." She nodded toward her suitcase and computer bag. "I'll unload the rest tomorrow."

Carter crossed the porch in two long strides, scooped up her suitcase and laptop bag as if they were weightless, and placed them at her feet. As she stood, her gaze swept Emma's body again, and her long fingers tugged at a chain resting against bronzed skin at the neck of her shirt.

"You'll need a fire."

Carter probably lit a lot of fires—in women's fireplaces, in their bedrooms. The last thing she needed was another lothario. Her words stuck in her throat. "I…I really mustn't impose on you any further. I'm sure you have other things to do."

"It's no imposition. It's my job."

"I'm certainly capable of…" She had no idea how to set logs for a fire. Might as well own it. "I'll figure it out. Sorry, didn't mean to snap. I'm a little edgy. I just get tired of people thinking…You certainly don't need to hear all that. Thanks for your help."

"You sure do apologize a lot."

"Force of habit." Emma hadn't meant to say that. It had just happened, like running into a spiderweb or falling down a hill. Apologizing was her first line of defense whenever she disappointed her parents, teachers, friends, or lovers, which was a lot.

"Bad habit, I'd say." Carter unlocked the door, handed the key to Emma, and stepped back. "Here you go, Ms. Ferguson."

"Call me Emma." Heat crept across her face as she turned to go inside, trying to keep from logging another of Carter's amused looks, but stumbled over her suitcase.

Carter caught her arm gently and steadied her. "I've got you."

Such a simple phrase, so confidently delivered that Emma believed it completely. Carter's words seemed carefully chosen, and Emma found herself clinging to every one. She'd enjoy listening to Carter's smoky voice for hours, mining the mysteries from her closely guarded words, but Carter West probably never talked for hours.

Carter guided her gently over the threshold and slowly backed away. "Need anything else?"

Reeling from their closeness, Emma could only shake her head.

"Very well. Have a nice stay, Ms…Emma." With a confident grin, Carter closed the cabin door softly behind her.

Emma dropped onto the closest piece of furniture, a sofa with wide wooden arms and leaf-patterned upholstery in autumn colors that belonged in the seventies. She sucked in some air and placed her hand over her stomach. Her heart was racing. Damn Carter West and her overly gallant reflexes.

After she caught her breath for a few minutes, Emma pulled the bottle of Riesling from her suitcase. Thank God it was nearly full. She unscrewed the cap, poured a hefty dose into a coffee cup she'd scrounged from the scantily stocked kitchen, and headed for the front porch. She quickly downed two gulps of the lukewarm wine and set the cup beside her rocker. The night was much darker than in the city and full of unfamiliar noises. She'd come here to do a job and unwind, but she couldn't relax, not at all now. She pushed her feet against the porch until the rocker pitched back and forth so violently she almost tipped out.

She was confused and agitated. She wasn't an immediate-attraction kind of woman, but she felt as if she'd met Carter before, as if she knew things about Carter she couldn't possibly know—the intimate feel of Carter's hands around her waist, the safety she'd felt in her arms, and the intensity of those chestnut-brown eyes. Emma was just vulnerable right now. Sure, that was it. Still, she couldn't deny the heat of her body's reaction to Carter West.

She stood and paced the length of the porch, taking another healthy sip of wine with each pass. She needed to go for a run to burn off some energy, but she had difficulty staying upright on city sidewalks, so she'd probably break something on the rough terrain of the park's gravel paths. Emma inhaled the smoky hint of a fire hanging in the air and listened to the crickets chirp as she scoured the star-filled sky. When the cool night air seeped through her thin jacket and she was no closer to an explanation for her strange reaction to Carter, she went inside.

Emma threw a cheater log on a pile of old newspapers already crumpled in the fireplace and lit a match to the stack. How considerate of the park to provide the necessities for non-camping types. *Any moron could start a fire with one of these things, Carter*

West. She loved the flickering flames, the occasional crackling that imitated real wood, and the cozy warmth the fire provided. It wasn't a Girl Scout fire, but it would do. All she needed was the ambiance and the rest of her wine to knock the chill off and relax her before sleep.

Settling on the sofa in front of the fire, she tucked her feet under her and examined the cabin for the first time. The living-kitchen space was about the size of a small loft, compact and snug, with a two-seater table tucked into a corner. A sliding barn-type door to the left led into the bathroom with a small shower and claw-foot tub Emma could imagine soaking in for hours. The other room on the right was barely large enough to accommodate a queen-sized bed and a valet stand for her suitcase. This would do for now.

She sipped wine. The quiet was almost disconcerting—no street noises, sirens, or voices from passersby, no television, music, not even the electrical hum ever-present in the city. The night was peaceful but not exactly soundless. Tree limbs brushed against the side of the cabin, leaves rustled in the wind, something scratched near the front door. Suddenly she didn't feel so peaceful or safe. Perhaps she'd become too accustomed to the sounds of civilization.

She downed the final dregs of wine and headed for the bathroom. She'd come here to examine her life without Sheri, to complete an assignment, and possibly make a professional decision about her future. Tomorrow she'd begin working on the business side of the problem, but the personal would have to wait. Her emotions were too raw. After a quick shower, she climbed into bed and reached for the earplugs usually reserved for raucous nights downtown. Tonight they'd protect her from peculiar sounds she didn't want to examine too closely.

❖

"Well, well, well, guess I don't have to ask why you're late. I'm sure it has something to do with the guest in cabin seven." Ann grinned as Carter entered the office.

"Please don't start." Carter wasn't about to admit her attraction to the high-strung Ms. Ferguson. Emma's wild red hair and sad blue eyes had caught Carter off guard. Damn it, even her crooked smile was unique and endearing. The fullness of Emma's breasts and the press of her hips as Carter had rescued her from a tumble toward the lake had ignited instant desire, but Emma's flash of annoyance at her clumsiness and Carter's laughter had set off drama-queen warning bells.

"You've got to admit she's a looker," Ann said. "It's like the Goddess sprinkled copper shavings all over her body with those freckles and set her hair on fire. I imagine she'd fly hot in a second."

"You have no idea," Carter mumbled. "Do we have to talk about this right now?" She rolled her eyes as her aunt launched into her next observation.

"I was just making conversation. If I know you, you didn't say a dozen words. She probably thinks you're mute." Ann gave Carter an apologetic shrug. "I'm sorry, honey. I didn't mean that. You know me, open mouth, insert both feet."

"It's okay, Ann."

"Redheads are sexy as hell and independent too. Your mama, Goddess rest her soul, was the same way. You couldn't tell her anything she didn't want to hear, especially when it came to my no-account brother. The more he chased, the harder she ran the other way. I think dating was a sport for both of them, but I do believe they really loved each other."

"Does this story have a purpose or are you just rambling?"

Ann pretended to ignore Carter as she locked the office, hung the emergency number on the door, and walked toward the Jeep. "So what are you going to do?"

"What do you mean, what am I going to do? Nothing. I just met the woman." Carter gave Ann a pleading let's-not-go-there look and twisted her necklace between her thumb and middle finger. "What's on my to-do list for tomorrow?"

"Stop with the diversion and fiddling with your necklace. You do it every time you get nervous. I haven't known you all your life without learning a few things. You must like this girl at least a little."

"I have a couple of errands to run and need to fit them into my day." Carter wanted desperately not to have a conversation about Emma Ferguson. If Ann got wind she was even slightly attracted to her, she'd do everything in her power to push them together.

"Carter Amelia West, listen to me. I'm the closest thing you ever had to a mama. I'm damn sure your aunt and only living relative, so you have to listen to me. I'm going to say my piece. You see something you like and haul tail in the opposite direction. All I ask is that you give yourself a chance for once."

"Maybe I don't want to." Flashes of Ann's thirty-six-year relationship with Cass played like a slow-motion trailer in her mind. She could never emulate their years of love and commitment, nor could she imagine the eventual loss of a love so deep. Maybe she was just afraid. She'd learned years ago that pain was a normal part of life and love.

"At some point you're going to have to settle down. These fly-by-night liaisons with tourists and townsfolk won't last forever. You'll eventually get lonely for something real, substantial. Trust me."

"How could I possibly be lonely if I have you?" Carter joked, hoping against hope to change the subject of her transitory but sexually sufficient escapades.

"That's just it. I won't always be here, and at the rate you're going, I'll find another girlfriend before you do. When was your last dalliance anyway? That one you met in certification training a year ago. What was her name?"

"Dalliance? Really, Ann?"

"Call it what you want. It was temporary. They all are with you. What *was* that woman's name? Bobby, Bunny…something weird." Ann thumbed the side of her jaw and looked at her expectantly. "I know you still hook up with her occasionally when you go to Charlottesville."

"Hook up? Where do you hear these words?"

"The kids keep me hip, but you're avoiding again. Tell me her name."

"It doesn't matter because we're not talking about her. You've got this harebrained idea about Emma Ferguson, a woman I just met. Let it go, Ann."

"Just promise that whatever reservations you have about a real relationship, you won't let me stand in the way of your happiness. I'd never forgive myself."

Carter swallowed against the tightness in her throat. What would Ann think if she knew Carter had ended more than one relationship because she was afraid of being hurt the way she'd seen Ann hurt? She'd call her a coward and demand she take charge of her life. "I don't know what you mean."

"You were studying to be a child psychologist at UVA, quit, and moved here, supposedly because you were bored with university and wanted something new. I think you were worried about me being here alone."

"It's not about you, Ann." What else could she say? Ann's safety and happiness had been part of her reason, but the truth was more complicated, and Carter would never hurt Ann by telling her.

"I'm not convinced, but whatever you say. Now get me home. It's cocktail hour, and there's a vodka tonic with my name on it."

"I love you, Ann." Carter reached over and patted her aunt's hand as she drove the short distance to their log home just outside the park property.

"Of course you do, honey. 'Cause I know best, always have. You don't live to be my age without getting a few perks. I'm never wrong, except that one time. Never mind. I knew I shouldn't listen to that crazy woman. I can't believe I lived with her for thirty-six years."

"You loved Cass as much as your vodka tonics."

"Course I did. Don't mean she didn't drive me crazy sometimes. That's another thing I know for sure. It's the ones that drive you crazy, claw their way right under your skin that we end up wanting, not the nice ones. Women in our bloodline need a challenge, honey."

"You need a vodka tonic in the worst way." She stopped the Jeep in front of their home that suddenly seemed huge compared to the small park cabins. "Do you ever think this place is too big for just the two of us?"

Ann looked toward the sprawling two-story house. "It was perfect when Cass was alive. We had a master suite on one side, and you had one on the other, perfect cohabitation property. I keep hoping you'll bring someone special home one day…and not kick me out."

"Never happen." She'd definitely never kick Ann out. And she'd probably never find that special person who made her want to commit to forever. "Let's get you a drink."

"That's my girl." Ann laughed and followed Carter toward the house. "Any woman would be lucky to have you."

CHAPTER TWO

Each step of Emma's walk to the park office next morning jarred her pounding head and churned her morning coffee perilously in her stomach. When she opened the door, Ann stood behind the counter, a straw hat decorated with fishing hooks and lures covering her head.

Ann smiled broadly and waved.

"Morning, Ann. Do you have anything for a monster headache?" Emma dropped her messenger bag on the floor and leaned against the counter. "I was going into town, but I don't think I'll make it like this. I could be a hazard to the motoring public."

"What's the matter, honey? You look a little blanched. Rough night?"

"You could say that. I'm not really an outdoors person, and I heard lots of strange sounds outside my cabin. Guess I over-medicated with the wine."

"And maybe it's not the setting. You looked a little unsettled and your eyes were puffy when you checked in yesterday. I thought a quiet night in nature would help, but..." When Emma gave her a quizzical look, Ann added, "I usually save my personal observations for day three. I don't mean to pry, but you can talk to me...if you want."

"I'm sure I was a fright yesterday if I looked half as bad as I felt. I'm sorry."

"Nothing to be sorry about. Happens to the best of us. My offer is always open."

Ann's words had the ring of sincerity, and her concern touched Emma. "Thanks, but just the meds, if you have anything." She wasn't in the mood for conversation, especially about the reason for her puffy eyes yesterday or her wine-induced disposition today.

"Got what you need right here." Ann busied herself for a few minutes with an electric kettle in the kitchenette a few feet behind the counter and then proudly offered her a smelly concoction in a white Styrofoam cup. "Drink it all right down or it won't work. Don't sniff it or you might not make it."

Taking one whiff of the brew, Emma pushed it aside. "Not a chance I'm drinking that stuff. Are you trying to kill me?"

"Oh, no, ma'am," Ann replied without a hint of levity. "Just because I wear weird clothes and see things a little differently doesn't mean I'm a whack job. This really works. It's only herbs, nothing artificial. It'll cure what ails you, the headache and your—"

"My what?" Emma was intrigued and a bit amused.

"Your...you know...your frustrations." Ann waved her hand toward Emma's middle like she should know exactly what she meant.

"What do you know about my frustrations?"

"Honey child, I've lived a long time. There are not many looks a woman has that I can't name. I lived with crazy Cass Calloway for thirty-six years. Mood-reading was a means of self-preservation. Now you, Ms. Ferguson, you've got that—"

"No need for details." Emma raised her hand to stop what would probably have been an accurate assessment of her preoccupation with Ann's niece. "I'll drink the medicine." Emma held her nose and downed the vile mixture in several quick gulps. It didn't taste as bad as it smelled, with a slight hint of coffee, a touch of cinnamon, and some indescribables thrown in.

"How's that?" Ann smiled, wiping her hands down the front of her Burning Man sweatshirt.

"Not bad, not bad at all. Let's just hope it lives up to your claims."

"It will, but you might want to wait a few minutes before you head out. Come over here and have a seat. That concoction's been known to cause strong reactions in folks. Might not bother you though. You look like you have a pretty robust constitution, if you get my drift."

Emma joined Ann in the leather recliners beside the wood stove. It could be a full-time job keeping up with all Ann's drifts. "So, you lived with a woman for thirty-six years? Did you? I mean were you—"

"Lovers? Is that what you're trying to ask? You don't seem like the beat-around-the-bush type to me. Spit it out, child."

Emma's face flushed. "Yes, but I didn't want to pry. You don't even know me."

"You weren't prying, honey. I know you writers are a curious lot. And I take every chance I get to talk about my Cass. It keeps her alive in here." Ann patted her chest. "We were friends, lovers, fighters, partners, Mrs. and Mrs., and everything else that goes along with loving another woman."

Emma was fascinated, and more than a little impressed, that a woman of Ann's age and experience would talk so openly about a lesbian relationship. The subject was bound to have been taboo in her youth. "Have you always lived here in Patrick County?"

"Oh yeah. I was probably the first full-blown lez-bean this county ever knew about for sure. Sometimes I felt like a local attraction, the way people pointed and stared. But it didn't bother me. I didn't try to hide my feelings for Cass from day one. No, sir. What you see is what you get with Ann West."

"How old were you when you met?"

"Cass and I knew each other all our lives. We went to school together and lived right next door to one another. I had a crush on her from about age ten. She was in the kissing booth at the fall festival when I was fifteen, and a couple of boys dared me to kiss her. That kiss changed my life. You ever had anyone kiss you like that?"

Not even close. Emma kept her response to herself. The look in Ann's eyes told her she wouldn't believe her. "Why did it take so long for you to get together? If my math is right, and I'm guessing your age close at all, that leaves a lot of years unaccounted for."

"Cass wasn't quite as good at snubbing decorum as I was. She tried to convince herself she wasn't *that way*, as it was called back then. She spent a long time dancing around the whoopee pole."

"I'm sorry?"

"Going with men, being married, being straight, or being whatever everybody thought she ought to be."

Ann's eyes suddenly lost some of their vibrancy. Cass's decision to remain closeted and not commit to their relationship had obviously affected her deeply. Emma understood the longing for a truly loving commitment. "I'm sorry, Ann. Where were you all this time Cass was so undecided—in a convent?"

"Oh, no. I could take a hint. No way was I staying in this rinky-dink town watching the woman I love be passed from man to man. Most of them were uglier than a sack of smashed assholes and dumber than a stump. I joined the national guard soon as I was old enough. They'd take you as a nursing trainee at the time. I ended up in a MASH unit and traveled the world. Honey, I sampled some of the world's best feminine cuisine. You couldn't tell it now, but I was quite a catch at the time." Ann raked a hand through wavy gray hair, lifted her chin, and winked.

Emma couldn't help but laugh. "So, did it help you forget Cass?"

"Nothing can make you forget your soul mate—not someone else, not time, not distance. You seem smart enough to know that."

Emma was completely out of her depth. If she'd ever experienced the kind of love Ann felt for Cass, she might've been able to identify with what Ann was talking about. Her heart ached with the realization that she had not, maybe never would. She stood.

"I'm feeling better, Ann. Thank you for the medicine and the chat. I should get moving, or I'll pass the whole day here with you." She started toward the door and turned back. "Maybe we can talk about my story some other time."

"I'd be honored. Just tell me what you need." Ann gave a thumbs-up.

"I need to locate Fannie Mae Buffkin first. I understand she lives downtown."

Ann broke eye contact and wiped her hand across the spotless countertop. "Yeah. She lives in the mansion on the hill in the center of town, overlooking the old furniture factory. You can't miss it. If you don't mind me asking, why her?" Ann sounded a little tense.

"She's hired me to write an article, so she's my initial stop."

Ann nodded as if satisfied with her answer, but her expression was still strained. "If you want the busiest busy-body in town, you need to talk to Harriett Smoltz, the librarian. You can't miss her. She looks like a frumpy old maid, always wears the most unflattering clothes. If she doesn't have what you need, her meddlesome twin sister, Hannah, will. She's the historian for the county. The jobs couldn't have gone to a better pair. They started out as telephone switchboard operators in the day and held on until the last gasp. The town had to come up with other jobs that allowed them to remain respectably nosy."

"That sounds perfect. Who knows? This history piece may be sprinkled with a little excitement after all."

Ann mumbled something she couldn't quite make out.

"Sorry?"

"I said good luck."

Emma turned toward the door just as it opened, and Carter strolled in. She looked as surprised as Emma felt to bump into each other again so soon. Her pressed uniform hugged her toned body, and her eyes swept Emma slowly. God help her, but she liked being visually caressed by the sexy ranger.

"Now here's exactly what you need," Ann said. "Carter, give Emma a ride into town and show her around."

Emma's insides tightened and her pulse pounded at the possibility of being confined in a vehicle with Carter for any amount of time. "That's really not necessary. I have my car."

"And I really need to—"

"You need to take care of our guest. There's nothing earth-shattering on your schedule today, unless you're partial to unblocking a toilet." Ann's eyes twinkled, and Emma suspected that her match-making gene had taken over.

"I'm sure Ranger West has better things to do, Ann. I'm quite capable of getting to town and locating contacts." Emma cast a glance at Carter and prayed she'd object more fervently.

"Well, I guess I could spare part of my day, but we need to get going." Shrugging at Emma, Carter held the door like a perfectly mannered hostess.

"Really, I'm sure I can find—"

"It's not a problem," Carter said.

Emma looked from Carter back to Ann, who smiled sweetly.

"Thank you. I do get lost easily in unfamiliar places," she grudgingly admitted.

The short ride to downtown Stuart felt like a stint in a sauna, and Carter's musky perfume mingled with the freshness of outdoors. Emma wanted to lick her to see if she tasted as good as she smelled. *What?* She'd never had thoughts like that about anyone. What had Ann put in that concoction? A love potion? Carter gave no sign of being affected at all. She spoke little, but her body exuded heat and a wild energy that made Emma edgy.

"You might've been a little more forceful with your aunt and saved yourself a trip."

Carter kept her eyes on the road. "Wouldn't do any good. It's pointless to argue when she gets something in her head."

"And what exactly has she gotten into her head?" Years as a reporter had taught Emma to read people's body language and nonverbal cues. She could tell by the way Carter fidgeted that she was going to sidestep her question.

"I guess she just likes you. What do you do for a living, Emma?"

Carter's lips formed a perfect pucker as she said her name, almost in a whisper. It took a second to recall what Carter had asked. "I'm a reporter doing a story on the history of Stuart, and that wasn't much of an answer to my question, Ranger."

Carter squirmed again as they pulled in front of an old two-story brick building. A wooden shingle dangling from a rusty pole identified the Stuart Library.

"This is our stop. I've got some errands to take care of, and then I'll be at the school gym later this afternoon." She pointed toward the end of the street, scribbled her number on a Fairy Stone Park business card, and offered it to her.

When Emma reached for the card, their fingers brushed and she jerked away. Her skin burned, and she remembered touching a hot stove for the first time. That burn had been painful, but this one left her fingers tingling for the stimulus again. What would Sheri think about her visceral reaction to another woman? She'd accused Emma of being cold and unresponsive, but she felt anything but cold around Carter West. Or maybe she was just emotionally sensitive and imagined a connection. She looked, and Carter's eyes searched hers. Emma quickly glanced away. It was as if Carter could see everything she felt.

"Call me when you're finished or just come by the school. Everything else is in pretty close proximity to the library. You shouldn't have any trouble finding your way around."

If she didn't get her mind back on work, she wouldn't be able to find her way across the street. "I think I can manage." Emma closed the Jeep door with too much force and immediately regretted her sharp comment. Carter was only trying to help. It wasn't her fault Emma found her totally distracting.

"But thanks for the ride."

Emma almost missed Carter's low, sarcastic prompt as she walked toward the gym.

Great. Now they both sounded like a couple of pouty teenagers. She watched Carter swagger down the street. The woman was infuriating. She said little and offered less in the way of nonverbal clues. Not even her deep-brown eyes indicated what she was thinking or feeling. Emma hefted her messenger bag onto her shoulder, determined not to be distracted by Carter West one second longer.

Carter could've strangled Ann for suggesting she give Emma a ride into town. The woman had a car of her own, and Carter had a job and not as a taxi driver or tour guide. But she'd been happy to see Emma a little less stressed this morning. Some of the dark circles under her eyes from yesterday had lightened, and the puffiness had disappeared. Carter had wanted to ask why she was upset, but it wasn't her concern. She wouldn't appreciate a stranger meddling in her private life.

Emma's fiery red hair was styled so it hung straight and fell across her shoulders and down her back, not bushy and unruly like the night before. If she'd met the Emma Ferguson who checked in at the park in a bar, she'd have stopped, tried to cheer her up, maybe even asked her to dance, slow. Today Emma wore snug jeans, a clover-green sweater that flaunted the swell of full breasts, and sensible shoes, not the heeled ones she'd fallen in last evening. If Carter had seen this woman, she'd have passed her by, knowing she was out of her league.

The trip to town had felt endless, probably because Emma's eyes had threatened to lay her bare. Something in her look made Carter want to open up. Was it the azure color of her eyes or her crooked smile that suggested she knew Carter wanted to talk, or maybe just the undeniable chemistry sparking between them?

When their fingers had touched, Carter turned away so Emma wouldn't see the surprise she was certain showed on her face. Her heart pounded. She felt breathless, and her mouth watered as if she were starving. She'd been attracted to women before, but nothing like this.

Emma's responses had been just as telling. Carter appraised women like scholars studied history or the classics. Emma's lips had parted as if she'd been shocked, and her crooked smile had turned into a perfect *O*. She wouldn't meet Carter's gaze, and her freckled cheeks had flushed the most gorgeous shade of pink. Yes, the lovely Ms. Ferguson had been attracted to her as well. No way to hide chemistry that strong.

But Emma had also been sharp and sarcastic, questioning why she hadn't challenged Ann about giving her a ride. There was fire in more than Emma's hair. If she didn't want to spend any time with her, that suited Carter just fine. She'd briefly entertained the idea of a quickie with an out-of-town reporter, since she'd be leaving as soon as she finished her boring story, but Emma was proving to be the complicated type, and she didn't want complications.

"Hey, it's Carter." An eleven-year old named Nico ran toward her when she opened the door of the school gym.

"What's happening, dude?" She gave him a fist bump and joined the other five kids waiting on the bleachers. "Sorry I'm a little late. Had to give a lady a ride into town."

Mitch, one of the other boys, chimed in. "Yeah. We saw you in front of the library. Is that your girlfriend?"

Why were kids so grown up these days? "No. She's just a lady staying at the park who needed a ride. Now, let's get started. Have you chosen teams already?"

One of the girls, Maddie, raised her hand and waited patiently until Carter called on her.

"Yes, Maddie." She was so polite and had come further than any of the others in the program.

"We've got three boys and three girls today, but we decided all by ourselves that we should mix it up and then switch again for the second half of the basketball game. How about that?" Her green eyes sparkled, and she placed her hands on her hips in a very adult pose.

"That's excellent planning, but let's tidy up the gym. Then we'll play, and talk last." She'd had considerably more luck getting the kids to open up about problems when they were tired and their defenses were down.

She stood in the center of the circle, tossed the ball, and watched the two tallest kids jump for it. As the game got underway, she forgot all about Emma Ferguson and focused on doing what she loved, helping kids.

Chapter Three

Emma glanced between the Stuart library and the large Buffkin house overlooking downtown. Plunge in cold or do preparatory research? She'd been too distracted by her breakup and moving out to give Fannie Buffkin more than a cursory pass before leaving Greensboro. Knowing as much about her subject as possible would help her ask better questions and all the ones necessary to write a thorough narrative. She took a deep breath and grabbed the polished brass handle of the heavy wooden library door.

Harriett Smoltz descended on Emma the minute a door chime announced her entrance. Ann's description had been so precise that Emma would've recognized the woman in a lineup. Her lackluster brown hair was swept back in a tight bun at the base of her skull, making her sharp features more severe. Harriett was younger than Emma imagined, probably early fifties, but wore a circa 1960s flowered tent dress and clashing blue sweater that successfully camouflaged any hint of a feminine shape.

"Good morning, ma'am. May I be of assistance?" The fingernails-on-chalkboard voice made Emma cringe. "I'm Harriett Smoltz, head librarian. And you are?" Harriett wrung her hands as her prurient eyes searched Emma's face and then her clothing and shoes.

"Yes, Ms. Smoltz, I'm Emma Ferguson, a freelance reporter, and I'm doing a public-interest piece on the establishment and growth of the town of Stuart. Could you direct me to the historical reference section?"

"A reporter, you say? Anything special you're looking for? There's a lot of useless history in those files." Harriett tucked her hands into deep side pockets and bobbed her head up and down in agreement with her own statement.

Harriett's determination to be of assistance made Emma more cautious than Ann's earlier warning had, but since she had nothing to lose and everything to gain, she indulged the librarian's over-helpfulness. "Just basic information right now, Ms. Smoltz."

"Please call me Harriett. Makes me feel younger." Harriett led her to a dark back room that was much cooler than the main lobby and smelled of musty books. "I keep the temperature down and the lights off to help preserve the older copies. The wood and acid combination in paper wasn't conducive to preservation until after the 1970s." She pulled on a pair of white gloves, reached for a book just beyond her grasp, and then stepped onto a stool to retrieve the tome.

Emma noticed the well-developed calves of Harriett's legs when she stood on tiptoes and wondered why she wore such unflattering clothes. If the rest of her body was in as good a shape as her legs, she should be proud. Emma certainly would be. She shook her head. When had she started staring at random women's legs? *Damn you, Carter West.*

Harriett started to hand her the book but stopped. "Glove up, please."

Emma stifled a giggle. *Glove up?* This wasn't brain surgery, but she did as instructed and accepted the work Harriett placed gingerly in her hands. "What's this?"

"The official history of Stuart, Virginia, complete with some impressive illustrations. When you finish that, I'll get you another great resource. Should keep you busy for a while."

Emma had the feeling Harriett was trying not only to keep her busy but also to manage the information she received. Maybe her suspicious reporter's nature was simply working overtime because

Harriett Smoltz had been nothing but gracious and helpful. "If I need old documents, do you still use microfilm?"

"Of course. Most of our historical information is still stored that way. Microfilm can last more than 500 years if it's kept under the right temperature and humidity. It's a far better archival medium than digital, which can suffer bit rot. I'm so glad I didn't let the town council talk me into going digital when the craze first hit."

Archival material and bit rot, indeed. Harriett Smoltz was more current than her outdated clothes and unattractive hairstyle suggested, and Emma respected her acuity a bit more. She'd be a great resource as her story progressed. "Thank you for your help, Harriett. I'll start reading, and when I'm finished, maybe you could point me in the direction of the historian, Hannah Smoltz."

Harriett's tight-lipped smirk reduced her eyes to thin slits. "Why don't I give you the abbreviated version of Stuart, and you can read this another time?" She took the book and placed it delicately on a table. "Now you come right over here and have a seat. When we finish you won't need to see Hannah. My sister is a good historian, but she's not available today." Harriett stood a little straighter, placed a hand in the center of her chest, and launched into her dissertation. "My family was one of the first to settle here back in the early 1900s…"

Four agonizing hours later, during which her mind wandered frequently to quiet, gorgeous Carter West, Emma extricated herself from the clutches of Harriett Smoltz, having gained a painfully thorough verbal history of the highlights and lowlights of Stuart. She also received the formal address of the Buffkin house on the hill and an editorial comment not to take her too seriously. Fannie, according to Harriett, had suffered a nervous breakdown after her husband died and hadn't been quite right since. She left the library thinking Ann had certainly given her a gold mine in Ms. Smoltz, if she could just sift through the silt to the nuggets.

Emma walked to the center of town, stood beside a fountain carved out of buff, reddish-brown, and gray sandstone, and turned in a circle. Ann and Harriett had been right about not being able to miss Fannie Buffkin's home. She debated visiting her immediately, but after her marathon with Harriett, the growl of her stomach reminded her she hadn't eaten dinner the night before or breakfast this morning. She headed toward the Stuart Diner with its red-and-white awning near the post office.

When she entered the diner, everyone in the place stopped talking and turned to look at her. She'd forgotten how curious people in small towns could be and how unabashed in their expression of that curiosity. She gave her best howdy-y'all smile and headed toward an empty seat at the far end of the counter. Several men smiled, two winked, but the women watched her with almost palpable hostility. Maybe an announcement that she was a lesbian and had no interest in their husbands would help, but that might scare some folks away, and she needed their cooperation.

"Morning, hon. What are you drinking?" A gray-haired, seventy-ish woman with a fantastic smile and popping chewing gum held a pencil in one hand and an order pad in the other. Her nametag read *Loretta*.

"Coffee, please, lots of coffee."

"I heard that," Loretta said, and handed her a menu. "Give me a nod when you're ready."

Not a single healthy choice on the Stuart Diner menu. She nodded to Loretta. "I'll have two poached eggs, hash browns, and crispy bacon." She signaled for Loretta to lean closer and whispered, "Is it always this quiet in here?"

Loretta straightened and raised her voice so everyone could hear. "Oh, heavens no, hon. The diner is a hotbed of conversation and gossip. It's never quiet unless there's someone new. Everybody's straining to pick up any scrap about the reporter staying out at the Fairy Stone Park. By the time you've eaten breakfast, half the town will know what you had, and the other half will be speculating on what you'll have for dinner. Ain't that right, boys?" Suddenly the room buzzed with conversation, and nobody was looking at Emma.

"Thank you." Emma added Loretta to her list of interesting Stuart characters. Ann had topped that list, and Harriett Smoltz came second. None of these women had a problem speaking their minds, which Emma found comforting.

"Here you go." Loretta set a plate of eggs, hash browns, and bacon in front of Emma, and the aromas wafting off it made her mouth water.

"Guess you've met Ann and Carter West?"

Emma reached for her fork and nodded. "When I checked in yesterday."

"They're good people. Don't let anybody tell you different."

"Why would they?"

"You know, small town, small minds. Some folks hold to old ideas and bad information, but you look smart enough to make your own decisions."

Emma never resisted exploring a cryptic comment, but another customer called for coffee, and Loretta grabbed the pot and made her rounds at the tables. Emma took the opportunity to inhale her breakfast. The hash browns were a golden shade of burnt, the bacon exactly crispy enough, and the poached eggs were perfection. No wonder the place was packed. Her last bite was a double forkful of hash browns slathered in egg remnants. She almost moaned aloud.

"More coffee?" Loretta asked, waving the pot in her direction.

"Thanks, I'm good, Loretta. If I'm not being too nosy, not that it wouldn't be encouraged, but why do you work here?"

Loretta laughed, and the loose skin under her neck wiggled with the rest of her. "You mean because I'm older than dirt, because I should be enjoying my golden years in a rest home, or because I should have lots of money saved up from my years working in a now-defunct furniture factory?"

Emma purposely wrinkled her nose and shrugged as if the options were too complicated to choose.

"Let me save you the trouble of exercising your oxygen-deprived brain while digesting that plateful of food. I love being around people, but not the ones who give up on living. This place makes me laugh. I get to meet new folks and keep up with what's happening. I'm too young for canasta or shuffleboard. Don't you agree?"

"Absolutely." She couldn't picture Loretta sitting around in a nursing home. Besides, the people at the diner would miss her motherly humor and overall good nature. "Thank you for a great breakfast and some insightful tidbits." She placed her money for the bill, along with a hefty tip, on the counter.

When she reached for the door handle, a man in a company shirt bulging with muscles and wearing khakis called out to her. "And be quick with your little project. There's work to be done around here."

Emma turned toward him. "Who are you and why are you so interested in my job?"

"I'm the project manager of the construction company that's going to get rid of that eyesore at the edge of town and replace it with a strip mall and more jobs. Best thing to happen to this place in years."

"Guess that's a matter of opinion." She waved and smiled sweetly as she left the diner and started toward the Buffkin house.

The sprawling residence occupied an impressive piece of real estate overlooking Main Street and the old Thompson Furniture factory that the contractor was so anxious to raze. Harriett had told Emma that Buffkin's grandfather, Wilbur Thompson, had constructed the home the same year he founded the small furniture factory and built the school at the opposite end of the street. Fannie and a brother were the only two heirs to the Thompson fortune.

As she huffed her way up the steep driveway toward the house, Emma noted overgrown shrubs, untended flowerbeds, and peeling paint, as if the occupant had already given up on the property. Before she could knock on the front door, a stooped, elderly woman flung it open and motioned her inside. The smell of mothballs mingled with pine air freshener hung in the air.

"I've been expecting you. Harriett said you left the library some time ago." Mrs. Buffkin's appearance in a long evening gown, white gloves, and animal-fur wrap harkened back to Harriett's comment about emotional instability. "Don't you just love Harriett?" Without waiting for a response she said, "She's a sweet person, and she's been good to me since my husband died."

"Mrs. Buffkin, I'm—"

"You're Emma Ferguson, or you better be, and I'm Fannie. Just Fannie." The blue-haired lady led the way into a formal sitting room in which every surface was populated with dust-covered bric-a-brac and a few expensive-looking pieces.

"I'm looking forward to working on your family's history. I've already started gathering the background of Stuart, and as you said, Ms. Smoltz was very nice and tremendously helpful."

"Forget all that." Fannie picked up a picture from the piano and plopped into a huge wing chair. "It's about time somebody took me seriously around here. Is that going to be you?"

Emma was taken aback by the confrontational tone and accusatory stare. She stood in the center of the room, uncertain if she was staying or going. "I was under the impression you wanted me to—"

"I'm aware of what I said. I'm not senile yet, regardless of what half the people in this town think." She waved for Emma to sit. "How else was I going to get a decent reporter to talk to me if I didn't entice you with something? You people are notoriously picky and self-serving."

"I beg your pardon? I don't appreciate being summoned under false pretenses and then insulted. You know nothing about me or my professional abilities."

Fannie smiled and pushed heavy glasses up her nose. "Well, I see that red hair is indicative of something other than good looks. Nice to know."

"Mrs. Buffkin, there seems to be some kind of misunderstanding. I have principles, and you've violated the first one—honesty." She rose from her chair so quickly, it toppled backward and almost crashed into a table covered with Faberge eggs before she caught it. "Sorry. I'll reimburse your advance as soon as I return home. I wish you a good day, and I hope you find someone to write your story. A word of advice. When you do, be honest."

"Don't you even want to hear what I have to say?"

"I'm not sure I would trust you to tell me the truth, so no. I'm sorry, Mrs. Buffkin."

Fannie struggled out of her chair as Emma turned to leave. "You're being impulsive, Ms. Ferguson. At least listen to my pitch."

Emma headed toward the front door.

"Your father would be very disappointed in you."

She faltered as Fannie Buffkin's arrow hit home. No. No more lies. She straightened her shoulders and continued toward Stuart Elementary School at the opposite end of town.

As Emma walked away from Fannie Buffkin's house, she couldn't wrap her mind around what had just happened. She'd been deceived, not easy to do in her line of work. She'd taken an elderly woman's word about why she wanted to meet without conducting proper due diligence. If she'd researched the Thompson or Buffkin families more thoroughly, she'd have been better prepared for Fannie's abrupt shift of focus, but she'd been distracted by personal issues. One of the first rules of journalism was to know your source. Fannie was right. Her father would've been very disappointed, but how would Fannie Buffkin know that?

Her father, Emory Lowell Ferguson, had been one of the first embedded reporters during the Gulf War. His name meant bravery and power, and he'd exhibited both of those characteristics during his storied career as a war correspondent. He'd received journalism awards and, until his disappearance, had written for various newspapers and broadcast media. Near the end of his last tour, her father had been reported missing behind enemy lines while covering a prisoner-exchange story. In spite of all efforts by the family, Emory Ferguson had never been located. His fascinating career, combined with his disappearance, had been the deciding factors in Emma's choice of a journalism profession.

Had Fannie Buffkin known her father or some other member of her family, or had she just done her homework before their meeting? Damn, she hated being one-upped. She'd been unprepared and appeared incompetent. Double damn. She couldn't leave now without finding out why she'd been summoned to Stuart and why Fannie felt she had to use subterfuge to get her here. She sighed.

She'd listen to Fannie Buffkin eventually, if only to show Fannie she was no quitter…and to make her father proud.

The back entrance of the gym was propped open, and the screams and laughter of children playing poured into the street. She stood beside the door and let the happy noises lift her dark mood. Then she closed her eyes and imagined the scene inside from the sounds—a basketball bouncing erratically across a polished floor, sneakers squeaking in stop-and-go patterns, and the metallic reverberations of the ball bouncing off the rim of the net. As an only child, she'd loved school for the playtime with other kids, free from the pressure to perform in the classroom and at home. If she'd had more recreational time growing up instead of always trying to please her parents and teachers, maybe she wouldn't be so driven to excel.

"Okay, guys, that's it for today." Carter's throaty voice cut through the laughter, and the space quieted. "Grab a bottle of water and gather around."

Suddenly Emma felt out of place, like she was intruding on something personal, but she wanted to stay, to learn more about Carter, even if what she was doing amounted to eavesdropping. Interacting with children was a side of the quiet ranger she hadn't expected. She squatted beside the gap in the door and peered in. Carter sat on the bottom bleacher, and six children sat one up from her, looking down. The kids had the superior position, though she was pretty sure they didn't understand why Carter had chosen to sit below them.

"Does anyone have anything to talk about today?"

The children were quiet for several seconds, looking back and forth at each other, some of them staring at their shoes. One towheaded young girl raised her hand and waited until Carter called on her. "Yes, Maddie."

"I don't think I play basketball too good." The little girl fidgeted with her blond curls as she spoke, and Emma's heart ached for her. She'd been that little girl, clumsy and always picked last for the team, but she'd kept trying because she loved being around the other children.

"What do you think, guys?" Carter threw the question back to the group.

A dark-haired boy spoke up. "She caught a—"

"Tell Maddie, Nico," Carter said. "Remember, talk *to* each other, and be honest."

"Oh yeah. I forgot." He turned toward Maddie. "You caught a really crappy pass I threw. That was good."

A small-framed African American boy added, "Yeah, and you always try so hard."

"Thanks, guys." Maddie smiled and poked her tongue through a gap in her front teeth. "I do try really hard."

Carter's rich, deep laugh filled the gymnasium. "Good job, Nico and Reggie. And that's what life is all about, guys, doing your best. No one gets it right all the time, but that's how we learn. Nobody's perfect, and anyone who tells you different is confused or scared. The real gift is to learn to accept and love each other in spite of our imperfections. Right?"

"Right!" The group answered in unison and pumped their fists in the air.

Emma's throat tightened and she swallowed hard. How different would her life have been if someone had told her she didn't need to be perfect? She was very glad these kids had Carter. She stood to leave, lost her footing, and stumbled forward into the gym. When she looked up, seven pairs of eyes were trained on her. The children laughed, but Carter's expression showed no trace of humor.

"Can we help you?" Carter asked.

"I'm so sorry," she said, trying to stand with some degree of grace despite her tumbling entry. "I was…I'm…" She had no words and no excuse.

Carter turned back to the children. "Guess we're done for today. If you need to talk to me privately, I'll be here for a while." She high-fived each child and watched them leave before facing Emma. "Eavesdropping?"

Warmth raced across her face, the embarrassment too deep for a slow crawl. "I didn't intend to, but it just happened. I finished my work for today, came to find you, and voilà. The children's laughter pulled me in, and when you started talking, I…it was too late. You're not going to help me out, are you?"

"Not at all. I believe people should take responsibility for their actions."

Carter's candor caught her momentarily off guard. The woman didn't say much, but when she did, it was a zinger. "You're exactly right. I'm sorry. I should've had the courtesy to ask if I could watch the game and the decency to leave when it turned into something more serious. What was that anyway?"

Carter started collecting the basketball and other equipment scattered around the gym, and Emma thought she might not answer. "FACES."

"I beg your pardon?"

"The school allowed me to develop my own program, with emphasis on children's behavioral problems and social skills. I focus on preteen, at-risk students. We call it Kids' FACES. It's an acronym for fitness, abilities, confidence, emotional intelligence, and self-esteem."

Emma watched Carter until she finished tidying up and met her gaze. "You created it?"

"Is that so hard to believe?"

She hadn't imagined Carter around children, much less teaching them or crafting programs for their development. "I'm just surprised." Challenging children needed the kind of quiet temperament and patience Carter had just demonstrated. Emma sensed something damaged inside Carter that helped her relate to these kids.

"I've always wanted to help kids, especially those without adequate resources."

Emma felt as if her heart had suddenly opened and absorbed the healing warmth of the sun. The depth of her emotions surprised her. Carter's honesty and the tenderness she'd displayed with the youngsters moved her. Carter might pretend feelings at other times, but the emotions Emma had just observed were genuine. "Do you have some kind of training?"

Carter secured the equipment locker and pointed toward the back door. "I've almost completed my doctorate in child psychology."

Emma stopped so abruptly that Carter almost ran into her. "You've what?"

Carter's brown eyes tunneled into her soul. "I see. You thought I was just a dumb jock ranger with no other professional aspirations."

"That's not it at all. Rangers are usually well educated and dedicated, though not very well paid for their efforts. And I know the competition for job openings is fierce. I just wouldn't have imagined you with children. This is a different side of you, a very attractive and impressive side. I'm sorry if I upset you."

"No need to be impressed or to apologize. I'm used to people underestimating me." Carter turned abruptly and walked out of the gym toward the Jeep.

"Carter, wait."

"Let's go. It's getting late."

CHAPTER FOUR

Carter was quiet for the first half of the trip back to the park but slowly seemed to come out of her funk. "Productive day?"

"Sort of disappointing really. I don't want to bore you with the details." Emma just didn't know how to engage with Carter or to understand the unexpected feelings she provoked.

"I doubt anything about you would be boring, but as you wish."

"Did you have a good day?" The least she could do was be civil.

"Yes, thanks."

Emma was amazed at how comfortable Carter seemed in the ensuing silence. Many people preferred to talk when alone with another person, to fill the gaps with mindless drivel. But Carter wasn't like that. Emma was the one struggling to keep her mouth shut. Her natural instinct was to ask questions, because she wanted to know everything about this woman who'd invaded her thoughts without really seeming to notice her.

Emma took every opportunity to feign interest in the scenery while stealing glances at Carter's profile, the set of her jaw, her long fingers wrapped around the steering wheel, and the muscles that undulated along her forearm when she shifted gears. She couldn't remember ever being so interested in the small details of a woman's appearance, but she'd never met anyone quite like Carter West. Everything about this woman of few words intrigued her.

"Would you like to take a walk?"

Emma hadn't been expecting an invitation, especially after her eavesdropping episode, and was momentarily stunned. "Sorry?"

"I asked if you'd like to take a walk with me. Lookout Pointe is really beautiful this time of year. Ann said I should show you around."

Maybe she was feeling guilty about her earlier behavior and didn't want to seem rude, or maybe she really wanted to spend more time with Carter. "That would be nice. Thank you."

When they arrived at the office, Carter popped out of the truck. "I'm going to tell Ann. Be right back." A few minutes later, she reappeared with two bottles of water and a walkie-talkie. "All set?"

Emma nodded, took the water Carter offered, and followed her onto a path that seemed from their vantage point to go nowhere. "I'm really sorry about earlier. I'm just—"

"Curious. You're a reporter. You get paid to be inquisitive." Carter smiled and waved for her to go first around a huge boulder in the middle of the path. They walked in silence for a while, and then Carter stopped to lean against a tree trunk and take a drink of water. She studied Emma's face as if trying to make a decision. "Last night you said you apologize so much from force of habit? What did you mean?"

"I was hoping you didn't catch that." An image of her parents' dissatisfied faces at the dinner table flashed through her mind. She slowly unscrewed the cap from her water bottle and took a long sip. "My parents were…" How could she describe them without making them seem like overbearing ogres? "Strict and demanding. They expected me to be perfect and didn't take disappointment well. As you can probably tell, I'm a deeply flawed individual." She wanted Carter to laugh or at least sense her discomfort and move away from the subject.

"I wouldn't say deeply flawed, just human. As I told the kids today, nobody's perfect."

"My parents and teachers wanted me to be, and I hated to fail them. So, I apologized a lot, trying to make amends. Good manners went a long way with my folks." She'd tried her best, but her father's military connections and her mother's disciplinary streak always left her feeling she'd failed them. It had taken her years to shed their expectations, but the associated guilt clung as firmly as ever. "They had very high hopes for my future, and being a poorly paid journalist like my father wasn't in the cards."

"But you love what you do?" Carter's stare held firm, and Emma couldn't look away.

"Yes. It's very gratifying most of the time, and in a way, it keeps me connected to my father, whom I loved dearly. He had a very successful and rewarding career in journalism."

Carter took another sip of water. "Is that why you're not in a relationship? Because you're afraid you won't live up to a partner's expectations?"

"What?" Emma spat water across the trail and wiped her mouth. She hadn't expected anything so personal or insightful from Carter. "Probably. Did you miss the part about me being flawed?" This conversation was making her very agitated. She was used to asking the probing questions, not answering them. "So, why are you still single?"

"Who said I was?" Carter dropped her water bottle into a side pocket on her pants and continued down the path in long strides, as if suddenly trying to get away from Emma.

A good reporter was persistent. Emma hurried to keep up, but her steps faltered over the gravely terrain and through slippery moss. "You just seem like the strong, silent type who doesn't get involved easily. Are you...single?"

"Mostly. I see someone periodically, but nothing serious."

"Well...why?"

"Long story."

"I've got time." Emma tried to sound casual. She'd never felt so drawn to a woman so quickly, and if Carter was single and willing, why not explore a bit? "Does it have anything to do with Ann?"

"What do you mean?"

"You seem devoted to her, which is admirable. Maybe you think a relationship would disturb that balance?" Emma was shooting in the dark. "Am I being too personal now?"

"Shush." Carter stopped as she reached the top of a hill and motioned for Emma to join her. "You have to see this."

Emma wanted an answer to her question. She could've cared less about some view from a hilltop in the middle of nowhere. What could possibly be worth walking this far? When Carter helped her up to the crest, Emma's breath caught. Below them, between the soft hills, lay a small field of golden grain waving in the breeze. She'd seen pictures of places like this, but they didn't do the scene justice. "What is that?"

"Hay at its peak, ready to be harvested. In a couple of weeks the field will be stubble. I love this view and the quiet swishing of the wind across the seed heads. It's as soothing as the roar of the ocean."

Carter's brown eyes had a faraway look, and her face glowed in the afternoon sun. This view was worth every precarious step Emma had taken to the top. She watched Carter watching the hay and felt her first sense of peace and contentment in days.

She took Carter's hand, and when Carter looked at her with questioning eyes, Emma said, "I've never shared anything this beautiful with another person. It's magnificent. Thank you."

"Emma, I—"

"Base to Ranger One. You out there, Carter?" Ann's voice broke the silence, and Carter gently slid their hands apart and tugged the walkie-talkie off her belt.

"I'm here, Ann. What's up?"

"We have a guest checking in to cabin nine. Can you go by and see if he needs anything?"

Carter looked toward the field one last time and then at Emma before answering. "On my way." She returned the walkie to her utility belt and started back down the hill. Emma didn't follow. "You coming?"

"I think I'll stay a bit longer. You go ahead."

"Can you find the way to your cabin? It's a pretty straight shot. Just follow the path."

"I'll be fine, Carter. Go."

"Don't stay too long. It gets dark and cold in a hurry, and you're not familiar with the area." Carter seemed as reluctant to leave as Emma was to have her go.

"Take care of business, Ranger." She shooed her away and turned back to the hayfield that glowed more brilliantly in the last golden rays of the sun. She missed the weathered texture of Carter's hand and the way their fingers slid together as if they always had. How could something so simple and easy feel so special?

When the light began to fade, Emma reluctantly started toward home. The path looked well marked as far as she could see. Her knowledge of the outdoors hovered somewhere between little and nonexistent, but how hard could it be to follow a trail to the bottom of a mountain?

She settled into a steady rhythm of much-needed exercise, and the muscles in her legs burned from the rugged terrain. Ranger Carter, Jane of the Jungle, probably knew every tree, bush, flower, animal, bird, fish, and insect in this part of Fairy Stone Park. Carter herself was probably some wild variety of lesbian no one had ever discovered. She certainly had that exotic, untamed look. *Think about something else, anything else.*

Emma replayed her conversations with Harriett Smoltz and Fannie Buffkin. Harriett had been forthcoming about the town and its history, even willing to provide other sources for Emma to interview. She'd be a solid resource going forward. But why had Fannie misled her in their initial conversation? What was she trying to hide, and why present the story as a public-interest piece if there was something more substantial?

She'd been too hasty in her retreat from Fannie's, but she couldn't abide dishonesty. She'd give Fannie time to stew over her error of lying, and then Emma would present her terms—no more lies if she reconsidered doing the story. She'd get back on Fannie Buffkin's payroll, because she needed the money. Maybe that wasn't the only reason, but it was a start.

When Emma finally decided on her approach with Fannie, she looked up from the path to find she was in a thick stand of trees and the sky had darkened around her. The well-worn path that had been outlined by regularly placed rocks and an occasional sign was nowhere to be seen. Making a three-hundred-sixty-degree turn, she studied each direction for something familiar. All the trees looked the same. Why hadn't she paid more attention? Which side had the sun been on when they started? How did she think she could make this excursion alone with her awful sense of direction and aversion to anything outdoors?

❖

Carter's visit to the new occupant in cabin nine took longer than she expected. He'd asked questions about his neighbors and park rules regarding outside campfires and hunting. He worked for the construction company contracted to raze the old factory, had checked in alone, and was staying indefinitely. His muscular physique and rugged appearance made her think he could take care of himself in the woods. She wondered why a single man preferred the isolation of the park to the Riverside Hotel but was happy for the park's bottom line.

On her way back to the office, she thought about her ride into town this morning with Emma and about their walk this afternoon. The two events had evoked very different feelings. Being in a confined space with Emma this morning had been stimulating and bothersome. Every time a breeze blew through the window, it had swept Emma's long hair across Carter's arm where it rested on the gearshift and left goose bumps. The tingling followed a familiar path up her arm, over her chest, down her middle, and all the way through her. She couldn't have talked to Emma if she'd wanted to. Her mouth was dry, and she couldn't think of one nonsexual thing to say.

She'd caught Emma glancing her way, eyes lingering on her arms and breasts, but she'd remained quiet as well. If they couldn't even have a normal conversation, they probably shouldn't consider anything else. How ridiculous. Neither of them was considering anything else. Were they? She wasn't so sure after their walk.

They'd both asked personal questions, and Carter had seen a bit of the vulnerability Emma hid behind her professional façade. Emma's face had flushed with the wonder and joy of a child seeing something magnificent for the first time when she saw the hayfield. And when Emma took her hand, the gesture felt beautifully spontaneous and natural. The softness of her skin and the possessive way she curled her fingers around Carter's was both intimate and arousing. Carter had struggled not to pull her in and kiss her. On the walk down the mountain alone, she'd convinced herself they'd both been overcome by the beauty of the view. Nothing more. She shook her head and raked her fingers through her hair before heading into the office to check in with Ann.

"That sure was a long walk up the point. You and Emma talk about anything interesting?" Ann asked with a smug grin.

"You are in so much trouble. I told you not to push this woman at me, and what's the first thing you do?"

Ann swatted at her and kept talking. "She was in no condition to drive this morning, and you weren't doing anything else. You just getting back from the walk?"

"You asked me to go by cabin nine. The guy's settled in." Ann was dancing around something and would get to it sooner or later. Carter was always better served to let her arrive there on her own. In the meantime, she stripped off her gear and headed to the restroom.

When she returned, Ann started again. "I thought you'd just come back from Lookout Pointe."

"Why? Has something happened?"

"Are you messing with me, Carter? If you are, it's not funny."

"Why would I do that?" Ann was taking far longer than usual to get to the point, and it was starting to annoy her. "If I need to take care of something up there, tell me before it gets any darker."

"Emma came in here this morning looking a bit on the peaked side, wanted something for a headache. You know she really is a nice person. We had a long chat about me and Cass and—"

"Ann, for goodness sake. Get to the point. What has that got to do with our walk?"

"She hasn't come back yet. I thought she was with you."

"What? She said she knew the way. Guess I better go find her. It's already dark. Give me a couple of flashlights and another bottle of water." She should probably be more annoyed that Emma hadn't come back with her or at least admitted she didn't know how to get back to her cabin, but the thought of finding her in the shadowy woods had a certain appeal. A lady in distress might be very grateful. She immediately regretted the thought. Emma deserved better.

Ann gathered the supplies, stuffed them into a backpack, and slid them across the counter. "Want me to call one of the boys to go with you?"

"Let me try first. She can't be too lost, but be on standby in case I need help."

"You've got it."

❖

Emma finally saw a small light through the woods that looked like a cabin. She prayed she was right and started to run, stumbled, and rolled the rest of the way down the slope. When she came to a stop, she was almost in front of the park office in a different direction than she and Carter had started. She stood, brushed leaves from her clothes, and headed to the office.

She was happy to see Ann through the window still puttering around in the office. "Jeez, it gets cold up here after dark, Ann. Got any coffee handy?" She hugged herself and rocked back and forth, trying to warm up.

"Are you all right?" Ann rubbed Emma's back while pulling leaves from her hair.

"A little cold. I obviously didn't wear enough layers, but I didn't expect to be out this late. I got a little disoriented somewhere between Squirrelville and Possum Trot."

"Come sit down and warm yourself by the fire. I'll get something for the insides."

"I can hear Madam Wilderness now saying a smug 'I told you so' because I strayed."

Ann stopped searching under the counter and turned to her. "Then you haven't seen Carter?"

"No, why?"

"Oh, brother. She's going to be as mad as a whore in church. When I told her you weren't back from the Pointe, she got pretty fired up. She left over an hour ago looking for you. By the way, how did you find your way back?"

"I may be a self-proclaimed nature-phobe, but I've got pretty good common sense. I did get kind of lost, but I listened for sounds of civilization and watched for smoke from the cabins. I'd been going around in circles for a while, so I wasn't far away at all."

"I knew you were a gutsy one, Emma." Ann handed her a tin coffee cup and clicked it against her own. "Here's to self-sufficient women."

"Amen." She took a sip, and the strong liquid stole her breath. "Good Lord, Ann, what is this? More of your concoctions?" Emma gasped as alcohol burned down her throat and brought tears to her eyes.

"It's just a little touch of brandy I had stashed away in the back for medical emergencies. Seems to me this qualifies. Don't you agree? I used to drink Geritol, supposed to be good for old folks, until I found out it was addictive."

"I like the way you think, Ann. I guess you should call Carter on the radio and tell her I'm back." Emma inhaled the smoky fragrance from the wood stove and took a much smaller sip of the lukewarm liquid.

"Well, normally that would be a real good idea, but I can't." She pointed to a radio sitting on the counter. "She was in such a rush, she left her handheld. Nothing to do now but wait. Care for another shot?" Ann asked, not waiting for an answer before refilling Emma's cup.

"Should we send someone after her?" The warming effects of the brandy lulled Emma into a more relaxed state. "Will she be all right?"

"Few people know these parts better than my Carter. She'll be just fine."

Emma removed her tennis shoes, reclined, and raised her socked feet toward the wood stove. She scrutinized Ann from the corner of her eye, wondering about her and Cass and about Carter's past.

"Spit it out, Emma," Ann said. "I can hear those wheels turning, but your mouth isn't engaging. What do you want to know?"

"You're much too intuitive for your own good. I really don't want to meddle."

"Of course you do. It's an occupational hazard. I just whet your appetite this morning about Cass. I know you're itching to pick the cobwebs for the rest of the story. Fire away. In a few more minutes, neither of us will care." Ann waved her cup in an air toast.

Emma wasn't sure what to ask first. She needed to work up to her questions about Carter. "What happened to Cass while you were away with the national guard?"

A painful look crossed Ann's face as she tilted her head. "I was gone close to four years before I came back for a visit. She'd already been married once and was heading for her second husband." She took another swig. "This one was harmless enough. He drank some and didn't make many demands on her…to be a real wife. At least that's what she told me the one night we spent together."

Emma stopped pulling at a leaf stuck to her sock as she realized the implications of Ann's comment. "You mean you actually got to sleep with her?"

"Wasn't any sleeping going on, but if you mean sex, yeah. We finally did the deed. I hate to sound like a cliché, but I loved everything about Cass. Her skin was the color of pure ivory, and when I touched her, I burned in places I didn't even know I had. I spent that night loving her with my body, mind, and soul. For the first time in my life, everything was perfect."

Emma's skin warmed too quickly to blame the fire or the alcohol, and she loosened the top button of her corduroy shirt. What would it feel like to love someone that much and to make love to them with your entire being? "So the two of you went away together, right?" There was no way this story didn't have a happy ending.

"Nope. She said she loved me with all her heart, couldn't imagine anyone else ever touching her, but she couldn't leave with me. Her family was here, her mother was ailing, and she'd given her word to this man that she'd marry him."

"But Ann—"

Just then the front door flew open and Carter rushed in, face red, brows furrowed. "Ann, I can't find her. She's good and lost." Then her eyes focused on them. "What the—"

"Look what the cat dragged in, Carter," Ann said too loudly, rising too quickly and grabbing the counter for support. "She made it back all by herself."

Carter walked to the recliner and glared down at Emma, her eyes scanning her body. Temporary relief washed over her face but was replaced almost immediately with anger as she looked from Emma to Ann and back again. "You two have been drinking? I was out there scouring half of the mountainside, and you're here getting plastered around the woodstove."

"Don't be so hard on her, Carter," Ann said.

"And you stay out of this," Carter snapped.

"Wait a minute, young lady. Don't give me that tone. After all, she made it back safely."

Emma rose to her feet cautiously. "It's okay, Ann." Then she turned on Carter. "I'm so sorry I spoiled your Tarzan rescue. Pardon me for not waiting helplessly in the woods for the liberation."

Carter's shocked expression almost made Emma smile. Part of her liked Carter's Neanderthal protectiveness, but Carter didn't need to know that.

She pulled on her shoes and took Ann's hands in hers. "Thank you for your concern and your hospitality. Don't think I'm going to let you get by without telling me the end of the story." She kissed Ann on each cheek and brushed past Carter on her way out.

CHAPTER FIVE

*D*amn *you, Carter West.* Emma had tossed and turned for hours after the unpleasant exchange with Carter at the office and then been unable to sleep at all. Maybe she'd overreacted and been ungrateful to boot. Carter's protectiveness had been a turn-on. Who was she kidding? Everything about Carter fascinated her.

She rolled out of bed and schlepped into the tiny kitchen for her morning caffeine fix. When she found only one remaining pack of complimentary coffee, she added grocery shopping to her to-do list for the day. She ate a flattened protein bar she'd found in the bottom of her computer bag, then showered and dressed in comfortable jeans and a blouse. First, she'd go see Fannie and hopefully begin researching her new paying project.

Emma stuffed her notepad and phone into her messenger bag as she opened the door and pulled it closed. As she bent to insert the key into the lock, she backed into something firm and unyielding. Strong hands encircled her waist. She whirled around, stumbled backward, and came face to face with Carter's deep-brown eyes and inviting lips. Her hands still rested on Emma's waist, and their bodies pressed together at the most distracting places.

Carter backed away quickly and almost stepped off the side of the porch. "Sorry. I was going to knock, but…" Her eyes held Emma's stare, showing no signs of discomfort.

Emma fought to keep her face from blazing as red as her hair. "No problem." She turned back to the door and locked it slowly, giving herself time to recover. When she finally looked at Carter again, she almost gasped. This was the first time she'd seen her out of the unflattering ranger's uniform. Tight, faded blue jeans covered her long legs and broadcast every ripple of her muscular legs. A crisp white cotton shirt covered firm, compact breasts but clearly showed her erect nipples pressing against the fabric.

Carter followed Emma's gaze but made no attempt to pull her black leather jacket together as she stepped back. "I wanted to apologize for my behavior last night. It looks bad for the park if someone goes missing...and I was worried about you."

Emma's heartbeat quickened at Carter's admission. Her words resonated with honesty and concern. "I overreacted, and you were right. I should've come back with you. Besides, it is your job to keep the visitors from walking off the side of a mountain."

"Yeah, but it was more than that." Carter twirled her necklace between her fingers and scuffed her boot against the edge of the porch. Emma had the feeling Carter was about to say more, so she waited. "Could I offer you a ride to town? I have to go. Plus, I'd like to make up for being such an ass last night."

Emma regarded Carter unabashedly for the first time. Carter didn't seem nervous or shy, but her words didn't come easily, as if merely speaking was an effort that required concentration. And that vulnerability tugged at Emma's heart. She longed to understand and protect this woman who seemingly needed no protection. Her heart pounded wildly, and she realized Carter was waiting for a response.

She cleared her dry throat and tried. "Uh...I need to go by the grocery store, but I don't want to inconvenience you."

"I don't mind dropping by on the way back."

"Okay, if you're sure it won't be a bother."

"No bother."

On the short ride, Emma watched Carter's agile fingers maneuver the steering wheel and gearshift. She imagined those hands on her body. What effect would they have? Would she be as unmoved as she'd been with Sheri, or could Carter summon her passion? She took a deep breath and found her reporter's voice. "So, do you have other family besides Ann?"

Carter gave her an almost pained look. "No."

Emma hesitated, not wanting to cause discomfort but unable to suppress her need to know. "What about your parents?"

"No. It's just me and Ann." Another artful dodge by the private ranger. "What about your family? Are they nearby?"

"My father disappeared during the Gulf War, and my mother lives on the opposite side of the country. My father was an embedded journalist, and my mother was an architect, retired now. I see her a couple of times a year."

"Did you move around a lot as a child? I always wondered what it would be like to travel, like Ann did when she was with the national guard. Seems exciting." Carter's voice had a faraway sound, like she was picturing herself in some exotic locale.

"We followed my dad to assignments all over the world. I guess some of it was exciting, but you miss a lot too."

Carter looked over at her. "Like what?"

"A permanent home with family traditions, getting to know classmates, forming strong friendships and relationships. My father was seldom home, my mother worked long hours, and I was often with a sitter, at summer camp, or at boarding school. My last birthday party was when I turned five. We lived in Germany. My mother had decorated the dining room with balloons and streamers, and we were waiting for my father, who'd promised to be there." Her chest tightened with a flood of sadness. "I'm sorry. It was a… long time ago."

Carter reached over and squeezed Emma's hand where it rested on her lap. "You don't need to apologize, Emma. You have nothing to be sorry for. I'm sure that hurt a lot."

"Thank you. Distract me. What about you and your family?" The atmosphere in the Jeep noticeably shifted from sparking chemistry to strained discomfort. Carter obviously didn't want to discuss her family, and Emma longed to know more about them.

"No time." Carter parked on the street near the library.

Their ride was already over, and she hadn't even scratched the surface of Carter's defenses, while exposing some of her own. "Okay."

"Shall I pick you up here around four?"

"I'll see you then, and thanks for the lift." She exited the Jeep before either of them had to say anything else.

On the walk to Fannie Buffkin's house, Emma considered tactful ways to revisit the conversation with Carter and, if that failed, how to pump Ann for information. Fannie's door opened as if she'd been expected, but she didn't see anyone. She poked her head inside. "Mrs. Buffkin?"

"What are you waiting for, an engraved invitation? Come in."

Emma followed the sound of Fannie's voice to the same sitting room as before. "How did you do that?"

Fannie, dressed today in housecoat and slippers, smiled as if she had a secret she wasn't going to share, but then said, "I have special powers. Crystal, my part-time helper, saw you coming from the center of town. There are advantages to living on a hill. Nobody can slip up on you." She gave Emma an appraising glance. "Had a feeling I'd see you again. What brought you back? Your father's memory and a bit of personal pride?"

"You piqued my curiosity. How did you know invoking my father's name would work?"

"Calculated risk. He was an honorable man. My husband and I followed his coverage of the war religiously. His disappearance was a great loss to the field of journalism, as I'm sure it was to your family. I knew if you had half his courage and professional dedication, you'd come around."

"And your risk paid off."

Fannie sat regally in the worn chair as if holding court. She brushed at wrinkles in her frayed housecoat like it was a designer dress. She clearly hadn't been expecting guests today. Emma felt sorry for her and knew Fannie would hate that.

"If you're willing to lie to get me here, this story must be important."

"Does that mean you'll write the piece?"

"That depends on the subject and your promise to be truthful with me from now on. I have to warn you that I will cross-check everything you tell me through other sources."

"I understand. Let's get to it. My brother, Theodore Wayne Thompson, was murdered thirty-seven years ago, and no one has bothered to find out who did it or why." She retrieved a framed picture from the table behind her and handed it to Emma. "I've raised hell, talked to every lawman ever elected or hired, called every politician local and state, and written every newspaper in the country begging for answers."

Emma stared at the photograph of a distinguished-looking man as if he might speak. "A *murder*? That's certainly different from a history piece."

"I have no interest in the history of this place! My family *is* the damn history."

Emma's mind hummed with excitement, but her reporter's instinct urged caution. The world was full of people who couldn't accept hard facts and wanted a reporter to write a story, as if it could change the outcome. "I'm so sorry about your brother, but I have to ask why you think he was murdered. Wasn't an investigation conducted at the time?"

"If you can call it an investigation. The lawmen around this town couldn't investigate their way out of an outhouse with directions on the door. It was a sham."

"Did you get a copy of the police inquiry, and could I see it?" Emma needed something concrete to add credence to Fannie's allegations.

"I'm telling you there wasn't any inquiry—just a missing-person's report." Fannie snorted with disgust and pushed her thick glasses up on her nose. She dug under the cushion of the discolored wing chair, produced a brownish piece of paper, and shoved it toward Emma. "This is all I've got. It's a few statements from people in town that don't say much."

The paper contained barely visible handwritten notes on official-looking Patrick County letterhead. Coffee stains and grease obstructed most of the content. Emma strained to make out any legible comments but couldn't. She handed the paper back.

"A missing-person's report? I thought you said he was murdered." The more Fannie talked, the more confused her story became. Why hadn't Harriett mentioned anything about a murder or disappearance? Surely it would have made news in a small town like Stuart, even if it didn't make the papers.

"Why don't you tell *me* what's fishy about this, Emma? My brother was only thirty years old and heir to half of what our granddaddy built in this town, which was considerable. He was a happily married man, expecting his first child, a church-going pillar of the community, and just a decent hard-working man and boss.

"The night he disappeared was a strange one. Theo was going to the factory to close after second shift, around ten thirty, but Sandra, his wife, volunteered. She was planning to check on her mother anyway. He agreed but then left shortly after her and didn't say where he was going. Neither of them came back. I figured Sandra had to stay with her mother. That happened sometimes. But they both just disappeared without a word to anybody. Doesn't that strike you as strange?"

"I have to admit it doesn't make sense. What was the official conclusion?"

"Sheriff said he just disappeared, no sign of foul play, nothing to indicate he didn't leave of his own free will. And they left it at that, but I can't."

"And what about his wife, Sandra? What did she say?"

"Turns out she'd gone to the hospital that night—miscarriage. Afterward she lived with her mother, who passed on a few months later. Sandra said she never saw Theo after that night. She and I grew apart after he disappeared...and the baby...nothing to bind us anymore."

"I'll want to talk with her."

Fannie shook her head. "She's dead, and I'm seventy-one years old and don't have a lot of time left to find answers." A tear trickled down her face, sliding her thick glasses to the end of her nose. She pushed them back up and looked over at Emma.

Fannie's eyes reminded her of her mother's as she'd waited for news about her missing husband. She and Emma had reminisced for hours, trying to remain hopeful. Even through her mother's laughter and words of encouragement, Emma saw the look of hopelessness—the same look Fannie Buffkin wore. She'd been unable to ease her mother's pain or answer her questions about her husband's disappearance all those years earlier. Maybe she wouldn't fail this time. Could she possibly find out what happened to Fannie's brother? "Why didn't you tell me this was why you wanted me to come here?"

"After my husband died I couldn't bring myself to do much of anything. Then I decided to try one last time to get to the bottom of my brother's case. I hadn't gotten anywhere telling the truth before. I was afraid you'd call up here first, and they'd tell you I was just a crazy old lady who couldn't accept that her brother had probably run off with some mistress he'd been hiding. So, I offered to pay handsomely for an article about the history of my family and this town." Fannie sniffed, clutched the picture of her brother to her bosom, and tilted her bun-coiffed head to the ceiling in defiance. "It's a damn shame when the story of some rinky-dink town is more important than a man's life."

The pain in Fannie's words was a hot blade fusing Emma's resolve. "I'll check into this, but a lot depends on how many people are willing to talk to me, how much they feel comfortable divulging, and how much they remember. And to be honest, when people have been quiet this long, they're not usually inclined to break their silence without some real motivation." Emma leaned forward to soften her words. "I have to warn you, when you uncover the truth, it's not always what you want to hear."

"I understand. My brother wasn't always kind or considerate, even to me, but he was my brother. All I ask is that you try, Emma. And if it helps, I'll offer a reward." Fannie rose, indicating their time was up, and escorted Emma to the door.

"You purposely chose me, didn't you? You must've known I'd be compelled to follow up since your brother and my father both disappeared without a trace."

"I prayed you would." Fannie grabbed her hand and shoved something into her palm. "And thank you for coming back. Please keep me informed."

"What's this?" Emma looked at the small silk drawstring bag.

"Some of my brother's hair. Maybe it'll help guide you to the truth."

"Fannie, I can't take this. It's too personal. You should hold on to it as a keepsake."

"Don't worry. I have more. It'll make me feel better knowing you've got a little piece of Theo to inspire you. Promise me you won't stop until you find the truth."

Emma looked around one last time. Layers of dust had collected on family heirlooms, and priceless antiques stood in noticeable disrepair. The opulent surroundings obviously didn't mean as much to Fannie without someone to share them. She wanted to help this lonely woman find the truth of her brother's disappearance, so she consciously chose not to consider her odds of being able to do so. "I promise."

Emma's cell phone vibrated as she walked back toward the center of town, and she read the new text message. Harriett Smoltz had sent the names of the folks for her to contact about Stuart's history. There were only two: Sheriff Sam Echols and Sylvie Martinez, manager of the Riverside Hotel. She was disappointed, but Harriett hadn't steered her wrong so far, and Emma had asked about residents with historical information, not witnesses concerning a missing person or homicide. She texted a brief thank you and headed to the sheriff's office.

Her first priority was a legible copy of the missing-person's report. Once she was satisfied there was nothing unusual about the circumstances of Theodore Thompson's disappearance, she could report back to Fannie. She didn't really expect to find evidence of foul play, but her gut and her commitment to Fannie's cause mandated she be thorough.

The two-room sheriff's office was very utilitarian. A metal enclosure on one side of the space served as a holding cell, while an antique desk with its JUSTICE OF THE PEACE/SHERIFF placard took up the rest of the area. The middle-aged man sitting behind the desk rose with effort and offered his hand as Emma entered. His genuine smile crinkled the sun-weathered skin of his face and lifted his handlebar mustache just enough to reveal slightly irregular teeth.

"Good morning, ma'am. I'm Sheriff Echols. You must be the reporter Ms. Smoltz has been telling everybody about."

"Guilty as charged, Sheriff. Emma Ferguson. It's nice to meet you."

"I understand you're doing a history piece on our little town," he said, motioning to a chair beside his desk.

"That's what I thought too, but I'm actually here on another matter. Something came up rather unexpectedly today during an interview. I'm hoping you can clear it up for me."

"I'll do my best." His truth-seeking eyes never left hers, and she felt almost uncomfortable under his scrutiny.

While Emma relayed her conversation with Fannie and her allegations of foul play, the sheriff's expression remained deadpan. "I've been expecting this. I called the county seat yesterday where the archives are housed and had them fax a copy of the original report." He shuffled through some papers stacked on the edge of his desk and handed her a file. "I'm not sure it's going to shed much light on the situation. Theodore Thompson's case appears to be a missing person, though I have to admit it seems odd. People who have as much to live for as Theodore don't usually disappear without a reason or a trace."

"Thank you, Sheriff." Emma slid the folder into her messenger bag. She'd examine it closely later and make notes. "I think that's why Mrs. Buffkin is having such a hard time accepting it. Did you notice anything unusual as you read the file?"

"Not really. The interviews probably aren't up to today's standards, but the officer was inexperienced and dealing with prominent members of the community. He probably got his marching orders from them or some politician and was reluctant to step on their toes."

"Just one more question. Have you heard any gossip around town about this case? You know how tales can grow through the years."

"No, ma'am. I can't say that I have. Anybody who's still alive and saw or heard anything tells the same identical story they gave to the officer that night."

That should've raised red flags then and now. In her experience, fabricated stories seldom deviated while a witness's truthful version shifted through time. "Thanks, Sheriff." Emma stood and Sheriff Echols followed her out.

Emma dug a bottle of water from her bag and settled near the fountain at the center of town, recalling her conversation with the sheriff. He had no real stake in Theodore Thompson's case, but he'd obviously read the file and familiarized himself with the details. And if he hadn't heard anything through the years about the disappearance, how did he know the original witness statements hadn't changed? Was he withholding something or just trying to save her a lot of useless work?

She pulled the folder out of her bag, opened it, and stared in disbelief at the meager contents. The first page was a basic missing-person report on Theodore Thompson that included a statement from Sandra, his wife, followed by a single-page witness statement from Sylvie Martinez. Both pages contained a maximum of three paragraphs and provided nothing significant. How had the police failed to thoroughly investigate the disappearance of the most prominent man in town? Even a rookie would've done more follow-up than this. Her curiosity morphed into full-blown suspicion.

She scanned the quiet street and tried to imagine what this small town might've been like thirty-seven years ago as a vibrant furniture hub with a close-knit community. Her thoughts drifted to Carter. She would've been a small child. What had happened to her parents? Emma's questions about her family had made Carter withdraw, and the more she withdrew, the more Emma wanted to understand why.

Her own parents hadn't been around much during her childhood, and she'd struggled for perfection in school because it was the only thing her parents seemed to value and praise her for. She'd felt more like another cog in the family wheel than a child. She'd missed the warm familial feeling some of her friends enjoyed with their parents. Had Carter had that connection to her parents? How would her own life have turned out if she'd been raised with a strong family bond and in a place where community really mattered?

Emma stuffed the disappointing folder back into her bag, finished her water, and walked to the Riverside Hotel to talk with Sylvie Martinez. The bold geometric lines of the front door and the impressive stained-glass windows emphasized the building's Art Deco theme. Like much of downtown Stuart, the Riverside had been meticulously tended and refurbished through the years. When she stepped inside, she noticed that the contrasting wood inlays and heavily lacquered surfaces had a comforting feel. The soft, lush surfaces were swathed in vivid colors, beckoning visitors to sit and relax. Why hadn't she booked a room here?

She took a seat in the lobby and watched the bustling activity, getting a feel for the place, how it was run, and who was in charge. She'd already spotted Sylvie Martinez floating from station to station, patiently answering questions, efficiently handling problems, and cordially interacting with the staff. When she approached the manager, Emma already had a sense of her character.

"Mrs. Martinez, I'm Emma Ferguson. I wonder if I could have a few minutes of your time? I can see you're busy, so I promise to be quick."

Mrs. Martinez shook her hand and led her to an office behind the reception desk. "We'll be more comfortable in here, Ms. Ferguson." She directed Emma to a seat in front of the desk with a nameplate that read THE BIG KAHUNA. "My staff's idea of a joke," she said, noticing Emma's smile. "How can I help you?" Her soft, pleasant voice imparted an immediate feeling of confidence, and

Emma understood why her employees would follow her. "I hear you're a reporter? What could possibly be newsworthy in Stuart these days? The last big headline in the paper stated MAN HITS DEER WITH CAR AND LIVES."

"I'm looking into a missing person's report from thirty-seven years ago."

Mrs. Martinez's forehead wrinkled, and the lines around her mouth tightened. "You must've been talking to Fannie Buffkin. She keeps that story alive. I'm afraid I can't offer any more than I told the officer that night."

"I'd appreciate it if you'd go over what you saw again for me."

Sylvie settled back in the chair and cocked her head to the right. "I was working here, as I have been for the past fifty-five years, helping my father get ready for the next day's breakfast and closing for the night. I was putting the specials' board on the front porch and looked across the street toward the train station. Nothing captures a kid's attention like trains going to distant places. I saw Sandra Thompson pass by the station and go into the furniture factory. Either she or Theodore closed the business every night after the late shift and janitor left, but I never saw Theo that night. I went back inside, and we locked the doors and went to bed. There weren't many people out because of the bitter cold."

"What time would you say it was when you saw Mrs. Thompson go into the factory?"

"A little after ten thirty. We closed the lobby at ten, and it usually took about thirty minutes to straighten up and get out."

"And you didn't see anything unusual that night?"

Sylvie studied the papers on her desk with too much concentration before replying, "Don't think so."

Emma considered Sylvie's hesitation and noncommittal response before pressing further. "Please think carefully, Sylvie. It would really be helpful."

"Well, I wouldn't really call it unusual."

Emma tightened her grip on her pen until it quivered between her fingers. "Please. Anything could be important."

"I'd left part of the easel inside the hotel and went back in to get it. When I came out, I thought I saw Harriett Smoltz going toward the factory, but I was wrong."

"Why are you so sure you were wrong?"

"Because she was on the telephone switchboard that night. Then I remembered Hannah, her twin sister, was relieving her at eleven, so it was obviously Hannah I saw heading to work. The next day I asked Harriett and she clarified it for me, exactly what I thought."

"And why did you think it was Harriett? They are twins."

Sylvie shook her head. "You *have* seen how Harriett dresses, right?"

Emma nodded.

"Well, that's never changed. Hannah is a bit more stylish, which isn't saying much. But it was bitterly cold and she was wearing a heavy coat."

"And how can you be so sure this was the same night Mr. Thompson disappeared?"

"Because he didn't show up to open the plant for first shift. It's a big deal around here when folks can't get to their jobs. And Mrs. Thompson was in the hospital the next morning. She miscarried their baby. There was a lot to remember about that day. Folks were real concerned about Sandra. She was a lovely soul, but everybody could've lived just fine without Mr. T."

"Why do you say that?"

"I hate to speak ill of the missing or dead, but Theo was nothing like his father or his grandfather. He'd rather cheat you out of money than come by it honest. He dreamed of buying up the entire Main Street block and converting it into retail shops and restaurants. He was always after the property owners to sell, sell, sell, especially Daniel Tanner. Dan's drugstore sat right smack-dab in the middle of Theo's planned strip mall."

"Aside from being an ambitious man, he was okay?"

"All I can say is what I know for sure, Ms. Ferguson. Anything else is pure hearsay and not worth the breath it takes to pass along.

He treated the people who worked here back then like we were subhuman. You don't forget how a person makes you feel."

Emma's enthusiasm waned as the adrenaline vanished, along with the possibility of uncovering some hidden clue. It wasn't a crime to be a horrible person, but it might be a motive for murder if she found proof of foul play. She stood to leave. "Thank you, Sylvie. I appreciate your time."

As she exited the hotel, Emma felt her disappointment like an oversized piece of clothing. She'd allowed herself to become excited about a real investigation, but nothing was panning out. Sylvie Martinez was the first person to say anything uncomplimentary about Theodore Thompson, so maybe their clash had been personal. Time would tell.

Chapter Six

Emma held her breath and quietly opened the library door so the bell wouldn't ring. No sign of Harriett. Excellent. She still had time to do some research regarding the days surrounding Thompson's disappearance before meeting Carter for their ride home. As she tiptoed down the hallway and rounded the corner toward the microfilm section, she heard footsteps behind her.

"Can I help you, ma'am?" a soft, younger voice asked, obviously not Harriett.

Emma sighed with relief and faced the woman, her pencil-thin frame topped by pigtails protruding from her head like a schoolgirl. "Is Harriett here?"

"No, ma'am. She pops in and out at will, but I'd be glad to help."

"No thanks. I need to look through some old files."

"You know how to operate the equipment then?" The young attendant blushed, obviously eager to end the face-to-face encounter and return to her bookish chores.

"Yes. I'm familiar with it. I'll let you know if I need anything." The comment brought a genuine smile as the girl retreated to her desk surrounded by books and files stacked just high enough to hide behind, should she choose to do so. She felt sorry for the painfully shy girl and the daily torture it must be for her to work side by side with extroverted Harriett Smoltz.

Emma settled at the computer and began her search in the fall of 1978. There had to be something in the paper about the disappearance of a prominent businessman, especially in a small town like Stuart. It didn't take long before an article captured her attention.

The headline read LOCAL MAN GOES MISSING, but the article mostly recounted his numerous positions in the community. Mr. Thompson was an heir to the Thompson Furniture fortune and president of the local Lions Club, but no mention of any outstanding contributions to the area other than employment opportunities. Practically everybody in town had speculated about how and why Thompson disappeared. Theories ranged from alien abduction to murder for hire, but Emma found no mention of evidence or an investigation to determine the real facts.

In an effort to put closure on her inquiry, she fast-forwarded through the paper for the next several years. Occasionally a Waldo-type article raised the question of where Theodore Thompson might be, and a contest at the town fair offered a prize for the most creative essay on the subject.

Emma smashed the fast-forward key and let the machine slowly wind down. Her eyes were glazing over. Just before she gave up, a partially displayed article in the lower corner of the screen caught her eye. She rolled it into view and read the caption, BONES FOUND AT OLD FACTORY, 1985. A light tingle raised the hairs on the back of her neck, and she zeroed in, scanning the article more closely. "Children playing in an old furniture factory found bones of unknown origin. The sheriff was contacted and the bones were collected."

That can't be all. She scoured the rest of the year for further information but found no mention of the mysterious bones or their possible origin. Emma made a quick copy of the article and dashed from the library toward the sheriff's office. Her instincts told her there was indeed a story here, and it involved the disappearance of Theodore Wayne Thompson.

"You ready to go?"

Emma had been so engrossed in thought as she hurried along the sidewalk she hadn't seen Carter pull alongside her in the Jeep.

"Actually, would it be a terrible imposition if I asked you to wait? I need to pop into the sheriff's office for just a second." Emma had to know the answer to this question now.

At Carter's agreeable nod, she charged into Echols's office waving the article in her hand. "Do you still have this evidence somewhere?"

Sheriff Echols leaned back in his chair and stared at her without responding for several seconds. "Evidence of what, Ms. Ferguson?" She handed him the article, and he glanced over it before handing it back. "This is far from evidence of anything. There was a lot of speculation about whether those bones belonged to Thompson or even to a human being."

"What about now, Sheriff? Technology has progressed significantly." Emma's voice had an edge, and she breathed deeply to maintain her professionalism. Why hadn't someone followed up on this since the discovery?

"I hope you're not creating trouble where there isn't any. Folks in this town have enough to gossip about without help from outsiders, no disrespect intended."

"I'm not trying to dig up trouble, Sheriff. I'm trying to put it to rest."

"Contrary to what you city folks think, not all small-town law enforcement officers are hicks who eat doughnuts, drink coffee, and chase women with their blue lights."

"I think you're a very professional law-enforcement officer who'd like to get to the bottom of an outstanding old case as much as I would. If you know anything about these bones, I'd be very appreciative." Apparently, her flattery worked because the sheriff sat a bit straighter in his chair and nodded.

"When this discovery was made in 1985, the coroner said the remains were from a male about the age Theodore Thompson would've been when he disappeared. The large bones were mostly intact and showed no signs of trauma, but the smaller bones of the hands, feet, and even the skull were either missing or in so many pieces we couldn't tell anything for sure."

"What about clothes, personal effects?"

"Nothing, no other evidence, no suspects. We were optimistic it was Thompson but couldn't prove it. Fannie hounded us for years, but the technology wasn't there to conclusively identify the remains."

"So you actually worked this case?"

"Not the original, of course, but the recovery of the bones was mine. It was my first big challenge as sheriff. I called in the Virginia Bureau of Criminal Investigation to help with excavation, and agents worked for days trying to recover the full skeleton."

Emma felt a little guilty for doubting the sheriff but still needed more. "And?"

"This is the embarrassing part. At night when we closed the site, townsfolk snuck in and dug around in the rubble. We didn't have the manpower for proper security. In the morning they'd walk into the office with bits of bones and hand them over, just trying to help. This kept up for almost a week, and by the time we finished there was a pile of bones twice the size of a human skeleton, and almost everyone in town had contributed to the stack."

"So much for the chain of evidence," Emma muttered.

"Exactly, and we never have been able to clear a single resident completely. So you see why this little story of yours won't help even if you find out it was Thompson and even if he was murdered. We'd need an eye witness or a full confession to bring charges."

"I understand, but humor me, Sheriff. I need to do this. Where are these bones now?"

"State crime lab, if they haven't been destroyed. They don't keep stuff this long."

"Can you call and see if they still have them? Now, please?" Emma was starting to feel hopeful about at least verifying Thompson's death.

Sheriff Echols scratched his head. "Even if they still have the bones, they won't run an analysis without a law-enforcement request, and I see no reason to issue one at this point."

Emma started to object, but the definitive expression on Echols's face convinced her it would be futile. "Thanks for your help, Sheriff."

Emma rushed outside, held up her forefinger in Carter's direction, and ran into the post office next door. She scribbled a quick note, stuffed and addressed the padded envelope, and slid it across the counter to the postmaster. "I need this to go overnight priority, please." She paid the postage and hurried to the waiting Jeep.

"Still need to make that grocery run?" Carter asked.

"If you have time, that would be great. My complimentary supplies are dwindling, and I can't survive without coffee."

"There's a Food Lion on the way."

A few minutes later, they were walking side by side like a married couple as Carter pushed a shopping cart around the grocery store. She'd imagined Carter would be uncomfortable doing such domestic chores, but her shoulders were relaxed and her pace suggested she was in no hurry.

"Do you do this often?"

"Not really." Carter glanced sideways at her and grinned. "But you've probably guessed Ann does the cooking and grocery shopping around our house. I'm occasionally coerced into emergency runs for things I can easily identify and not mess up."

Emma reached for a bag of whole Colombian coffee beans, remembered she didn't have a grinder, and grabbed the ground instead. "I find cooking therapeutic but don't do it often anymore." Emma regretted her comment when Carter stopped the cart and waited for her to explain. She'd cooked for Sheri initially, but she hadn't been around much as their relationship deteriorated.

Carter's gaze held hers for a beat, and then she smiled and pushed the buggy forward. "You don't have to talk about it. But just for the record, you can cook for me anytime you need therapy. I'm a good guinea pig. Cast-iron stomach." She patted her abdomen, and Emma had to laugh.

"I'll keep that in mind."

As they approached the meat counter, the burly butcher waved enthusiastically. "Hey, Carter, Ms. Ferguson, how are you today? Something I can help you with?"

Emma gave Carter a questioning glance.

Carter leaned close and whispered, "Small town. Everybody knows your name already."

Everybody? She was exposed, a deer in the headlights. No. Wait. She reconsidered her knee-jerk reaction. The warmth in the butcher's greeting made her feel something different—like she belonged. Being known, she decided, was a good thing. She returned the butcher's wave and even smiled. "I'm good…"

"Peter," Carter whispered, even closer to her ear this time, her breath sending chills down Emma's spine. She wanted to close her eyes and savor the feeling, but Peter was waiting expectantly.

"Peter." She pointed to the meat display. "Could I get one of those small roasts and a couple of the salmon fillets, please?"

Peter nodded and reached for her items.

"You've just made his day," Carter said.

"How's that?"

"You called him by name."

"Doesn't everybody in town know Peter the butcher?"

"Yes, but not everybody is kind or thoughtful enough to address him by name. His father had a little run-in with the law last year, and the family is still paying the social tab. Some folks in this town think they're better than others. You're the new girl, and you acknowledged him. That means a lot."

Carter's observation surprised Emma. She hadn't expected Carter to be so attuned to the feelings of other people. One more thing she appreciated about her. But the realization that people were petty in small towns as well as in cities was disappointing. Maybe she was being naive, but she wanted to believe that camaraderie, cooperation, and mutual support existed here, in the kind of place she'd always wanted to live.

When Peter handed the carefully packaged items across the display case, Emma smiled. "Thank you, Peter. I look forward to seeing you again soon."

While Emma checked out, four people greeted Carter; two inquired about Ann and two others asked about her children's group, FACES. Carter and her aunt were obviously an established and respected presence in Stuart.

As she paid the cashier, Emma wondered if her parents had exchanged greetings with people while walking through a grocery store in any town they'd lived in. Had her mother known the name of her local butcher or the shopkeeper down the street? Did her father know the given names of the soldiers he'd shadowed during battle? The sobering thought made Emma long for a connection she'd never experienced. Her somber mood carried over to the ride back to the park.

"You're quiet this afternoon," Carter said after several minutes in silence.

That's certainly the pot calling the kettle black. But their morning trip had been tense enough. Emma didn't want to spoil this time by airing her personal miseries. "Yeah, this story is more complicated than I imagined."

"Really? How complicated can history facts be?" Carter asked with a sympathetic grin.

"Different people have different perspectives. I have to sort out what's true and what's just perception."

"I like learning about the past," Carter said. "I believe it keeps us from repeating the same mistakes."

"Why don't you regale me with your knowledge of Stuart past and present?" Emma mostly just wanted to hear Carter's words roll off her full, luscious lips. She warmed as she remembered Carter's over-protectiveness last night and her contrition this morning when she apologized. She'd never met a woman who possessed such strength and vulnerability and who guarded both so fiercely. Carter was a paradox, and Emma planned to unravel her with the same vigor she devoted to the stories she pursued.

"Anything special you want to know?"

Emma watched Carter's lips move and imagined them closing over hers, stealing her breath. She wet her lips with the tip of her tongue. She'd never fantasized so freely nor been so willing to consider her hopes, but her timing was horrible.

"Emma?"

Her named rolled so casually off Carter's tongue that she wanted to hear it over and over again as Carter took her in her arms. She shook her head to dislodge the image. "I'd like to know everything. Could you come by the cabin later? Say around eight, if you don't have plans."

"Love to, but I can't. It's kids' night," Carter replied as she drove up to Emma's cabin.

"Kids' night?"

"I host the kids in my FACES group every other month. We usually have a cookout, play games, and just talk." She glanced over at Emma. "If you want, you could join us. You might enjoy it."

Emma weighed a night alone in the cabin against spending more time with Carter in any situation. Plus, she loved children—hearing their laughter and experiencing their honesty before all innocence was socialized out of them. "I'd love that. Can I help with anything?"

"Nope. Just show up at the picnic area beside the office at five thirty. Dress warmly and leave your insecurities at home."

"Uh, okay." What did that mean? As she walked toward the cabin, she wondered if she was making a mistake. How uncomfortable could a cookout with Carter and half a dozen kids be? She looked at her watch. Still time to do a little work.

Emma made notes about her conversations with the sheriff and Sylvie Martinez before calling her contact with the Virginia Bureau of Criminal Investigation. She and Rick Hardy had known each other since college, when he'd had a huge crush on her, even after she told him she was a lesbian. They'd kept in touch through the years, and Rick joked they'd marry when he divorced his gorgeous, rich wife and Emma lost her mind.

"Hello, handsome. Miss me?"

"Always." No matter when she called, Rick sounded happy to hear from her. Their friendship was the only unconditional love she'd ever experienced, and she felt their closeness every time they spoke. "Is this business or pleasure?"

"It's always a pleasure to talk to you, my friend. How are you and Carolyn?"

"Excellent as usual, but we miss seeing you. Promise to visit soon. Now, get to the point. I hear some anxiety in your voice. You're on the trail of a story."

He was the only one who could read her just by her tone. "Yes, I have a professional need." She explained the story and the article she'd found in the archives. "I overnighted a copy of the newspaper clipping along with some of Theodore Thompson's hair for comparison, if you find the bones. You should get it in the morning mail."

"The connection sounds thin, Emma. Even if the bones haven't been destroyed, I'm not sure I can justify looking into it, especially with no new evidence. Why the interest?"

"An elderly lady has been missing her brother for thirty-seven years. She won't live forever, and I'd like to help her."

"Could your helpfulness have anything to do with your father?"

They'd been best friends in college, shared their hopes, dreams, insecurities, and cried together over losses. After all those years and his continued support, she couldn't lie to him. Even if she tried, he'd know. "Probably. They both disappeared and left family members searching for answers."

He was quiet, and she waited for him to think things through in his logical and methodical manner. "I'll get started on locating the bones. If I find them, and when I get the information you sent, I'll work up a petition for review. If, and that's a big if, I get approval, I'll have to submit a request to the DNA lab for analysis. You know how backed up those folks get. It could be a while before we hear anything."

"Come on, Rick. A contractor is salivating to tear the factory down where the bones were found. We have to work quickly." She pictured his surfer-boy good looks and stroked his ego. "Somewhere in that DNA lab a poor defenseless damsel toils daily, just praying you'll walk in and ask her for a favor."

"Stop with the hand job. Maybe I could have it in a few days—"

"Please. You know I love you." She said the magic words.

"Okay. I'll try to get it back to you as soon as possible. Be careful. If there is a connection between these bones and your missing person, you could be in danger. People don't like strangers digging up the past."

❖

Carter skidded the Jeep to a halt in front of the park office and then cursed her lack of control. She didn't need to broadcast her excitement about seeing Emma later, especially around Ann. She steadied her breathing and opened the office door. "You ready to go home?"

"What's got your knickers in a twist?" Ann motioned toward the front. "You stirred up enough dust out there to create an environmental hazard. What's the hurry?"

"I'd just like to get home and change clothes before…" She'd stepped in it now.

"Before what? Got a hot date?"

Was it a date? Had her invitation to the cookout been a date cloaked in business attire? And if so, did it matter? And why was she so reluctant to admit it to Ann? "Maybe. I'm not sure. I just asked Emma to come by the cookout with the kids. I thought she'd enjoy it. You know, stranger in town, no friends."

Ann eyeballed her as if she were a rare species. "Really? That's what you're going with? You're attracted to each other. Of course it's a date, no matter what you call it." Ann grabbed her coat and followed Carter to the Jeep. "Just do me a favor and be careful."

Carter pulled out of the park and drove faster than usual toward home. "I thought you liked Emma."

"I do." She placed her hand gently over Carter's, where it rested on the gearshift. "You know I love you, but your track record with women doesn't bode well for long-term relationships. You've been seeing a married woman off and on for a year, and Emma seems like she's going through something right now. I'm just asking you to be careful, for both your sakes."

Carter rolled her eyes. "FYI, she's not married."

"She has a partner. I don't condone that sort of thing."

"Her partner runs around too, but we're not serious anyway. I never am."

"You could be, if you let yourself care enough…for someone special," Ann said.

And that was the part Carter wasn't worried about. She had built-in safeguards to ensure she didn't overstep—Ann, her job, the occasional rendezvous with an unavailable woman, and her work with the children in the community. She'd never abandon her responsibilities for a long-term relationship, especially not with an out-of-towner. She wasn't denying her attraction to Emma, but it would only be sex, just like the others. "Can we please talk about something else?"

"Fine. What did you do in town today?"

"Went grocery shopping."

Ann turned sideways slowly and pinned Carter with her stare. "I have to practically beg you to pick up a carton of milk from the store. Were you kidnapped, forced at gunpoint, or seduced inside by a gorgeous woman?"

"Emma needed a few things for the cabin, and we stopped on the way home. No biggie."

"No biggie except for the fact that you hate shopping of any kind."

Carter absently tugged at her necklace and then quickly dropped her hand. "It wasn't so bad." She'd actually liked perusing the aisles that were nearly as foreign to her as they were to Emma, locating the items she needed, and chatting with locals as if they were at a social. Normally the thought of doing anything so domestic with another woman would've given her hives, but she'd felt at ease with Emma, even enjoyed their closeness and sharing a new experience. But it had been a necessity and just a little fun. Seriously, no biggie.

"Do you need any help tonight? I left the hot-dog buns and marshmallows on the counter, and the dogs and fixings are in the fridge."

Carter dashed around Ann and into the house. "I'll be fine. Thanks." She rifled through her closet, chose a pair of faded jeans, and tried on three shirts before settling on a gray-plaid flannel. "Jeez, Carter, you're going to a cookout in the woods, not a fancy restaurant." She laughed. Her jeans and flannel would be considered dressy in any Stuart restaurant. She wiped her sweaty hands down the front of her jeans, kissed Ann, and drove back to the park.

As she collected the supplies from the office and set up the fire, Carter kept glancing toward Emma's cabin. Why was she so nervous about seeing her again? They'd be with six energetic and highly observant children. Any chance of private time or even a furtive glance without being noticed seemed unlikely.

If this were a real date, Carter would've planned it much better and definitely without an audience. Her seduction would be carefully choreographed from cocktails and appetizers to dinner, dessert, and a slow progression to the bedroom. She'd undress Emma—a spear of arousal shot through her, shattering her carefully imagined plan. A date with Emma Ferguson would never follow anyone else's agenda. Something about that realization excited Carter more than her seduction scenario.

CHAPTER SEVEN

Okay, guys, quiet down." Carter waved her hands to get everybody's attention, and four eager faces turned in her direction. "Let me introduce our guest this evening." She turned to Emma and almost lost her train of thought. Emma wore a bright-green sweater that set off her red hair perfectly. Her jeans were so tight, Carter wondered if she could walk in them.

"Well…who is she?" a chubby African-American girl asked.

Carter smiled at Simone, the latest addition and least trusting of the group. She loved the girl's frankness and curiosity and vowed to nurture it. She doubted anyone else would. "This is Ms. Emma Ferguson. She's a freelance reporter."

Simone leaned over to another child but spoke loud enough for everybody to hear. "That means she makes stuff up."

Emma stifled a laugh. "You're right, Simone, and if I'm lucky, they pay me for it."

Simone eyed Emma suspiciously. "So, you Carter's girlfriend or what?"

Carter would've paid money for a picture of Emma's face. Her eyebrow arched, mouth dropped open, and she glanced at Carter. "She's a guest in the park and doesn't know anyone, so I invited her to the cookout. You guys are fun, and she needs to have some fun."

Simone seemed to consider her answer before finally nodding. "Okay. That's cool."

"Any more questions about Emma?" No one spoke up. "Is everybody okay with her being here, because if you're not, I'll ask her to leave. This is your night."

"You'd do that?" Simone squinted as if divining the truth from her.

"Of course I would. We made a deal when you joined the group. We respect each other's feelings and talk about anything that makes us uncomfortable. Right?" Every time Carter met with these kids, her admiration and affection for them grew. Each one had come to her broken and afraid for various reasons and had gradually opened up to her privately. Some of them still had issues with groups, but all were making progress. "Last chance. Any objections?"

All the children shook their heads.

"Okay, when I call your name, raise your hand so Emma knows who you are. Emma, meet Maddie."

A young blonde with curls and an eagerness to please raised her hand. "Hi. If you need any help tonight, just ask."

"Thank you, Maddie," Emma said.

"Reggie." Carter pointed to a shy, skinny African-American boy who barely raised his hand and picked at his UVA basketball T-shirt.

"Hey, Reggie. I like your T-shirt," Emma said. The boy sat taller and almost smiled.

"Nico."

"That's my name. Don't wear it out." He grinned at Carter and winked at Emma.

"I thought you said there would be six." Emma looked toward the activity bus that had dropped the kids off and now waited near the office.

"A couple couldn't make it." Carter turned back to the kids gathered around the campfire. "We need to go over the safety rules. Who wants to help?" Three hands shot up. "Nico."

"Don't play with the fire."

"Right," Carter said. "Reggie."

"Uh…I got it. Don't wander off in the woods."

"Excellent. Maddie."

"Don't go down to the lake without an adult."

Carter nodded. "You guys are so smart. And what's our number-one rule, Simone?"

"If something doesn't feel right or you don't understand it, ask." Simone pumped her fist in the air. "I got that."

"You sure do," Carter said. "Okay, guys, choose sides for a quick game of cornhole. The light will be gone soon."

She left the kids talking about how to divide the group into fair teams and walked to where Emma was unwrapping paper plates and plastic forks. Carter heated under Emma's hungry gaze. "Are you all right? They can be a handful."

"I'm more than all right. Thank you for the invitation." Emma lightly touched Carter's arm before returning to her task. "The hot dogs are in that container by the grill, and all the fixings are in the cooler. I'll finish laying the table when you give me the two-minute warning."

"Two-minute warning?"

"I assume you're the grilling chef, right?"

Carter nodded.

"Then yell when the dogs are two minutes from done, and I'll put everything else out."

Carter grinned but couldn't speak. She had a sudden image of her and Emma maneuvering around each other while preparing a meal in Ann's kitchen. She felt a rush of warmth because in her vision she and Emma were both older, with threads of gray in their hair and defined laugh lines around their mouths. *What? Where did that come from?*

"Yo, Carter," Simone called out.

"Yeah? Sorry. Ready to play?"

Maddie stood with her hands on her hips, the way she always did when she had something she considered important to say. "We've decided that you, Reggie, and I are on one team, and Nico, Simone, and Emma are on the other."

"Sounds good," Carter said. Then she heard a choking sound behind her. When she turned, Emma was flapping her hand in the air in a stop motion, her face bright red.

"Nooooo…" Emma coughed again and pointed to her throat. "Sorry…water…windpipe. Not good." She finally pulled a deep breath and motioned for Carter to come closer. "I can't play cornhole. I don't even know what it is." She waved her hands down her body. "Look at me. I'm not a sporty girl." She nudged Carter back toward the kids. "You guys have fun."

Simone kicked up a pebble that skirted across the ground. "It's because of me, ain't it? You don't like me for some reason."

Carter's heart ached as she saw the pain etched so clearly on Simone's gorgeous face. She started toward her, but Emma caught her arm.

"Oh, Simone, it's not about you, really," Emma said. She stooped to the child's level and lowered her voice to a near whisper, but the others were close enough to hear. "Can I tell you a secret?"

Simone shrugged.

"I'm awful at sports, never learned to play anything. I'd just hold the team back."

"Is that all?" Simone snorted, took Emma's hand, and escorted her to the boards. "Don't worry. Me and Nico got this. Right, dude? Besides, nobody is great at everything. I bet you tell a good story."

Carter watched as Maddie and Nico hugged Emma, and Reggie fist-bumped her. Emma's shoulders visibly relaxed as she stepped behind the raised platform with a hole in one end.

"Somebody tell me the rules," Emma said, hefting one of the corn-filled bags in her hand.

Nico took another bag and swung it back and forth. "You just throw the bag and try to get it in the hole on the opposite board. One point if it lands on the board, three if it goes through, and the first team to reach…" He scratched his head as if trying to remember.

"Twenty-one wins," Reggie offered from the other side where he, Maddie, and Carter stood. "But we got Carter, and she has the longest arms."

Carter pulled a coin from her pocket. "We'll flip to see who goes first. Call it, Reggie."

"Heads." He watched the coin tumble through the air, land on the ground, and then shook his head. "They go first."

Emma tried to hand the bag she held to one of her teammates, but neither would take it. "Guess I'm first?"

Carter watched as Emma swung the bag back and forth, each swing stretching the fabric of her sweater tighter across her full breasts. The image vanished when Maddie pulled her sleeve and motioned toward Emma, who was still swinging the bag. "Throw it, please."

Emma heaved the bag toward the board Carter, Maddie, and Reggie stood behind, and they scattered as it overshot the mark and sailed in their direction.

"I'm sorry. Is everybody okay?" Emma started toward them but stopped when Carter waved her off.

"We're fine. A little less force, more finesse might work better." She motioned for Reggie to take his first throw.

He aimed carefully, made the toss, and the beanbag skidded very close to the hole. "One to zip."

Emma missed shot after shot. Each time, the desperation in her eyes grew, and she tried to back out of the game. Her last pitch didn't make contact with the board either.

Emma threw her hands up. "I'm sorry. I told you I was no good at sports. I'll leave you guys to it."

"Nobody quits," Simone said, stepping up beside Emma.

"Yeah," Nico added. "You just need to change your point of view." He looked toward Carter, and she gave him a thumbs-up. "Get down on your knees, at our level. Adults don't always have the advantage."

Emma knelt and started her swing to toss the beanbag.

"Relax your shoulders and just go with it," Simone said. "This ain't no contest. It's a game. Have fun."

Emma took a deep breath and let the bag fly. It sailed through the air, hit the board, bounced, and disappeared into the hole.

"Did you see that?" Simone was jumping up and down pointing toward the board at Carter's end. "Emma hit a bull's-eye." She gave Emma a high five. "We'll make an athlete out of you yet. Stick with me…and Nico. Three to one."

"That was awesome, Emma. Well done." Carter gave her a wink that she hoped relayed how proud she was. They played several more rounds before she stopped the game. "Guys, I'm calling this one at a tie. It's too dark to play anymore. Go to the bathhouse and wash up while I start the fire and get the hot dogs going."

"Guess I should wash up too," Emma said, and started to follow the kids.

"Hold up a second, please?" Carter stepped in front of Emma and took her hands. "You're a natural with these guys. You seem to understand what they need."

Emma's shy smile almost brought Carter to her knees.

"Everybody needs the same thing. Understanding, acceptance, and love."

"You're exactly right." Carter kissed Emma's cheek and lingered, fighting the urge to dip lower and softly touch her lips. She stepped back, releasing her hands. "I could use some help getting these guys fed."

"Roger, Ranger." Emma headed for the bathhouse, and Carter smacked her backside as she passed, remembering her earlier image of them fixing dinner together.

By the time Carter finished cooking the hot dogs, Emma had set the table with paper plates tucked neatly inside straw holders and napkins, a bag of chips, and a cold drink at each place. She'd arranged all the fixings in the center of the table and taken a seat at one end. She and the kids sat with their plastic forks and knives raised on either side of their plates, ready to dig in.

"All right, all right. Here you go." Carter forked out two hot dogs for each person before taking her place at the other end of the table. She was very proud that everybody waited patiently until she was seated. "Emma, it's our tradition to express gratitude before eating." When everybody around the table had joined hands, Carter said, "We are grateful."

Emma felt tears gathering as Reggie and Maddie, who sat on opposite sides, reached out to her. "Yes, I am," she said quietly, dabbing the corners of her eyes with her napkin. She wasn't sure she'd make it through the meal without breaking down completely. The whole evening had been like a fairy tale of sorts. She'd played games, laughed, been clumsy and imperfect but at the same time felt included and accepted. Carter and these children had given her a wonderful gift.

As they ate, she watched Carter engaging with each child, inquiring about his day, his life, and offering encouragement. She was a woman of depth and character, a soul who understood how to reach children with emotional issues. Where did that knowledge come from? She was totally lost in considering the possibilities when Maddie nudged her and pointed to her messenger bag. The other kids were staring at Carter.

"What?" Then she heard her cell phone ringing. When she reached for her bag, Carter shook her head. "Let me turn this off. Sorry, guys."

"Somebody want to tell Emma why we don't bring cell phones to our outings?"

Maddie raised her hand and waited patiently, though she practically vibrated with excitement. When Carter nodded, she cleared her throat and began. "Several reasons really. It's just good manners to leave your phone off during a meal. It's respectful of other people, says you think they're important and you like them. And you can't really do two things at once and be equally good at both. There." Maddie nodded and reached for her drink.

Emma patted Maddie's shoulder. "You said that beautifully, and you're exactly right. Thank you for reminding me." She glanced at Carter, and her wide smile as she looked at Maddie could not have been any prouder.

"Okay, guys, it's time to say good night to Emma while I take care of the fire. I'd like a few minutes alone with my favorite kids before you go."

When Emma stood, the four children swarmed her and wrapped their arms around her waist. As each one hugged her good-bye, his and her parting words burrowed into her heart.

"Good game tonight, Emma," Simone said. "You can play on my team anytime."

Maddie said, "You're a good person. I can tell these things. Come out with us again."

Olive-skinned Nico hitched his pants up and kissed her on the cheek when she bent to hug him. "Remember, cornhole is just a game. What's important is to play fair and have fun."

Shy Reggie hung back until the other kids moved away. He motioned Emma closer so he could whisper in her ear. "I like that you write stories. Maybe you can read mine one day. I want to be a book writer."

"I'd love that, Reggie." Emma stood, so full of emotions that when she saw Carter coming toward her, she knew she couldn't talk to her right now. "Thank you, everybody. I had a great time tonight." She grabbed her bag and ran toward the cabin.

She made it to the other side of the ridge, out of sight of the office, before falling to her knees and sobbing tears of complete joy. From the mouths of babes she'd heard some of the best advice, and she'd had one of the most enjoyable nights of her life. Children had a way of drawing a line under what was really important. She cried away some of her old sadness, then continued toward home.

The return uphill was much more grueling than she remembered, and she picked her way slowly along the poorly lighted path. Her legs burned and ached, but she finally saw her cabin in the distance. As she drew closer, someone ducked around the side of the house. Maybe Carter had finished with the children and had come by to check on her. Adrenaline-fused excitement pumped through her.

"I'm here." But there was no response. Maybe she hadn't seen anyone at all.

When she crested the last ridge at the road, car headlights blinded her, and she lost her footing on loose leaves, tumbling down the embankment. Pain radiated from her left ankle, and she grappled for a handhold to stand. Before she could steady herself, someone grabbed her from behind.

"What the—" She struggled.

"Relax, Emma. I've got you. You fell, again." She recognized Carter's teasing voice.

Still a bit disoriented, Emma realized Carter was carrying her toward the Jeep. "Put me down, Carter. I can walk, for goodness' sake."

"Your ankle is sprained, if not broken. Calm down and don't make this any harder than it has to be."

The pain in Emma's ankle convinced her that Carter was probably right, so she relaxed into her arms, not an entirely bad place to be. Laying her head against Carter's chest, she heard the strong pounding of her heart and smelled the delicate scent of her perspiration. Her arms were sure and her steps unwavering. But Emma felt vulnerable and helpless, something she'd never allowed herself to accept before.

"Where are you taking me?"

"To the hospital, of course. You might've broken something."

"No. Take me back to the cabin. I'll be fine. It's just a sprain."

"And how would you know that? Do you have medical training?"

"No, but I can tell. I've taken enough falls in my life to know when I break something."

Carter stopped by a raised boulder beside the path, shifted some of Emma's weight onto her knee, and reached into her jeans' pocket. "Then I'm calling Ann. She's a nurse."

"Don't disturb her. I mean it, Carter. I'm really fine."

Carter shoved her phone back into her pocket and took a different path around the incline toward her Jeep. "You're really stubborn."

"So I've been told." She relaxed against Carter's chest again. No one had ever held her like this, and she loved how safe and comfortable she felt.

When they reached her cabin, Carter waited while she unlocked the door, deposited her on the sofa, and started back out. "Stay put until I get back, and I'll examine your ankle."

"Carter, wait. I saw someone snooping around the cabin. Don't go out there."

"I left the Jeep running. If somebody's out there, I'll find him."

Carter closed the door, and Emma searched within her reach for anything that could serve as a weapon. She didn't want to be alone in these woods with some unknown person lurking nearby. She heard a rustling noise outside near the door but didn't dare open it. She called out to Carter and got no reply. A sharp crack pierced the still air, followed by something crashing against the side of the cabin. She burrowed deeper into the sofa. She'd give anything to hear the warbling wail of a police siren outside her door.

After what seemed a spooky millennium, Carter knocked on the door. "It's me. Don't shoot."

"Get in here," she demanded before the door could close behind Carter. "What in blazes is going on out there? What was that awful crashing noise? Are you all right? Did you find anyone?"

"Number one, the crash you heard was a dead tree limb falling right outside your window. Number two, I'm fine, thank you for asking. Number three, I didn't find anybody. It was probably a teenager who slipped out after his parents went to sleep. You should be used to prowlers. You live in a city." Carter placed a pillow under Emma's swollen appendage and kneaded the tender flesh until she grimaced. "Sit still and I'll get some ice."

"Are the cabins beside me occupied?"

"Just the one to your left, number nine. He's from out of town and works construction. Seems nice enough."

Carter dumped the old-fashioned ice trays into the kitchen sink, filled a plastic bag and wrapped it in a dishcloth, and then knelt in front of Emma. She gently positioned the pack on Emma's ankle and gave her a questioning look.

"What?"

"Are you always—"

"Clumsy? Uncoordinated? In a word, yes. And I did warn you."

"I was actually going to ask if you're always so unpleasant when you're hurt?" Carter grinned.

"You can stop teasing me now. It's embarrassing enough that you saw me do the Jack-and-Jill tumble again." Few things annoyed her more than making a fool of herself in front of others. "And yes, I'm a very bad patient."

"Your clumsiness is sort of charming." Carter wrapped the dishcloth around Emma's ankle so the ice pack was secured.

The sight of Carter's long fingers moving gently over her flesh caused a different kind of pain deep inside Emma. She flinched.

"Does it hurt?"

"Uh…" It took a second to realize Carter was referring to her ankle. Her face flushed with heat. "Mostly numb."

"I was worried when you left the cookout so quickly. I thought maybe I did something wrong, because you seemed to get along great with the kids."

"You wanted to talk with them alone. And I was just overcome with the joy and wonder of children that adults seem to lose somewhere along the way."

"Tell me about it. We'd all be better off if we could keep that childish curiosity forever."

Emma studied Carter as she knelt in front of her, her well-defined legs bulging against the taut fabric of her jeans and her tailored flannel shirt outlining developed chest and arm muscles. She didn't often feel safe or even necessarily comfortable when other women violated her personal space, like Carter had when she'd carried her.

Carter glanced up and caught the direction of her gaze, and a tiny smile tweaked the corners of her mouth.

Emma didn't want to pretend she hadn't been looking, and she sucked at subtlety. "You have a very nice body, Carter. So strong and capable."

Carter twisted her necklace. Emma's words warmed her almost as much as touching her had. "Thank you." She usually paid the compliments, not the other way around. "When I saw your tumble, I turned into Super Ranger, savior of lost children, protector of baby animals, and champion of lame reporters."

Emma grinned. "I'm sure there are rewards for saving small children and helpless animals, but not for rescuing a poor struggling reporter who's fallen and can't get up."

"My reward was holding you." *Did I just say that out loud?* Emma's pupils dilated and she licked her lips. Carter unconsciously mimicked the action. *You'll only be a rebound. Perfect. Short-term is all you want.* Her internal argument continued, while her eyes remained locked on the woman lying in front of her. Damn it, even her clumsiness made her seem vulnerable and more endearing.

Emma reached for her.

Carter stood quickly. She was attracted, sure, but she didn't want to take advantage. "Why don't I start a fire? It feels like it's going to rain. I'm even getting a little chilly." Fire was the last thing she needed, but building it provided distance to regain control of her feelings. Why was she resisting the pull toward Emma?

She worked slowly, creating a base of balled-up paper and twigs and a tepee of loosely placed small limbs. When she was satisfied with the final product and certain she'd harnessed her emotions, she turned back to Emma. "Prepare for the fire-lighting ceremony." She held a fireplace match in front of her, poised to hit the striker.

"What? No rubbing of sticks or shaving of flint? You're actually using a match?"

"I save my best tricks for the wilderness. Are you ready?"

Emma sat straighter. "Is there a ceremonial speech at least?"

"I could bore you with the history of fire or the park, or I could just toss a little foofoo dust and we could make silent wishes."

"I vote for the latter."

"Me too." Carter sprinkled imaginary dust on top of the stack and lit the match. Flames hopscotched from one piece of paper to the next until the base and tepee of twigs crackled and blazed. When she turned away from the fire, her eyes met Emma's again and held for several seconds, a familiar feeling settling deep in her gut.

"What is it?" Emma asked.

Carter fumbled with her necklace and scanned the room. For the first time, she actually felt shy with a woman. Something about

Emma made her want to share things she'd never told anyone. "It's just…you…in the firelight. You look so beautiful."

Emma crossed her arms as if to protect herself from the feelings Carter's words evoked and stared into the fire. "I…it's…"

"I'm sorry. I don't usually blurt." What could she possibly say that would explain the strange blend of feelings Emma stirred? "You just make me want to…"

"What, Carter?"

"Never mind. I better take off and let you rest."

Emma reached for Carter, but she was too far away. "Don't." She had no idea where to start explaining herself, or if she even wanted to try. But she did want this soft-spoken ranger with dark, searching eyes to stay. "Don't go, Carter." She owed it to herself to explore the possibilities that life presented. Didn't she?

Carter didn't move.

"Carter?" Emma reached out again, then stopped. Maybe she'd been reading Carter's intentions wrong.

"You really shouldn't look at me like that. Those blue eyes are saying things to me you might regret."

"They speak too loudly sometimes."

Carter knelt in front of her. Time shifted to a slow, sensuous crawl as Carter raised her hand and lightly traced the outline of Emma's mouth with the tip of her index finger. Then Carter leaned close and kissed her so softly Emma would have questioned whether they'd really touched, except her lips tingled and heat flashed through her. She threaded her arms around Carter's neck. She wanted her. For the first time, she actually hungered for another woman, this woman. She wanted to rip her flannel shirt open and caress flesh she knew would be smooth and hot. *This* was what she'd missed in previous relationships, this burning need to consume and be consumed.

Carter's lips suddenly stilled, and she gently loosened Emma's arms from her neck. "I think it's best if I stoke the fire and leave you to rest."

"But…" She wanted Carter to stay and make love to her, but God, she didn't want to sound as desperate as she felt. Every nerve in her body sparked, every hormone raged. She wanted this woman. Now.

"I'm sorry. I shouldn't have kissed you," Carter said.

Carter apparently didn't want her. Emma looked toward the fire and tried to breathe normally before answering. "I'm the one who should apologize. I practically choked you." Nothing about this situation was humorous, but she needed to get back on stable ground. "Thanks for the cookout and for getting me back to the cabin. You really went beyond the call of duty."

"Don't put much weight on your ankle for a while. Do you need anything before I leave? Would you like something to eat? Can I help you to be…" Carter squeezed Emma's hand lightly. "Strike that last part."

"I'll be fine. Thanks. I should be comfortable here with the fire." She pulled the blanket from the back of the sofa and snuggled in. The way her body was humming, comfortable was the last thing she'd be tonight.

"I'll check on you tomorrow." Carter waved from the doorway and disappeared in a blast of cold air.

Emma tried to sleep, but the ibuprofen she'd taken hadn't eased her ankle pain or the ache of Carter's abrupt departure. Their kiss had ignited a fire, a passion that wouldn't be so easy to extinguish.

CHAPTER EIGHT

Emma woke from a dream of pitchfork-wielding hillbillies to a light tapping on the cabin door. Her aching ankle reminded her of last night's tumble, and her hand pressed between her thighs reminded her of Carter's kiss—the sexiest, hottest kiss of her life. Another knock prevented a total free fall into her feelings.

"Yes, who is it?"

"Emma, are you all right?" Ann's voice was laced with concern.

"Just a minute and I'll let you in."

"Don't get up. With your permission, I'll use the pass key."

She rolled her legs over the side of the sofa and put a little pressure on her ankle. Not happening. "Please do." She checked her cell, surprised she'd slept until after noon.

Ann slowly entered, balancing a pot in one hand, and nudged the door closed with her foot. She wore a bright-green tent dress decorated with tiny red tassels that made her look like a walking Christmas tree. "How you feeling today?"

"Like I can't be trusted to walk on my own. My ankle is stiff but not broken."

"Carter should've called me last night. I gave her hell." Ann placed the pot she was carrying on the kitchen table, settled at the end of the sofa, and lifted Emma's foot onto her lap.

"Don't be too hard on her. I wouldn't let her call. I'm not a very good patient."

Ann gently probed Emma's leg from mid-calf to toes, paying special attention to her swollen ankle. "I think you're right. You probably need to rest at least another day before walking on it, and then be careful. Do you have an anti-inflammatory?"

Emma pointed to her bag resting at the end of the sofa.

"And no more tumbling down hills or running on these gravelly roads. Got it?"

"Yes, Nurse Ann." Emma nodded toward the kitchen. "So... what you got there?"

"I thought you might need some food." Ann stood and headed toward the table.

"I'm starving. The hot dog I had at the cookout is long gone."

"And how was the cookout? Did you enjoy yourself?"

"Ann, it was so much fun. I haven't laughed that much in years. Those kids are pretty special, and Carter is absolutely magic with them. It's like she has a direct line into what they're going through. Know what I mean?"

"She's definitely found her calling, if I can just get her to follow it."

"What do you mean?" Emma rose on an elbow and looked toward the kitchen.

"Nothing. I'm just rambling." Ann pointed to the pot as she retrieved a bowl from the cabinet. "This is a guaranteed-to-heal-anything concoction—specialty of the late, great Cass Calloway. The woman was nutty as a fruitcake, but she had talents."

"So, do I eat it or rub it on my ankle?"

"Blasphemy!" Ann clasped her hands together and looked toward the ceiling. "Don't listen, Cass. She didn't mean it. For your information, Ms. City Slicker, this is the number-one jambalaya recipe in the history of the free world. Cass had a knack for exotic cuisine. It was her attempt to wean me off travel and other foreign delicacies."

"I love jambalaya."

"A word of caution before you try it. Any failure of the recipe to perform its intended purpose—to take your mind off your ankle while it sets your insides on fire—is entirely my fault. I'm a mediocre cook, nothing like my Cass."

"I'm sure it will be delicious. Sit with me while I eat?"

"Sure. I'm off today, nothing else demanding my attention." She handed Emma the bowl of jambalaya, the aroma making her mouth water. "Carter will be by later. She was coming this morning but had to go out on something. It's probably another murder—spider suffocation or fish drowning."

Emma eagerly dug into the bowl of steaming goodness, as much to cover her reaction to possibly seeing Carter again as to quench her hunger. She moaned when the blistering spices hit her tongue. "So good. Would you tell me more about Cass?"

"Glad to. She just happens to be my favorite subject. Let's see. Where did we leave off last time?" Ann pulled a straight-backed chair from the dining area and propped her high-topped tennis shoes on the corner of the coffee table.

"You'd come home for a visit, spent the night together, and made love for the first time. She wouldn't leave with you, so you left town again."

"You really were paying attention. When I finished my stint in the national guard, I came back. She was hooked up with fiancé number three. He was meaner than a rattlesnake in a burlap sack. She couldn't even look at anybody else without him flying hot. He hit her too."

"What did you do?"

"Nothing. She was standing on the platform at the train station the day I returned. I walked up to her and said, 'Ms. Calloway, nice to see you again. You look beautiful as ever.' With tears in her eyes, she made some remark about no longer being a Calloway. I smiled and said, 'You'll always be Cass Calloway to me, and I'll always love you. I'll be waiting when you're ready.' Then I walked away."

"And she followed, right? Or came to you later?" She took another spoonful of the soup, her eyes never leaving Ann's face.

"Not exactly."

"So you gave her some time to think and then went after her?" This story had to have a happy ending. Emma could see how much Ann loved Cass even after all these years.

"Couldn't. I had responsibilities. Besides, she had to come to me. It wouldn't have worked any other way. I already knew what I wanted."

Emma struggled to hold back tears. Clearing her throat, she asked, "How long did it take for her to do that?"

"About two hours, best of my recollection. Her no-account fiancé gave her a belting when he found out I was back in town and that we'd spoken."

"That worthless son-of-a—" Emma muttered.

"My words exactly. She came to my house that night, and we talked for hours. She needed me to tell her everything would be all right if she married this low-life bastard, that she could change him and make him a better man."

"Did you give her the lie she needed to hear, Ann?"

"I told her to let her heart be her guide, and it would never betray her. I wanted to wrap her in my arms, take care of and protect her, but I couldn't. She kissed me, told me she loved me, and went back to him. We didn't speak for two more years."

"What?" Emma accidentally stamped her foot in disbelief and flinched.

"Steady, girl." Ann eased her leg back onto the sofa. "Stay put and finish your lunch."

"But why? She said she loved you, and you let her leave? I don't get it."

"You know how complicated love can be—new feelings, other people, expectations—and two women trying to navigate those waters was unheard of in our day. She was committed to this man, and when Cass gave her word, she stuck to it regardless. She needed the security and status of marriage. Somehow she thought that could right all past wrongs. Anyway, I had obligations I couldn't ignore and nothing of any substance to offer except my heart."

When Emma finished the jambalaya, Ann pulled a deck of cards from the pocket of her Christmas dress and dealt them each a hand on the coffee table. The sun dipped lower in the west as Emma talked about her childhood and her father's disappearance while they played blackjack for matches.

"You're a shark, Ann West." Emma pushed her final match chips to Ann's side of the table and dropped her cards.

"I've been accused of that before." She seemed to study Emma for a second. "What else is on your mind, Emma?"

"I was just wondering. What could possibly have been more important than the woman you love?"

"Okay, you two, come out in the name of the law." Carter's voice accompanied a loud banging on the front door.

"That child's timing has always been impeccable or atrocious." Ann smiled at Emma. "But I love her just the same."

Ann rose to answer the door, but Emma grabbed her hand. "You truly are a special woman, Ann West. I can hardly wait for the next installment of your love story. I just hope I don't have to sprain another ankle to get it."

"Any time, Emma." Their hands slid apart as Ann moved to the door.

"It's about time. What have you two been—" Carter stopped as Ann shook her head. "I'm sorry. Should I come back later?"

"Of course not," Ann said. "I've done my duty here. The woman's been medically evaluated, fed, and robbed of all her matches. The rest is up to you." Ann smiled as she grabbed her jacket and started toward the open door, where Carter stood in a pair of blue jeans and a teal turtleneck sweater that hugged her compact breasts like plastic wrap.

"Thank you so much, Ann, for everything. You did the recipe justice." Emma flashed Ann a reassuring glance. She'd gotten the message that Ann wasn't going to share any more in front of Carter.

❖

Carter headed for the kitchen with the two bags of groceries she'd brought. "Guess it's my turn to take over the care and feeding of the invalid." After her lapse last night, Carter had tried to convince herself to stay away for both their sakes. But she couldn't very well desert Emma when she was injured, could she?

Emma looked pensive as she stared after Ann.

"What was that all about?" Carter asked. "I feel like I stepped into the twilight zone."

"She was telling me more about Cass and how they got together. I love a good romance. Do you know their story?"

"I lived their story." Carter turned back to the kitchen and started unpacking the groceries. She was more comfortable answering difficult questions while doing something with her hands and avoiding eye contact. "Cass moved in when I was still a child." She placed a carton of milk in the refrigerator. "I've always had questions about how she came to us at that particular time." She stared at the bag of chips in her hand, not really seeing it. "Ann just said we became a three-woman family. That was her only explanation."

"That's the first personal information you've shared with me. Thank you. I love the sound of your voice, and when you share intimate details, you're quite enticing." Emma slapped a hand over her mouth. "Sometimes I engage my mouth before my brain. Sorry if I made you uncomfortable."

Uncomfortable wasn't really how Carter would describe the heat that scorched her body. She slowly finished putting away the groceries while she calmed.

In the living room, she sat in Ann's chair by the sofa. She needed to clear the air and then keep things professional. "Sorry about last night. You were injured and vulnerable, and I took advantage."

Emma's blush consumed the spattering of freckles across her nose, and she looked at the floor. "I should apologize for flinging myself at you. I suck at relationships. It was my fault—the kiss, I mean. Don't worry about it."

Carter released a long sigh. Was she relieved or disappointed? *Too much analyzing.* "So, how's the ankle?"

"Much better. Ann said another day's rest should be enough. The jambalaya definitely took my mind off it for a while."

Carter laughed aloud, remembering the first time she'd eaten the concoction. "She fed you Cass's red-hot, gut-busting jambalaya?"

"It was delicious." Emma's eyes narrowed and the space between her brows wrinkled. "How did you come to live with Ann?"

She was going for the jugular. The question smashed against Carter's chest like a deployed airbag. Breath gushed from her lungs, and she swallowed hard. "You're the most direct person I've ever met."

"I'm a reporter, and I'd like to know more about you."

"It's a short and boring story." Carter felt the lines around her mouth tighten. She wasn't going to offer any more information unless pressed. She prayed Emma wouldn't do that.

Emma scooted to the end of the sofa and touched Carter's arm. "You interest me, and I ask questions about things that interest me. Besides, I'm a captive audience."

The energy from Emma's touch shot up Carter's arm and through her body. She felt helpless to resist Emma's requests, no matter how painful.

"I don't remember when I didn't live with Ann." Her voice sounded so timid she was reminded of the weeks and months she'd been totally without words. Carter rose, stoked the embers in the fireplace, and added more wood before returning to sit near Emma. "I was two years old when my parents were killed in an accident with an eighteen-wheeler on the interstate. I survived only because my mother covered me with her body just before impact." She spoke coolly, emotionally disconnected, like reading the story from a newspaper.

Emma clutched her throat as if she couldn't breathe, and her blue eyes, never leaving Carter's, clouded with tears.

She'd tried to tell her story to Cass many years earlier, but she'd been too young and traumatized to say much or to even cry. She didn't want to talk about it now. She could recite the details dispassionately because she'd heard them so many times through the years, but she couldn't stop the resurgence of emotions as she gave voice to the horrific event. She felt frozen, her lips stiff to prevent any hint of tremble.

Emma slid closer, took Carter's hands, and urged her to the sofa. "Come here."

Carter shook her head. "You don't have to…"

"I want to. Please?" She tried again, and this time Carter moved beside her. Emma eased her head onto her shoulder. "Let me hold you for a few minutes. You don't have to say anything."

And she didn't. She couldn't. She'd cried all her tears years before, but the comfort of Emma's arms gave her the courage to speak the whole truth. "The hardest thing about living with Ann and Cass was how they were treated. They chose to love each other in a time when it wasn't acceptable for two women to do that. Everybody knew about them, but no one talked about it. People just gave them a wide berth and looked at me with pity."

Her limbs were heavy and weak as time passed, and she clung to Emma. "I've never even said that to Ann. It would hurt her too much." As the fire flickered and dimmed, she realized it was almost dark outside. She eased from Emma's arms, embarrassed by her meltdown. "I'm sorry."

Emma placed her fingers over Carter's lips. "Don't ever be sorry for sharing your feelings with me. It's a gift, and I'll treasure it always. I'm sorry I brought up something so painful. I never want to hurt you."

"It was a long time ago. Ann took me in because she was my only relative. I couldn't have asked for a better mother." Her eyes filled with tears, and she clenched her jaw to keep them from falling.

"Ann was a godsend. I'm so very sorry about your parents. Is there anything I can do?"

"You listened, and you…held me. I haven't been held in a nonsexual way in years. And, in case you haven't noticed, I don't open up often. So thanks for that." Time to lighten up. "I just hope what I've said doesn't end up in your story." She smiled and brushed a strand of hair from her forehead.

With her fingers, Emma crossed her heart. "You have my word as a journalist."

"Great." She gave Emma a quick hug and rose before she got too comfortable again. "I'm acting like I don't have anything to do. Since I knew you wouldn't be mobile today, I brought the makings of a pretty decent dinner. Are you brave enough to risk my cooking?"

"There's always Cass's leftover jambalaya."

"So you don't trust me?"

"With my life. If you were going to kill me, you'd have let me die on the side of the mountain instead of rescuing me—twice."

Carter stepped into the small kitchenette, sliced cheese and French bread, opened the olive jar, and washed grapes. She arranged everything on a dinner plate and placed it on the coffee table in front of Emma. "Do you like red wine?"

Emma's azure eyes widened. "Um…"

"You don't."

"Well…I like it very much."

"So, what's the problem?" She couldn't resist teasing Emma.

"It…makes me…"

"Horny?"

Emma's blush turned her face crimson and she looked away. "How did you know?"

"It's a scientific fact. Alcohol in small amounts increases libido. It stimulates the hypothalamus, which regulates body temperature, hunger, hormone levels, and sex drive."

"How do you know that?"

"I may be a lowly park ranger, but I'm not uneducated."

"But why would you specifically know about wine and sex drive?"

"Uh…" She didn't consider her personal observations scientific proof, and she never boasted about her sexual liaisons.

"Experience. I see. Have you been with very many women?"

Emma's stare held, and Carter was afraid she'd peer into the darkness of her soul. No one had asked that question before, so she'd never actually counted, wasn't even sure she could remember them all. "A few." She retreated to the kitchen before Emma detected the truth in her eyes.

"More like a few hundred, I'd guess." Emma said.

"I'll bring you a glass of wine to go with the munchies until everything else is ready."

"Actually, I'd like to take a shower. I'm starting to feel like my clothes are permanently attached. Do I have time?"

"Take it easy." Carter rushed to Emma's side as she tried to get up from the sofa. "Can you manage?"

"If you'll help me into the bedroom, I can manage from there." Emma slipped her arm around Carter's waist and leaned against her as they made their way slowly into the bedroom. "In the top of my suitcase." She pointed to the bag resting atop the luggage valet. "Pull out the red lace teddy and a pair of sweats."

Carter eyed her sideways as she bent to retrieve the items from Emma's luggage. Being close to Emma again so soon after her epic control failure made Carter's body sizzle. She wrote it off to a couple of sexual aphrodisiacs—emotions and adrenaline—and went for humor. "Something this sexy," she raised the teddy, "should not be hidden under sweats."

"Come on, Ranger. I'm dying here."

So am I, but for entirely different reasons. She escorted Emma to the bathroom door and reached for a button on her blouse. "Need help getting into the shower?" She grinned. "I am a full-service ranger."

"I wouldn't let you touch me with your worst enemy's hands right now. Out." Emma slammed the door, leaving Carter aching on the other side.

CHAPTER NINE

The cool-shower spray needled Emma's skin, but even as she hugged herself to stop shivering, the intimate moments she'd spent with Carter had her burning inside. What was happening to her? She'd taken the Stuart assignment to work and escape a commitment-phobic woman, not engage another one. But Carter had shared her deepest pain when she was normally so guarded, and her vulnerability tugged at Emma. Maybe Carter was the antidote to her lazy libido, at least one dose, or maybe she was something more entirely, something Emma hadn't imagined she could have.

If nothing else, Carter's concern and obvious attraction were releasing some of the self-doubt Sheri's betrayal had raised. Maybe Carter could appreciate her imperfections and understand her quirky ways. Was she willing to make another move and risk a rejection like she'd received last night? She was heading down a very slippery slope, probably alone. She finished showering quickly and dressed, deciding to let the evening unfold naturally.

When she hobbled back into the living space, Carter was still scraping and chopping vegetables and humming a tune that sounded a bit like Elvis's *That's All Right, Mama*. Emma settled on the sofa and took the first sip of wine, enjoying its aggressive acidity and subsequent warmth. The smell of spices mixed with sautéing vegetables drifted through the cabin, and her stomach growled in response. "That smells fantastic. What is it?"

Carter turned from the stove. "You should've called. I would've helped you."

"I'm good. So…what are you cooking?"

Carter waved a spatula in the air like she was creating air art and turned back to her cooking. "It's my turn to ask questions."

"Shoot. I have liquid courage."

"So, what about you and your girlfriend?"

Emma spluttered part of her wine back into the glass so she wouldn't choke. "What? What girlfriend?"

"The one who gave you that fresh-road-kill look."

She flashed back to the scene in her bedroom and fiddled with her wineglass, unable to immediately find the words to describe her relationship with Sheri or its demise.

"You seemed upset when you arrived." Carter returned to the living area and sat beside her on the sofa. "If I'm being too personal, you don't have to answer."

Emma considered the offer for a moment. "No, actually I want to. I might be able to let go if I talk about it." She took a gulp of wine while trying to decide how much of her ineptness in relationships to reveal. She weighed that fear against her desire to be as open as Carter had been and began.

"I came home from work early to tell Sheri I'd reserved this awesome little cabin beside a lake in Virginia for a romantic getaway. She'd complained our sex life needed…a boost." Carter would pass on a tryst for sure with that admission. Why was she exposing her faults to the only woman she'd ever found sexually attractive?

Carter took her hand and waited until Emma summoned the courage to look at her. "No judgment. I promise."

The memory of that day settled like a culmination of all her relationship failures, and Emma struggled for a deep breath as the walls closed in on her. "I walked into the bedroom. They were in *our* bedroom, in *our* bed. Some brunette was going down on Sheri. If that wasn't bad enough, when Sheri saw me standing there… she didn't stop. She stared straight at me as her face flushed, her legs stiffened, and her body arched. I could've sworn she smiled when she grabbed the other woman's head and held it against her, screaming as she climaxed."

The small room was suddenly too quiet. She could almost feel the pity radiating from Carter. Emma choked down a sour taste with another gulp of wine. When she looked up, Carter was shaking her head.

"Seriously? In the bed you shared…and you watched?"

"I couldn't move. My body just wouldn't respond. I was totally shocked but, in retrospect, not all that surprised. She'd been complaining for months about our…I thought eventually I'd grow to love her and our sex life would improve—bad decision. If the attraction or chemistry isn't there at the beginning, there's not much chance it will do that. Lesson learned. I was never enough for her in that way. When I walked in on her with another woman, my confidence took quite a hit. And I was hurt, not about the sex part, but about the infidelity."

For the first time she admitted Sheri's betrayal had actually caused her pain, though she'd known for some time they weren't right for each other. Why had she waited, forced Sheri's hand? Why hadn't she had the courage to leave sooner? How would Carter interpret her story? She felt strange talking about Sheri with Carter, probably because she was more attracted to Carter than she'd ever been to Sheri.

"Were you in love with her?" Carter asked.

She shook her head. "We socialized in the same groups, liked some of the same activities, and things just happened. You know?"

"Absolutely. I'm sorry about the breakup. Nobody deserves that. And FYI, relationships are about more than just sex."

Emma hesitated, uncertain if she should probe deeper, but she couldn't stifle her desire to know more about Carter's past. "It sounds like you speak from experience."

Carter's eyes met hers and held. "Janice and I had been together three years when she told me she was in love with my best friend. I thought we had a good thing. Sex had never been a problem, but she wanted a commitment I couldn't give her. Needless to say, I lost both of them. Now I'm strictly casual."

"So you're a player?"

"Ouch. I wouldn't say that. I'm just not relationship material."

"Maybe you just haven't met the right woman," she said slowly. "Carter, I'd never experienced sexual chemistry with anyone until I met you. I'd always assumed my lack of interest was a physical defect or poor libido. Now I'm sparking like a downed power line."

Carter tugged at her necklace. "I see." She rose and poked the dying fire, churning the coals and laying on more wood. "I'm not sure I'll ever get used to your candor."

"Too much?"

Carter smiled. "Just surprising, in a refreshing way." She placed a large log over the top of the fire. "Are you hungry yet? I'm starving." She disappeared into the kitchen and returned moments later with a large bowl of spicy-smelling food. She placed the bowl on the coffee table and poured Emma another glass of wine. "Now, poor lame journalist, relax and let yourself be pampered."

Pulling a set of chopsticks from her back pocket, Carter unwrapped them. She sat cross-legged in front of Emma on the sofa and secured the bowl of food between them, scooting closer until their knees touched. Emma shivered in anticipation.

Carter guided the chopsticks carrying delicious-smelling vegetables to Emma's mouth and teased her lips apart. The act was intimate, nurturing, and sexy as hell. The first taste that hit her tongue was spicy, and as she chewed the crunchy vegetables, a sweeter flavor emerged, like the woman sitting across from her—a complex blend of sweet and spice and so addictive.

The next time Carter held the chopsticks to her lips, Emma gently steered her hand back to the bowl. Energy surged through their joined hands. She placed the container of food on the coffee table, uncrossed Carter's legs, and slid between them. She'd be humiliated if Carter stopped her again, but persistent desire pushed her past the warning of her frantically beating heart.

"I'm not sure this is a good idea, Emma." The darkening of Carter's brown eyes and the way she licked her lips betrayed her caution.

"Isn't this exactly what you want—no strings? I want it too, but I'm not sure if I can…how to…" Her voice sounded foreign, her tone raw with need. She'd never been so honest with anyone about sex.

Carter inched closer, pulling Emma's legs over her thighs. "What about your ankle? Does it hurt?"

"Other things hurt more." She wanted only two things—to cool the prickly heat consuming her and have her first orgasm that wasn't self-induced.

Carter threaded her fingers into Emma's hair and combed the length of it down her back. "I've wanted to bury myself in your hair since the first time I saw you. I love the natural waves, and it feels like gliding through water." She leaned forward and breathed in. "You smell like the woods at night. Delicious."

Emma caressed Carter's face and thrilled as her pupils dilated in response. The pools of deep brown were flawless expressions of desire, and she couldn't wait to dive in. She skimmed Carter's lips with her index finger and then slid it inside her mouth. "Suck this."

"Mmm," Carter moaned as she drew Emma's finger in and out excruciatingly slowly. The slick heat of Carter's mouth made Emma burn and moisten. Would Carter be as unvocal sexually as she was verbally? She'd love to be the one to make Carter scream her orgasm.

She nuzzled against Carter's neck, inhaled her distinctive scent of musk and the outdoors, and kissed her way up. She was in uncharted territory, more comfortable being the submissive partner, but something in her needed to be released. She rimmed Carter's outer ear with the tip of her tongue, dipped inside, and savored her quick intake of breath. Emma's nipples pressed painfully against the fabric of her sweatshirt as the rise and fall of her pelvis became more urgent.

Carter slowly pulled Emma's finger out of her mouth. "Emma."

"Please." Old memories of rejection, disappointment, and inadequacy flooded back. What if Carter reconsidered? What if Emma really wasn't enough for her sexually? Even if this was a one-night stand, she wanted it. She had to try. "Please don't make me stop."

Carter grabbed Emma's hips and hefted her onto her lap. "I want to be sure you're okay with this. I'd never take advantage."

"Trust me. You're not." Would Carter be uncomfortable if Emma took the lead? Would *she*? "Carter, I really want…" Could she even say the words aloud?

Carter met her gaze. "Tell me what you want, Emma."

"I need to know if I can…if I'm enough…for once." She broke eye contact, unable to bear any disapproval in Carter's eyes. "Would it be all right if I took the lead?"

Carter raised her arms as if to surrender. "I'm all yours. Do what you want."

"You might need to help me. I've never done it like this before."

Carter smoothed her hand down the side of Emma's face. "That makes two of us. We'll learn together. What would you like first?"

Emma grabbed the hem of Carter's turtleneck and in one motion swept it over Carter's head and tossed it to the floor. "You naked." Her bare breasts beckoned, their nipples puckered with excitement. She'd never seen anything so beautiful as the rise and fall of Carter's chest with each urgent exhale.

Emma lowered herself slowly, watching Carter's mouth open and close in anticipation, gasping for precious air. This exquisite woman wanted *her*. She lay exposed and waiting for *her.* She'd never had this effect on a woman. It was a heady feeling.

When she closed her mouth around Carter's compact breast, she arched and threw her head back. Muscles along her rib cage tensed, and her belly hollowed—so stunning and graceful in her need. Carter's responses fanned Emma's desire. She licked the base of each breast to its point and sucked a nipple into her mouth. She savored the lightly salty taste and silky smooth texture as she poked and teased with her tongue.

"Is this all right?" Emma asked, desperate to arouse and satisfy.

Carter cupped the back of Emma's head, urging without words. Her body conveyed exactly how she wanted to be pleasured. Emma felt like the conductor of the world's most sensuous orchestra.

Carter pulled her closer, her lips leaving a trail of fire on Emma's face and down the side of her neck. She smoothed her hands under Emma's sweatshirt and tried to remove it.

"Not yet. Can I take your jeans off?"

"Please." Carter lifted her hips.

Her acquiescence fueled Emma's confidence, and her own body heated more. Emma rose on her knees, unzipped Carter's tight jeans, and tugged them off. "I'm going to touch you now."

"Yes."

Emma slid her hand down the plane of Carter's abdomen and marveled at the tantalizing feel of skin against skin. When her fingers stroked the edge of pubic hair, her crotch dampened. This kind of deep, burning arousal had always eluded her.

"Please, Emma."

She checked Carter's expression. "Did I do something wrong?"

"Not at all. I'm trying to let you go at your own pace, but it's really hard."

Emma smiled, enjoying the urgency of Carter's need. Emma settled alongside Carter and tangled her fingers in the moist patch of curls between Carter's legs. She was rewarded with the satiny warmth of Carter's arousal, and her fingers glided easily into her.

When Carter's muscles pulled her fingers deeper, Emma almost lost control. She quivered and clenched her abdomen to stave off a powerful wave of desire. She didn't want to come until she'd proved she could satisfy her lover. Emma plunged deeper and massaged Carter's swollen clit with her thumb.

Carter closed her eyes and pumped slowly against Emma's hand, then clenched her jaw and moved faster, trying to control the pace. Emma stilled inside her, and Carter's eyes flew open. "What're you doing?" Her voice was raspy, her eyes hooded and dark.

"I really want to make you come. Please let me."

"It's not easy to be still while you're doing that."

Emma smiled. "Doing what?" She circled Carter's clit with her thumb. "This?"

Carter groaned. "Uh-huh."

"Or this?" Emma penetrated her with a slow, firm thrust.

Carter bit her lip, her eyes pleading.

She enjoyed teasing Carter, facilitating her reactions, but she also loved feeling her own body respond so readily and powerfully for the first time. Confidence was a potent aphrodisiac, but Carter's willingness to let her explore and set their pace touched her deeply. Pressure built between Emma's legs as her lace underwear rubbed painfully against her clit and nipples.

Carter held Emma tighter as her labored breathing deteriorated into erratic panting.

Emma eased herself onto Carter's thigh and almost came with the first firm stroke. "Take my shirt off."

Carter peeled the garment up and threw it behind her. "So beautiful." She teased Emma's breast with her fingers, and Emma's clit twitched, ready for release. "You are so responsive."

Emma ground slowly against Carter's thigh, savoring the tingling buildup that rose from her toes and coalesced in her crotch. When Carter tightened around her fingers, Emma increased her pace. Penetrating Carter and commanding her pleasure made Emma wild. "Come for me, Carter. Now."

"Oh, yes." Carter claimed Emma's mouth and thrust her tongue inside. She rode Emma's hand faster as spasms milked her fingers.

Emma clung to her, unwilling to pull out until she'd urged every ounce of pleasure from her. "That's right, baby. Let it all go."

"So good," Carter panted.

Carter's words and her last shudder freed Emma's release. She rode Carter's thigh and rubbed her breasts across her lips until she buckled in an eruption so intense her entire body went slack. Tears rolled down her cheeks as she collapsed against Carter, unable to move.

"I guess we're both fast learners."

"Uh-huh." Emma's body was limp, her muscles exquisitely drained. "So that's an orgasm with someone else. Totally unbelievable. Thank you."

CHAPTER TEN

On her drive to work with Ann the next morning, Carter still felt Emma's hands on her body, seared into her skin like a brand. The sex had been raw with a touch of vulnerability for both of them. Carter wasn't usually so passive, but she'd enjoyed it, sexually. Emotionally, she was unsettled that she'd trusted someone she'd just met that much. Who was she kidding? She'd never given up control to anyone. What made Emma Ferguson different?

"So, did you bed that feisty redhead or not?"

"Huh?" She'd totally spaced out. Not good. "Sorry, I was thinking about..." She couldn't come up with one single lie that would sound believable. She reached for her necklace but scratched her ear instead.

"You did! Spill." Ann tugged on her arm.

"That's none of your business." Her voice sounded harsh.

Ann's hand stilled as a look of surprise claimed her face. "Okay."

She and Ann had discussed sex since she was old enough to be attracted to girls, nothing off-limits. But she had no words to explain her reaction to Emma or the fact that she'd been sexually managed, quite satisfactorily, for the first time in her life.

"I didn't mean to snap at you." She hoped Ann wouldn't take her apology as an invitation to unleash a new volley of questions, because she didn't have a lot of answers.

"So it didn't go well? I can't imagine that. You two seem like a pretty good match."

"You think any woman I sleep with more than once is a good match, but you've jumped the gun with Emma. It was just sex."

Ann gave her a sideways glance.

"It was." At least that's what she kept telling herself as the familiar warnings about relationships returned. *Don't get attached. Love is dangerous. Nothing lasts forever.*

"It must've been different, because you've always talked to me before. Did she do something you didn't like? Though I can't imagine what a woman like that could do that I wouldn't like."

Carter looked out the window to keep Ann from reading the truth in her eyes. "She *was* different, and so open about what she wanted. I felt almost like I was with a virgin, or at least someone just learning about herself sexually. It was...well..."

Ann grinned and nodded as if it all made sense. "Intimate? Intense? A nice change?"

Carter's throat tightened and she looked down at her necklace, twisted into knots almost to her chin. Why had being with Emma felt so unusual? Emma had needed to take the lead, and for some reason, Carter had wanted to let her, but it went deeper than that. She'd connected with Emma on a level she hadn't with other women.

"Intimacy is good, Carter. Remember that. Women are complex creatures who crave connection. Intimacy makes you stronger, but it also helps you yield when necessary."

Ann made sense after what Emma had told her about Sheri. It hadn't sounded like she and Emma shared any real intimacy. "You're probably right."

"Emma took a more direct path with you than the others. Maybe she got to you a little."

Carter let Ann's words sink in as she pulled up to the ranger station. "I told her about my parents' accident."

This time Ann turned toward her in the seat. "You haven't talked to anyone about that since Cass." She squeezed Carter's forearm lightly. "Honey, it's good to share your life with people you trust."

"That's just it. I don't really know her yet. And she's a reporter. Should either of us trust someone who makes her living digging into other people's secrets?"

Ann swatted her arm. "Oh, please. Stop being so suspicious. Try something different. Give the woman a chance. You never know what might happen."

"All I know is I couldn't be there when she woke up this morning."

"Why, honey?" Ann's forehead crinkled and her eyes studied Carter.

She looked out the window and raked her fingers through her hair. How could she explain her feelings to a woman who had always known what true love felt like and exactly what she wanted? "When I woke up, Emma was practically on top of me, her head on my shoulder, our legs entwined, her arm across my middle." Carter faltered, and Ann was quiet for a few minutes, giving her time to think.

"And that scared you?"

"That's the weird part. It didn't. I know this is going to sound crazy, so don't laugh."

Ann put her hand on Carter's arm. "Honey, when have I ever laughed at your emotional struggles? I know how hard these things are for you."

"I didn't feel smothered or panicked like I normally would've. I felt…grounded. You center me in family and tradition, but this was different. In that moment, I felt emotionally anchored in something deeper. Does that make any sense at all?"

Ann smiled and nodded. "It makes perfect sense, Carter. So, why did you leave?"

"Because I didn't know what to say or how to explain my feelings. I was torn between apologizing for last night and asking for a date."

❖

Emma rolled onto her stomach, and tenderness in her crotch reminded her of last night—her first real orgasm, with Carter. She sprang upright on the sofa and scanned the room for the woman she knew instinctively would not be there. She rubbed her eyes and inhaled Carter's scent still strong on her fingers. The aroma ignited her. Sucking her fingers into her mouth, she tasted the delicate salty flavor and surrendered to the slow melting that spread through her. One by one she licked each digit until she found the last delicious reminder of Carter and her other hand was wet with her own arousal.

And then her anxiety began. She'd never been compelled to seduce another woman, but she'd needed to prove she could, to erase her insecurities. *And*, Carter found her sexually exciting—something Emma had given up on. Yesterday she'd had nothing to lose by putting herself on the line. She woke up thinking she and Carter were building something together. So why hadn't Carter stayed, or at least said good-bye, before sneaking out like a burglar?

She'd wanted to talk with Carter, to thank her and make sure things wouldn't be weird between them. If she'd read Carter right, she'd be second-guessing herself and worrying about having breached some invisible boundary. Emma had no such concerns. She'd done exactly what she wanted and been rewarded with the most delicious result. However, she needed Carter to know she wasn't just a means to an end. She'd trusted Carter enough to show her vulnerability and believed Carter would handle it with care—that spoke volumes about the rebound of her self-confidence.

The screeching of her cell phone startled Emma out of her self-satisfied state, and she scrambled for her bag. "Hell—o."

"Hey, darling. You sound hungover. " Rick Hardy's voice changed from business to concerned. "Are you okay?"

"I'm good. What've you got for me?" Emma secured the blanket around her and prepared for Rick's news.

"I put my magic powers to the test and got results. Your instincts were right. The remains are definitely human."

"And what about the DNA comparison? Anything you can tell me yet?"

"You were right about that too. There's a match between the bones recovered from the factory and the hair sample you sent. They both came from the same person. I assume that's the missing guy you're working on?"

Emma tingled with a surge of adrenaline. "Yeah, but—"

"I know where you're going with this, Emma. I've already got a team working on it. The medical examiner's staff thinks they have enough bones, minus the nonhuman additions, for a full reconstruction, but it'll take a bit longer. The forensic anthropologist they use is out of town. Even with that, we can't be sure it'll give you the answers you're looking for."

"I know, Rick. I just want to explore all the possibilities. If something on the skeleton indicates foul play, there's more than a story here. If not, at least I've done my best."

"I'll let you know as soon as I do. In the meantime, don't get yourself into a pissing contest with the locals. Okay?"

"I'll try to keep it low-key." If this turned into a murder case, she'd need all the help she could get from the locals. She'd try to keep on their good side.

She gingerly paced the small cabin floor, favoring her sore ankle. Should she call Fannie Buffkin? She'd want more than a handful of possibles and maybes, but she deserved to know her brother's remains had been found. She picked up the phone and dialed, praying for the right words to soften the blow.

"Hello. This is Fannie Buffkin."

"Fannie, it's Emma Ferguson. I need to tell you something. Should I come by?"

There was a brief pause at the other end. "Just spit it out. It's about those bones, isn't it?"

"Yes, I'm afraid it is. They're—"

"It's Theodore."

"I'm sorry, yes. The remains have been identified as belonging to your brother. I don't have anything else to tell you right now. A forensic anthropologist is doing a reconstruction to determine cause of death. As soon as I know, I'll be in contact."

"Thank you for calling, Emma."

"Again, I'm so sorry."

The line went dead.

Compared to delivering a death message to a loved one, her situation with Carter felt almost minor. Carter would probably continue to avoid her for the same reason she'd left before dawn. Emma couldn't do anything about that. In the meantime, her assignment was becoming more complicated. She didn't have all the facts yet, and to proceed without them was both unwise and unprofessional. She quickly showered, dressed, and walked toward her car.

Emma fumbled in her bag for the keys and dropped them. When she stooped to pick them up, she noticed her back tire was flat. She cursed under her breath for the delay a repair would cause. She checked the rest of the car, remembering the prowler she'd seen around the cabin, and found the front tire was flat as well. "Damn it." She wasn't sure AAA would respond to a place so far outside a major town.

When the park Jeep pulled up behind her vehicle, her stomach knotted as she mentally prepared a number of responses tailored to match Carter's mood. She looked even more delicious today than ever, maybe because Emma had tasted the goods.

Carter left the Jeep door open and approached, her eyes never leaving Emma's face. "Good morning, Emma."

Not what she expected, or maybe wanted. Carter's tone relayed no warmth or hint of familiarity, as if nothing had happened. Her eyes told a different story. She scanned Emma's face as if searching for something buried.

"Good morning," Emma said, trying to sound equally unaffected.

"I'm really sorry about leaving so early this morning. Not very chivalrous of me."

"I'm sure you had your reasons." Her departure had stung, and Emma wanted an explanation, but she refused to push. Pressuring a woman like Carter would be the equivalent of asking her to get married on the spot—quick exit in the opposite direction.

"Yes, but I'd rather talk about it later. Are you going into town?"

"I was, but…" She pointed toward her car tires.

Carter stooped and inspected both tires. "They've been slashed. I'm sorry I didn't think to check them the other night after the prowler incident."

Emma searched her messenger bag for her wallet. "Do you think AAA will come out?"

"Nope, but I'll have one of the guys at the service station take care of it. May I give you a ride? You probably shouldn't be driving until your ankle is stronger anyway."

Emma nodded and started toward the passenger side of the Jeep.

"Let me help you." Carter cupped Emma's elbow with one hand and hooked her other arm around her waist. "Lean against me."

Emma snuggled against Carter's side, and the passion she'd felt last night flared again. Carter helped her into the Jeep and reached across her for the seat belt. Emma inhaled the scent of her and was lost in the memory of their lovemaking. She heard a faint click, and then Carter's mouth was on hers. Carter's lips were hot and demanding. Her tongue probed deeply and she breathed with urgency. Emma eagerly returned the kiss as though it might be her last. When Emma reached to pull Carter closer, she backed away.

Carter stood outside the Jeep staring, her breathing rapid and her lips swollen and wet. "Sorry I left you alone this morning. I wanted to say things, but I couldn't. Forgive me?"

Emma couldn't think clearly enough to formulate words. She nodded and watched as Carter crossed in front of the Jeep and climbed into the driver's seat. As they rode silently into town, Emma realized her perception of Carter had subtly changed since they'd met. Her physical strength had initially called to Emma, but Carter's strength of character had given her the courage to reach out again. Carter wasn't a womanizer who seduced one minute and distanced the next. Something deeper held Carter's emotions hostage, and Emma vowed to find out what.

"Where should I drop you?" Carter slowed as they approached the town center.

Emma's stomach growled, and she remembered she hadn't eaten anything or even had a cup of coffee before rushing out. "Near the diner, please. Where will I find you later?"

"If you wouldn't mind, come by the school gym when you're finished." When Emma opened the door to leave, Carter added, "And stay off your ankle as much as possible."

Emma waved and headed toward the Stuart Diner, walking slowly in deference to her sore ankle and to the memory of Carter's kiss still spreading warmth through her. The diner buzzed with the lunchtime consumption of massive quantities of carbohydrates, sweet tea, and the exchange of gossip. The high-pitched roll of competing voices lowered a notch when she entered and surveyed the room for a place to sit. An older gentleman dressed in a colorful plaid jacket motioned to the only empty seat next to him at the end of the counter. The hushed voices fell to whispers, and all eyes followed her to the empty barstool. When she sat down, the man offered his hand.

"Afternoon, Ms. Ferguson. I'm Timothy Black, director of Black's Funeral Home."

"Mr. Black, it's nice to meet you." Emma shook his hand and eyed the plaid jacket, bright turtleneck sweater, and tan wool pants that weren't a stereotypical mortician's attire. However, his deep voice and focused attention were soothing and would probably be comforting during stressful times.

Emma plucked a menu from the clothespin that secured it to the side of the counter and searched the list of specials for something semi-healthy. "What do you recommend?"

"Loretta, give the lady a sweet tea and a number three."

"Hey, Emma. Nice to see you again." Loretta plopped a glass of tea in front of her. "I'm surprised you'd take meal advice from an undertaker, but it's your funeral." She wrote #3 on a ticket and clipped it with another clothespin to a wire strung across an opening to the kitchen. "Order up."

"Are you sure I want a number three?" Emma asked Timothy Black as she sipped the tea and calculated the number of calories being pumped into her system.

"It's the closest thing to healthy they serve, chef's salad. You having any luck on your story?" The room again became uncommonly quiet.

"As a matter of fact, it's become something quite different... and very interesting." Emma replied loud enough for the curious. Then she leaned closer to Mr. Black and whispered, "Perhaps you remember the disappearance of Theodore Thompson, the furniture-factory heir."

Mr. Black picked up on Emma's desire for discretion and replied in a hushed tone. "I remember it well."

She felt the renewed vigor that always accompanied the unearthing of fresh information. "How do you recall that particular night so long ago?"

"He disappeared the same night his wife ended up in the hospital. Nobody could find him. I was working late at the funeral parlor. My assistant and I were preparing someone for a wake the next day. It was a strange night all around, as I recall."

"What do you mean?" Emma turned her back to the other counter customers so the two of them could talk privately in the corner. Loretta slid a chef's salad down the counter in front of her, and Emma nodded before returning her attention to Mr. Black.

"Around eleven, Harvey Livengood from Maple Street called. His mother had passed, and he wanted me to collect her from the hospital."

Emma's initial surge of excitement dwindled to the dull thud of disappointment. "What's so unusual about that?"

"It wasn't the call, Ms. Ferguson. Harvey said he'd been trying to get me since about ten thirty and couldn't get through. It was a common practice that if somebody needed to contact the mortuary, ambulance, or sheriff, you'd give up the line."

Emma, obviously missing the point, shrugged and stared at Mr. Black.

"Several people shared the same phone line back then, a party line they called it, but in emergencies, you were supposed to surrender the service. Harvey said there was no one on the line. The operator never picked up. We found out the next day we'd had a glitch in the system. There were a lot of glitches in town that night. That particular one was very unusual. Never happened before or since."

Emma shoveled a forkful of salad into her mouth and chewed very slowly to mask her frustration. The things small-town people considered significant or unusual amazed her.

"How well did you know Mr. Thompson?"

"Too well." Timothy Black's pleasant expression turned dark, and he pursed his lips.

"What do you mean?" She tried not to get her hopes up again and took a sip of tea.

"It's not kind to speak ill of the dead, or in this case the missing, but he was a pain in the butt. Everybody in town disliked the man for one reason or another."

Emma's confusion must've been obvious because Mr. Black continued with his story. "The townsfolk loved Mr. Thompson Senior, the factory founder, and Junior. They were wonderful men, kind to everyone and always willing to help. Employees at the plant liked them and liked working for them, but that grandson, Thompson III, was cut from different cloth."

"I don't understand, Mr. Black. Most of what I've heard so far has been flattering." She kept Sylvie Martinez's comments to herself.

"Then somebody is rewriting history. Very few people could stand the man. His sister is the only person who missed him. When he disappeared, most of the townsfolk figured we'd leave well enough alone. He was gone, and we didn't need to sully the family name further. He'd seen to that quite well."

Timothy Black's voice held a hint of barely contained anger. What had happened in his relationship with Theodore Thompson to make him so annoyed? "What did he do, aside from trying to expand his already-handsome empire? Why did you dislike him so much?"

Mr. Black sopped up some gravy on his plate with a biscuit but spoke before plopping it into his mouth. "Theodore Thompson didn't have to work for his money and looked down on folks who did. He had no compassion and thought only of himself. He had quite a reputation as a womanizer and flaunted it in poor Sandra's face every chance he got. Is that enough? If not, I could go on. People in this town know what he was like. If they're honest, they'll tell you the same thing. I've probably said too much. It's not my place to pass judgment on people, only to pass them along." He finally ate the gravy-soaked biscuit and pushed his plate across the counter.

"Just one more question, Mr. Black. Did Thompson try to buy your property?"

"Many times, but fortunately mine wasn't high on his priority list." Timothy Black glanced at a pocket watch from his vest and rose from the barstool. "It's been a pleasure, Ms. Ferguson, but I have to get back. Loretta, put this nice lady's lunch on my tab."

Emma started to object, but Black shook his head. "I don't often get to eat with an attractive woman." As he approached the exit, he turned and announced, "If you have any more questions about Theodore Thompson, come see me and I'll give it to you straight." The voices in the diner shot up an octave after he left.

Emma finished her salad slowly, rehashing her conversation with Timothy Black and trying to understand what bothered her about it. The old phone system had been replaced years ago, and any record of outages or maintenance was probably long gone. She made a few notes on her pad, thanked Loretta, and stepped out into the afternoon sun.

She slowly browsed some of the quaint shops dotting Main Street, attempting to distract her thoughts from Carter West, Timothy Black's opinion of Theodore Thompson, and the highly anticipated call from Rick Hardy. If she mulled over any of the subjects too long, her mind spiraled in a circle of conflicting and incomplete feelings and data. She took a seat by the fountain to rest her ankle before walking to the gym to find Carter.

As Emma started toward the school, her cell rang, and she pulled it from the side of her bag. Rick Hardy's number showed on the screen. She hadn't expected a response so quickly, but his call would change the entire focus of her visit to this small town. "Hi, Rick. What news?"

"I've just gotten a call from the lab."

She recognized his curt tone, reserved for serious business matters. She gripped the phone tighter and waited.

"The medical examiner and forensic anthropologist agree the skull of your missing person definitely shows signs of trauma, probably from a small-caliber weapon. Point of entry was just above the glabella and exit between the superior and inferior temporal lines."

"Can you give it to me in English, Rick?"

"The entry and exit points of the bullet indicate a trajectory consistent with Theodore Thompson being shot between the eyes by someone shorter or possibly seated at the time. We won't be sure about other injuries to the rest of the skeleton until it's completely reconstructed, but this is enough to cause death pretty quickly. Looks like you've got yourself a murder story. I'm sending Agent Billie Donovan down there tomorrow to reopen the case on behalf of the BCI. She's new to my team, but she comes highly recommended."

"But—"

"I know how you are, so please stay out of the investigation. The agent knows you've got first dibs on the story when the case is closed."

"Rick, that hardly seems fair. After all, I dug this up on my own. Can't I just tag along? I've developed a rapport with the folks and could be an asset to the investigation."

"That's not a good idea. You've been asking general, non-threatening questions. Once folks find out this is now a murder investigation, there's bound to be resistance and evasion. My agent has the legal authority to manage that. Let Donovan handle it. Promise me you will."

She wasn't about to politely hand off the biggest story of her life to a buttoned-up BCI suit. She'd made a promise to Fannie and intended to keep it.

"Emma?"

She crossed her fingers. "I'll let your trained professional handle the case." She hung up quickly and continued toward the gym to meet Carter before Rick could hear the deceit in her voice.

Children's laughter reached her as she drew close to the gym and immediately made her smile. Laughing kids made everything brighter, or at least took her mind off her troubles for a while. She eased the back door open and glanced inside, hoping to catch Carter in her relaxed state, enjoying the children and doing what she loved. But the old metal door squeaked, and her four young friends from the cookout rushed her.

"Emma. Emma."

"Hi, guys. What's going on?"

Simone mimicked bouncing a ball and executing a jump shot. "We're smoking Carter at basketball."

"Really?" She looked toward Carter, who was holding a basketball and shrugging as if she had no excuse. "All of you against one?"

"She's like a giant," Nico said. "We gotta have some kind of advantage. This ain't golf, you know."

Emma laughed. "I guess you're right."

Carter sauntered over and started to put her arm around Emma but stopped. "You ready?"

Emma nodded.

"Okay, guys, put the equipment away, and I'll lock up. Good session...and great game. You won fair and square. See you next time."

Emma watched Carter lock the equipment room and turn off the lights while the kids collected their gear and filed out. It was a rote task, but Emma would be content watching Carter sleep, eat, read the paper, or any of thousands of mundane activities. She made everything seem effortless and sexy somehow.

With all the kids gone, Carter slid her arm around Emma's waist and escorted her to the Jeep. "You should really be careful looking at me like that in public."

She brought her hand to her chest in mock surprise and produced her most innocent face. "Like what?"

"Like you could eat me."

Carter stood at the door of the Jeep, and Emma almost grabbed her and pulled her in on top of her. "Now there's a great idea."

CHAPTER ELEVEN

The ride back to the park was as quiet as their first one had been, but for an entirely different reason. Carter constantly touched Emma's arm or leg, fanning the desire that had plagued her all day, and Emma couldn't keep her hands off Carter either. Carter didn't need words to express what she was feeling. Emma sensed her passion like a hungry beast hovering, ready to consume her, and it stirred Emma's blood.

But she and Carter were just beginning to discover each other, to really communicate, and she didn't want to blow it by being an insatiable sexaholic. She'd learned through journalism to be patient and take things slowly, but she seemed to operate on an entirely different level in relationships. Logic gave way to emotions, and she was out of her depth.

When they approached the park, Carter asked, "Where do you want me to drop you?"

The question took Emma entirely by surprise since they'd been fondling each other nonstop since town. She'd assumed they'd go directly to her cabin. "I…thought maybe we'd…"

Carter leaned over and gave her a light peck on the cheek, not at all what Emma hoped for, and said, "I've got to make rounds. Prowler, vandal. Be back in about an hour."

Emma stifled her disappointment and forced a smile. "Okay. I'll just chat with Ann, but what about my car?" When Carter showed no sign of understanding her question, she continued. "I should pay the guy who fixed my slashed tires."

"Don't worry about it. He owed me a favor."

"I'd still like to pay my own way."

"Can't you just accept a favor and say thank you?"

"Thank you, Carter, and I look forward to seeing you later."

Carter winked. "You bet."

When Emma opened the office door, Ann sprang from her seat behind the counter, her purple shirt and pink-scarf necktie a flash of bold color.

"Howdy, Emma. I've been wondering what happened to you today. I saw the service-station guy replacing your tires. Sorry about that. Seems like we've got a vandal on the loose. How's your ankle?"

"Much better, thanks. Do you have any of your special brandy left, or did I clean you out last time?"

"You bet." Glancing at the wall clock, Ann said, "Flip the sign on the door to closed."

Ann retrieved the tin mugs, filled them with her secret stash of apple brandy, and set one by Emma's chair while Emma removed her shoe from a still-tender ankle.

"Here's to whatever ails you...and to a speedy recovery."

Emma took a sip of the amber liquor and rolled it around in her mouth, enjoying the hint of dried apple and citrus.

"So, what's going on with you and my niece?"

Emma gasped and swallowed at the same time, forcing the potent liquid up and out her nose. She coughed and sputtered, trying not to choke but wishing she would. Ann offered her a napkin, and she dabbed at her watery eyes and nose.

"I didn't mean to send you into a tizzy. That's sure a waste of good brandy. I was just wondering what happened with you two. Carter was a bit light on details."

Finally able to speak, Emma said, "I think I understand what you're asking."

"Am I being too nosy?" Ann's voice held only a hint of real contrition. "Carter tells me I should mind my own business, but I have to admit, my business isn't near as interesting as hers."

"What did Carter say?" Emma wasn't sure how or even if she should answer.

"Not much, as usual. She's always been the quiet type."

Deciding she had nothing to lose, Emma dove in. "I'm not sure I know exactly what happened. We talked for a while. She fed me dinner with chopsticks, which was the most romantic thing anyone's ever done for me. And before I could stop myself, I was all over her." Emma's pulse pounded with the memory, and she fanned herself with the napkin.

"I bet that threw her for a loop. Carter has always fancied herself as the one in charge."

"And that's the other thing. I don't usually make the first move. It was like something foreign was driving me. I probably scared her, and I've no idea what she's thinking now."

"Who knows with that one, but it was probably good for her. She needed a new experience. I wouldn't worry about it too much. Just be yourself."

"I met her at the school gym to ride back home, and she was with the kids again. I'm so attracted to the woman I saw with those children that I couldn't pull myself away. She's amazing. They love her, and she obviously loves helping them."

Ann nodded and took a sip of brandy. "Carter has always wanted to be a child therapist. She would've had her own practice by now if she hadn't interrupted her studies to be here with me. She denies that's the reason, but I know the truth. She didn't want to leave me alone after Cass died. I couldn't talk her out of it."

"She said she's almost finished her doctorate work."

"She's been going to night classes at the University of Virginia and working on her dissertation in her spare time. I hope she'll get a full-time position when she's finished and leave this dead-end job."

Emma stretched her legs closer to the fire and sipped her brandy. "I didn't realize she was so nurturing."

"Protective is more like it. She's seen the harsh side of life and has appointed herself as protector—mostly mine. I've told her I can take care of myself."

"No doubt about that." Emma paused before asking her next question. "So what should I do, Ann?"

"It depends on your intentions, not meaning to sound old-fashioned. But if you care about Carter, give her time to think through what happened and how she feels about it. If you're just having a fling, chase her."

"I don't get it."

"When Carter figures out how she feels, she'll come to you if she's interested. If you chase her, she'll run faster than an eight-point buck in hunting season."

Emma considered Ann's advice and decided it made sense, based on the little she knew about Carter. "I'm not really sure what I want, but thanks. I defer to your insight about your niece and your expertise with women. Speaking of which, can I please hear more about you and Cass? I know we're close to the two of you getting together. You left off where she'd come to visit and told you she was going to marry husband number three. She kissed you good-bye, and you didn't really talk for two more years."

Ann topped up their mugs and settled back into her cushy recliner. "And Cass did exactly what she said. She married that man a week later. Things seemed to be going all right between them as far as anyone could tell. Of course, I never talked with her. We would pass on the street and exchange long glances, but she wouldn't acknowledge me. I didn't find out until years later that he'd threatened to beat her senseless and leave her and her mother flat broke if she ever spoke to me again."

"What a heartless animal. Was there nothing you could do?"

"Cass made her choice. I had to live with it."

Emma couldn't help thinking there was more, something else keeping Ann at bay other than an abusive husband and a half-hearted choice on Cass's part. Too many love stories had overcome greater obstacles. She didn't seem like the type to give up without a fight.

Ann tugged at her scarf necktie. "Anyway, the first year went along with no major problems. I heard news occasionally from friends. Toward the end of the second year of their marriage, all hell broke loose."

Emma leaned forward, certain this was the part where Ann finally got her woman.

"I heard that Cass was pregnant and—"

"Pregnant? No way." Ann and Cass had been plagued with a string of unfortunate circumstances that kept them apart for years. Emma's heart ached for such a strong love so long denied.

"That's pretty much what I said before I went on a week-long bender. I'd been living with false hope the marriage was in name only, that she really didn't allow the bastard to touch her, much less put his…You get my meaning."

Emma reached over and squeezed Ann's hand. "I'm sure that was devastating."

Ann's eyes misted. "That was it for me. I quit my job at the furniture factory and—"

"What?" Emma shook her head, unsure she'd heard right. "Wait a minute. Furniture factory? I obviously missed something."

"Guess I skipped over some details. As I've said before, things were difficult in my life too. I'd gone to work in Thompson's factory shortly after they got married."

"Which Thompson?" Emma's empty stomach pitched and churned, as much from Ann's news as from the brandy.

"Theodore Wayne Thompson, III, her good-for-nothing husband. He never did anything but siphon money from the business and make the workers miserable."

Emma's mind clouded, and her pitching stomach now churned. She tried to put the disjointed pieces together. Cass was married to Theodore Thompson? This couldn't be right. "I thought Theodore Thompson was married to a woman named Sandra."

"Sandra, hell. Her name was Cass Calloway. I was the only one allowed to call her Cass—short for Cassandra. Everybody else knew her as Sandra. He thought it sounded more high-society. My aching ass."

More pieces fell into place, and the implications made Emma queasier. She wiped sweat from her forehead and took another sip of brandy.

"Are you okay, Emma? You look washed out."

"I'm just a little hot all of a sudden."

Ann rose and adjusted the wood stove while Emma tried to compose herself. Questions whirled through her mind too numerous to count and too compelling to ignore. She considered leaving to avoid the inevitable conclusion of this story, but her professional curiosity forced her to stay and to question until the end.

"How could you work for a man you despised, Ann?"

"Like I said, things were complicated. The economy was tight. They needed workers at the factory, and I needed a job in the worst way. I had no other choice."

"I can't imagine what it must've been like for you to see him, knowing the woman you loved was in his bed at night."

"It was all I could do not to strangle him every time I was near him. He'd look at me with his smug grin, and I'd see blood. He was an awful boss too. If his tiny little pea brain were on fire, not one of us would've pissed in his ear to put it out. Except for my supervisor, I would've killed him several times over. He pulled me off him more than once and made me refocus on the big picture."

Ann had just uttered the words Emma prayed she wouldn't hear—a motive for murder. A knot gathered in her throat, and she struggled to swallow. "What was the big picture? What kept you so dedicated to a job you hated and to a woman you couldn't have?" She needed confirmation of the driving force behind Ann's commitment, afraid she already knew. She sensed a deeper purpose and feared what Ann might've done to achieve it.

"Maybe I was a slow learner?" Ann wiped her eyes and rose unsteadily to her feet. Worry lines creased her forehead.

"Did I say something wrong?" Grasping Ann's hands, Emma brought them to her cheek. "I'm so sorry."

"It's just that some stories aren't entirely mine to tell. I had financial responsibilities I couldn't ignore."

"Was it Carter? She told me about the accident and coming to live with you."

Ann hesitated. "What else did she say?"

"Just that her parents were killed in a car accident when she was two years old." Emma knew there was more to this story, but the conflict and pain on Ann's face stopped her from pushing harder.

"Yes. I had to work in Thompson's God-forsaken factory to take care of Carter. Her father was my only sibling. We're blood. I did what had to be done. Always have and always will. And I don't regret one single second I've devoted to that child."

Ann's responses raised more questions, questions Emma wasn't ready to ask. What if Ann had been involved in Thompson's murder? Did Emma really want to know? How would that fact affect her fledgling relationship with Carter and Emma's growing affection for Ann? What would it mean for her story? She rose from the recliner, drained the brandy from the tin mug, and handed it back to Ann. "You're an honorable woman, Ann West, and I can tell Carter loves you very much. That was a totally selfless thing you did." She hugged Ann. "Are you okay?"

"I'll be fine. Don't worry about me. Some memories will be painful as long as I live. Thanks for listening."

"Thanks for trusting me with your story." Emma stepped into the cold night air, and as tears sprang to her eyes, she wiped them with the back of her hand. She desperately wanted these two powerful stories—Thompson's murder and Ann's love—to remain separate, but they'd collided and entwined years ago. Emma's only hope now was to keep them from destroying the lives of two women she cared for deeply.

Carter paced outside Emma's cabin, debating whether to knock on the door. Her nerves knotted as she tried to calm down and breathe normally. Why did she feel compelled to talk to Emma about last night? She'd seemed perfectly fine during their trips to and from town, even anxious for a repeat. Carter had never explained herself to a woman after sex, but she'd never gotten entirely carried away before either.

She climbed the steps, a gangplank to the unknown, and shuffled from one side of the porch to the other. The argument raged in her mind. *Knock. Don't knock. Talk. Don't talk. Run.* She'd always been in charge of her emotions, always holding a little back for protection until she was certain she could trust. She wasn't there with Emma Ferguson yet. Carter turned to leave. Whatever she imagined needed to be said could wait.

Suddenly the cabin door opened, and Emma stood in the entrance holding a broom above her head. "Who the hell is out here?" she yelled, rushing onto the porch.

Carter raised her hands. "I give up."

"Carter? I heard someone walking around, and since the prowler and the slashed tires…Guess I'm getting paranoid. I'm sorry. Come inside."

"Are you sure it's not too late for visitors? I could come back another time." Carter secretly prayed she would say yes.

"Since you didn't show up after your rounds, I thought you were already having second thoughts." Emma closed the door behind them, leaned the broom against the wall, and waited.

Carter tugged at her necklace. Emma's pull was as strong as the outdoors and even more appealing. *I need to have my say and get out—fast.*

Emma stepped forward, so close Carter felt her body heat. Then she reached up and touched Carter's hand that was fingering her necklace. "I've been meaning to ask about this. It seems to give you comfort when you're anxious about something."

Was she ready to tell the story of this treasured piece, of the anguish she'd gone through to earn it? She slowly pulled the chain and its small ornament from her shirt. At the end of the chain, encased in a sphere of tiny silver threads, rested a cat's-eye marble. The clear-glass exterior protected eight veins of deep amber. Carter had worn the beautiful orb for so long she knew every flaw and nuance.

Emma took the small object between her fingers and rolled it over and over. "The hue of the veins matches the color of your eyes. It's beautiful."

"It's a peewee cat's eye. Cass gave it to me for my eighth birthday. We played marbles all the time, just the two of us. She said it would always watch over me. Her eyes were the same color too." Carter couldn't tell the whole story yet; her memories were too strong and emotive.

"You loved her very much, didn't you?" Emma took Carter's hand and led her to the sofa. "Sit with me."

"She and Ann were my family for thirty-six years. We were very happy." Carter's voice cracked as she allowed her gaze to settle on Emma's face. The tenderness in her eyes soothed and encouraged her.

Emma hugged Carter, nestled Carter's head against her breasts, and gently rocked. Time slipped by as Carter allowed herself to be comforted by someone other than Ann. Tension drained from her body as Emma stroked her hair. She'd shared two of the most intimate stories of her life with this woman. Being with Emma was so easy. When she finally stirred, Carter felt a lightness she'd never experienced and decided to tell Emma why she'd come by.

"Carter, I'm glad you're here. I wanted to talk about last night."

"Wait. Can I go first, please? I've been wandering through the woods for the past hour trying to get up the nerve to come in. If I don't get it out now, I never will."

Emma searched her face for a few seconds and finally nodded.

"I've never been one to just come out and say things, emotional things. I figure what is meant to happen is just going to, and we don't need to talk it to death." Carter rose and paced in front of the fireplace. "No, that's not right," she muttered to herself.

"Why don't you just say it, Carter? You don't have to be eloquent, just honest."

"I've always been a loner in the relationship sense. That sounded ridiculous. What I mean is, it's not easy to let people in. Ann says I've got enough scar tissue for several lifetimes."

Emma smiled and waited patiently.

"I…I think I have…feelings for you, and I've never felt like this. It's too soon. Last night you…that was another first for me. I don't know what to do with all these different emotions. Maybe I'm just imagining a connection. Don't get me wrong. I'm not suggesting anything serious, but maybe we could explore the possibilities…if you're interested at all. And you're probably not. You'll be gone in a few days, and I'll be a distant memory."

Emma smiled again, but this time her smile suffused her face with light. "Once you start you just keep going. Do you want my input, or would you rather continue your monologue?"

"Sorry, but this is scary." There. She'd said the word that summed up every insecurity, false start, ended relationship, and uncertainty in her life. Fear.

"Beginnings are always scary. I imagine it's especially so for you, to open up and trust."

"It's difficult for me to imagine…" Carter scrunched her face like she'd done since childhood when she was worried or unsure.

"I'm afraid of abandonment. Women always leave me, not the other way around," Emma said. "In your case, you're probably the one who ends it. Am I right?"

Carter couldn't look at Emma because she was right. Carter had never found a woman who made her want to commit to the long haul. She was the epitome of Emma's greatest fear.

"There's no shame in that, Carter, no judgment. We're all different. It would be so easy for me to get seriously involved with you," Emma admitted. "I'm very attracted to you, and it scares me too."

Carter stopped in front of the sofa and their eyes locked. Emma flushed a delicious shade of pink and looked at the floor. "Last night was different for you too?"

"I've never been that assertive before. It was something I needed to do, and you were strong enough to let me. And you were so responsive. I've never elicited that sort of reaction from a lover."

Carter wasn't sure what Emma had just said. Did she care about her too, or was she just having a fling, spreading her sexual wings? She paced from the front door through the small living area into the kitchen. Had she made a terrible mistake revealing her fledgling feelings? When she reached the table, she turned and started back.

After several trips conducted in silence, she couldn't bear the quiet any longer. "Does that mean you have feelings for me too?"

She stopped abruptly beside the kitchen table, resting her hands on the back of a chair, readying herself for Emma's answer. She stared at the stack of documents scattered across the tabletop. *What the hell?* Picking up a notepad, she scanned the notes and followed the drawn arrows toward two words circled in the center of the page. *Ann's motive.* She tensed as she turned to face Emma again. The warmth between them evaporated, replaced by a sheet of black ice, invisible but deadly.

"Carter, what's wrong?"

She shook the pages in Emma's direction. "What's this about?"

"What's what about?" Emma rose from the sofa and started toward her.

"Stop. I should've known better than to trust you."

"Carter, why are you so upset? Those are notes for my story."

She pointed to the papers. "Did you think I wouldn't find out?"

"Find out about my article? I haven't kept it a secret."

"Don't play innocent with me. You know exactly what I'm talking about. This is more than a history piece. You're rehashing the Thompson disappearance, aren't you?" The blood in Carter's temples pounded so loudly she could barely hear herself think. *Idiot! I told you not to trust her.*

"I'm looking into the possibility that it might be more than a disappearance."

"You don't have any idea what you're about to unleash, do you? Was Ann part of the plan all along or just icing on the cake? Pretending to care about her life with Cass was a nice touch. If you really have any feelings for her or me, you'll drop this before you drag us all through the mud. Our life may not have been Ozzie and Harriett, but it was ours."

Emma's eyes pleaded for understanding as she stepped closer and tentatively extended her hand. "Carter, why is this upsetting you? I know you're a private person, but this story is about Thompson. What am I missing?"

"I doubt very seriously you've missed anything. You're connecting all the dots, but in the wrong order." She held up the sheet of paper with *Ann's motive* in the center and waved it in front of Emma again. "Was this what last night was about too? Were you getting close to hear my side of the story?"

"Carter, no. It's my job to explore all the possibilities."

"No matter who it hurts."

"You asked if I have feelings for you—"

"And this is my answer." Carter flung the paper to the floor. "If you *do* care about me, you'll let this go. *Please*, Emma."

Emma held Carter's gaze. "I can't. I gave my word to a woman who desperately needs help. She's in the same situation my mother was years ago, and I couldn't help her. This is professional and personal. I have to see it through. But it doesn't change how I feel—"

"I don't need to hear any more."

"But Carter, please." Emma tried to stop her as she headed for the door

"Don't touch me." She glared at Emma before opening the door and stepping out. She barely remembered hearing the door close behind her before she ran into the woods.

CHAPTER TWELVE

Night passed slowly as visions of Carter's pained expression interrupted Emma's attempts to sleep. At dawn she forced her drowsy body from bed, showered, and consumed a pot of strong coffee. The caffeine kick was more like a stumble as she sat staring at the documents covering the kitchen table.

Carter's reaction to her investigation seemed over the top. Cass and Theodore Thompson had been married, and while she appreciated Carter's desire to protect Ann from any potential fallout, her response had gone beyond protectiveness to something more personal and immediate. Before she'd had a chance to find out why, Carter had stormed off.

The warm surge of attraction between them had turned to cold splinters. She'd struggled to speak but could only watch as the anger on Carter's face transformed into pain and settled in deepening lines that creased her forehead. Emma wanted—no, she desperately needed Thompson's disappearance and Ann and Cass's story to remain separate. One could help her resolve old issues about her father's disappearance and earn enough money to live for a while, and the other held the key to the possibility of a love she'd only imagined. But as Carter headed toward the door, she felt the latter being stripped from her.

Carter's overreaction and her protectiveness of Ann only fueled Emma's fear that Ann's relationship with Cass Calloway *was* connected to Theodore Thompson's murder. How connected remained to be seen. What was Carter hiding? For now, Emma was forced to push her feelings aside, get on with the task of finding a killer, and hope that somewhere along the line it would all make sense and leave those she cared about unscathed.

When she entered the sheriff's office, Echols glanced from his guest to her and shook his head. His furrowed brow and pink cheeks left little doubt to his state of mind. The attractive government-suited blonde seated beside his desk didn't acknowledge Emma and continued her conversation in whispered tones, leaning into the sheriff's body space. Emma stepped close enough to hear.

"Based on this information, Sheriff, we have no choice but to open a new investigation into the disappearance of Theodore Wayne Thompson. BCI Supervisor Hardy has sent me here to do that. I hope I can depend on your cooperation." She punctuated her final comment by placing a manicured hand on the sheriff's arm and flashing a surprisingly sincere smile.

Turning his attention to Emma, the sheriff stated, "And here is the person we have to thank for all this. You couldn't leave well enough alone, could you, Ms. Ferguson?"

The BCI agent turned to Emma and offered her hand, along with another devastatingly charming smile.

"Emma Ferguson, I'm Billie Donovan, Virginia Bureau of Criminal Investigation."

"Agent Donovan. So you're officially reopening the Thompson case?"

She nodded. "Agent Hardy's told me a lot about you."

I bet he has, Emma thought, but he didn't tell me anything about you. But maybe that's because you're just his type—petite, blonde, gorgeous, and oozing sex appeal.

"And I've been instructed to give you an *exclusive*," she emphasized the word, "when the case is closed."

Donovan's green eyes scanned Emma's body with an intensity that felt intrusive. Was it the law-enforcement appraisal or the one-woman-sizing-up-another that bothered her? "We might be able to help each other. I've been looking into this for a while."

Sheriff Echols rose from his desk. "Well, the two of you have a wonderful time tearing open old wounds. Folks around here would much rather handle their own dirty laundry." Casting a disapproving glance at Emma, he concluded their conversation. "If you need anything from me, Agent Donovan, I'll be around." He handed Donovan a business card and pretended to busy himself with a stack of unfiled papers.

Donovan aimed her practiced smile back on Emma. "Why don't we go over to the diner and compare notes?"

As they walked the short distance to the Stuart Diner, Emma contrasted Agent Donovan's feminine sway and demeanor to Carter's swagger and androgynous appeal. Carter's body moved with a confidence Donovan seemed to force. Her breasts seemed way too perky for a fiftyish woman. Implants maybe? Would Carter be attracted to Billie Donovan? She winced at the thought and pushed the image from her mind. Whatever had gone wrong between her and Carter couldn't be handled now, though the pain and uncertainty of it persisted.

When they'd settled into a back booth and ordered coffee, Donovan laced her fingers together around the cup and leaned across the table toward Emma. "It seems like you've stirred up a hornet's nest, Ferguson. Do you always create this much excitement?"

Emma disliked Billie Donovan more each time she spoke. The gorgeous smile that lit her face with simultaneous concern and curiosity grated on Emma's nerves. Donovan's investigations were probably exact and personally satisfying, which irritated Emma because of the seemingly perfect package it represented of Agent Billie Donovan. Nobody was that flawless. But maybe she was just being petty.

Whatever her reasons, she wasn't entrusting this case to Donovan, especially since it involved Ann and maybe even Carter. She wanted to be the one to clear Ann, if that became necessary, and to reassure Carter, not this BCI bombshell.

Best stay on track and keep it professional. "What else did Rick send from the lab? I already know the bones have been identified as Thompson's and he was shot. Is there more?"

"Not at this time. Anything new on your end?"

Donovan was slick, sidestepping Emma's question and turning it around on her. "No."

"Are you sure? It wouldn't be smart to withhold relevant information." Donovan swiped a drip of coffee from the side of her cup and licked it off her finger. Emma hated to admit she found the act sexy as hell. Billie Donovan was everything Emma wasn't: confident, model thin, blond with emerald eyes, and she radiated sex appeal. Carter would be a fool not to be attracted to this woman.

"Hell—o." Donovan waved her hand in front of Emma's face.

"Sorry."

"I asked where you're staying. I need a place to set up shop and sleep occasionally."

Emma took a sip of coffee while she decided how to answer. She didn't want Donovan anywhere near Carter, but they'd meet eventually. "I'm at the Fairy Stone State Park."

Donovan chuckled. "You don't seem like the outdoor type." She looked off in the distance, and her practiced grin turned to a genuine smile. "Fairy Stone Park. That's the one run by Ann West. Her niece, Carter, is a ranger there." Donovan's eyebrow shot up almost imperceptibly as she mentioned Carter's name.

Emma nodded, afraid to speak in case she revealed her feelings for Carter.

"I could stay out there, probably free, but woodsy and I don't get along."

Emma exhaled deeply and placed her hand over her queasy stomach. "There's a relatively nice hotel in the town center that's convenient to everything."

"Sounds perfect. Thanks." Donovan swiped a hand through her long, blond hair and brushed it away from her face. "You've been here for a week. Any leads on possible suspects?"

"I've just found out it's a murder case. Compiling suspects without all the facts seemed a bit premature. But most folks in town didn't care that Theodore Thompson was gone. A suspect list could be pretty extensive."

"Sounds like I'm going to have my work cut out for me. Why don't you fill me in on the rest of the gossip you've gotten from these fine townsfolk?"

As much as Emma disliked revealing her sources and intelligence, she didn't want to appear uncooperative. She filled Donovan in on the information from her interviews that seemed significant, carefully avoiding Ann's connection to Theodore Thompson. Repeating it all, she realized she hadn't uncovered any substantial leads in the case.

"Sounds like we're a little shy on suspects. Why did you dig all this up in the first place? Why not just leave it alone, do your little history piece, and go back to civilization?"

Fannie's tearful plea replayed in Emma's mind, and her eyes clouded. "It's just something I have to do. Something unfinished."

"Sort of like Carter West and me."

Emma clasped her hands together in her lap to keep from going after Donovan.

"That woman is absolutely gorgeous...and delicious, if you don't mind me being so bold. We've been having a little fling for a while up in Charlottesville. This might be the perfect time to take the relationship further. I've relocated to Richmond now, more convenient and available."

Emma felt her coffee clawing its way back up her throat. The image of Carter with Donovan—touching her, making love to her— made Emma want to vault over the table and...what was happening to her? She wasn't a violent or jealous person, but she'd never felt so strongly about another woman. She had to leave before she embarrassed herself by defending a relationship that didn't exist. Emma rose and grabbed her messenger bag, in the process spinning her cup across the table and sloshing coffee onto Donovan's pristine pale-blue blouse. "Sorry. I'm clumsy." Excellent addition, Emma thought as she tossed her a napkin.

On the way out, the same construction worker who'd questioned her before stepped into her path, his shaved head and face red with obvious irritation. "So there's two of you trying to stall our work now. When are you going to give up and let us get on with our business?"

Emma jerked her thumb in Donovan's direction. "Ask the BCI agent."

The walk to Fannie Buffkin's house was not one Emma wanted to make, but the time had come. Fannie didn't deserve to hear about her brother's murder from some gossipmonger. The news would be devastating, but it would be better than the continued agony of not knowing.

After the third knock, Fannie answered the door. Her eyes sparkled when she saw Emma, and she ushered her inside. "Emma, I wasn't sure I'd ever see you again. You have news, don't you? The gossip vine has been particularly active the past few days, but no one will tell me what's going on. Even Harriett Smoltz is dodging my calls. It's about Theodore, isn't it?"

"Fannie, can we sit down please?"

When they were seated in the drawing room, Emma struggled for the right words. The expectation on Fannie's face tugged at her heart. She'd seen that expression on her mother's face so many times over the years, and each time Emma had disappointed her.

"My brother was killed, wasn't he? I knew I was right but didn't really want to be."

"Yes, you were." Emma understood. Her instincts that Theodore Thompson had been murdered had also been right, and Fannie Buffkin wasn't loony. But from what she'd seen so far, few people cared, thirty-seven years ago or now. His sister cared and so did Emma.

"I'm so very sorry." Emma took Fannie's wrinkled hands and held them gently in her own. "You don't know how much I wish I had better news."

Fannie lowered her head, and tears dropped onto her pale-green apron. "I remember when those bones were found at the factory in 1985. I told the sheriff it was Theo. Why did it take so long to identify him? Couldn't something have been done before now?"

"The technology for a positive DNA analysis is a relatively recent development. The sheriff was right not to get your hopes up. When I discovered his remains were still in the state lab, I asked for a test against the hair sample you provided, and it was a match." She paused, not wanting to cause unnecessary pain and uncertain how much detail Fannie needed or wanted.

"What else? Tell me all of it."

"There was trauma to the skull, which indicates a violent death. The BCI has reopened his case. I'm sure you'll get a visit from Agent Donovan sooner or later." Emma took a deep breath and waited for one of the two questions to which she did not have an answer.

"But why? Why would anyone want to kill my brother?"

Emma chose not to divulge Theodore's questionable reputation around town. Fannie probably already knew what kind of man her brother had become but colored his life with a rosier brush for the sake of the family legacy. No matter what he'd done, his sister didn't deserve to suffer any further for it. Emma patted Fannie's hands and whispered, "I really don't know." And she sincerely hoped she didn't.

She sat with Fannie, offering whatever comfort she could until the older woman took a deep breath and rose from her chair.

"I really appreciate you telling me in person." As she walked Emma to the door, her frail hands held on tight. "Thank you for taking the time to care about Theodore. I know most people didn't, but he was family. You will see this through, won't you?"

She thought about the pained look on Carter's face and her plea for Emma to abandon the story, but she felt compelled to honor her promise to Fannie and now to keep Ann out of the investigation. "Of course."

"I mean, the BCI is probably very thorough, but I want you on Theodore's case."

She hugged Fannie and left her alone with her memories and whatever peace her news had provided.

Before heading back to the park, Emma stopped by the county historian's office to talk with Hannah Smoltz. The woman who greeted her held no resemblance to Harriett. "I'm looking for Ms. Hannah Smoltz."

"On vacation. Not sure when she'll be back." The young woman was the first person Emma had encountered in Stuart who seemed unfriendly, almost hostile.

"You mean she just told you she was going on vacation and didn't say how long she'd be gone?" Emma arched her eyebrows at the woman for effect.

"*She* didn't tell me anything. Her sister told me she'd left after the fact, and I'd be in charge until she showed up again. Harriett didn't offer any information about where Hannah had gone either, in case you were going to ask." The woman returned to her computer without asking if she could be of any further assistance.

"Thanks for nothing," she muttered under her breath as she exited. She crossed the street toward her car but turned back when someone called her name. Harriett Smoltz was standing in the library doorway, waving and motioning her over.

"Want to come in and rest a spell? From what I hear, you've been busy."

"I don't mind if I do, Harriett. I've just been over to the historian's office, but Hannah is out of town. Do you know when she'll be back?"

"She takes off a couple of times a year. Is there anything I can help you with?" She motioned Emma to her small office in the corner of the library.

"I wanted to inquire about her whereabouts the night Theodore Thompson disappeared. It's a general inquiry."

Harriett's eyes narrowed to slits. "I can answer that one for you. She was night-shift operator at the telephone company. She relieved me about eleven o'clock. So you've definitely decided to investigate this case?"

"My inquiries are strictly for my article. The investigation is with the BCI now. Theodore Thompson was shot, so they're reopening the case as a murder. An agent is already here."

Harriett's eyes flicked from side to side. "Isn't that interesting?" Her whole body seemed to bristle to attention as she fired questions. "Who would've believed we'd have a real murder right here in Stuart? Do you have any leads? Are there any suspects?" She edged closer to her desk phone, and Emma imagined her dialing the gossip tree with the latest update.

Emma provided a brief rundown of the story, omitting any classified information. "So you see, they really don't have any clear-cut suspects at this point. I'm going to ask around, touch base with any folks who were here then. You could give me a list, if it wouldn't be too much trouble."

"I'd love to help," Harriett responded, wringing her hands. "I'll have a list ready by tomorrow."

❖

Carter and Ann were pulling out of the park gate when Emma drove in around dusk. Ann leaned across Carter, waved furiously, and yelled, "Hey, Emma!"

"Can you stop that?" Carter snapped.

"Well, excuse the hell out of me. What's gotten into you?"

"Nothing. I just don't think it's a good idea to get too chummy with her."

"Now that you've slept with her, it's okay to treat her like road kill? You beat all, Carter West. You know that?"

"It's not about sleeping with her, Ann. There's more going on than you realize." Carter's body heated with the memory of making love with Emma. Then her chest constricted at Emma's refusal to let the story go. *How did I let myself get so twisted up in this mess?*

"Why don't you enlighten me then, because I sure don't understand."

"Just take my word for it and stay away from her. Can you do that for me?"

"No, Carter, I can't. Either you tell me what's going on, or I'll ask Emma."

Carter thought about her stumbling walk to the lake last night after her confrontation with Emma. She could usually find her way blindfolded, but Emma's betrayal had rocked her. The gravel path had been marred by groundcover, and soon she'd come to a small campsite a short distance from the lake. The grass around the fire pit had been worn away from frequent use during the season, and Carter had recalled some of her happiest and most painful memories there with Cass.

Cass and Ann. She'd let them down. She'd allowed Emma into their life and was afraid she might destroy what was left of their love. Wasn't it enough that the town of Stuart had surreptitiously tried to force them to leave when they discovered the nature of their relationship? Now Carter had let a stranger too close to their story. Emma was trying to connect Ann to Thompson's murder, something her aunt would never be involved in no matter how much she loved Cass or hated Theodore. And Carter was to blame.

Carter's knuckles whitened as she clenched the steering wheel. "If you must know, she's looking into the disappearance of Theo Thompson, but this time it's a murder investigation."

Ann raised her palms in the air and shrugged. "And…"

"And I want you to stay away from her. She's been pumping you for information since she got here, with her fake interest in your life. She's a reporter, and she'll spin everything you say into something else if it helps her story. That's probably why she slept with me anyway."

"Oh, Carter. Get over yourself. First of all, there's not a fake bone in the woman's body. If there were, I would've sensed it days ago. Second, she's free to use anything I told her about my life with Cass because it's nothing but a love story. And third, there are easier ways to get information than sleeping with *you*."

"But something's very wrong. I'm waiting for the other shoe to drop."

"Honey, don't worry. You're safe. You were only two years old when all this happened." Ann turned in the seat to face Carter. "Wait a minute. You're worried about me."

"What?" Something about that time summoned uneasiness bordering on panic inside her, but she couldn't resurrect exactly why.

"Do you think I had something to do with Theo Thompson's death?"

"No, of course not." She twisted the cat's-eye chain into a knot. "You do."

"No, I don't, but other people might. Emma Ferguson can influence other people's opinions. I saw her notes. She's already decided you had a motive to kill Thompson."

Ann laughed out loud. "Well, that's for damn sure. I'd put myself first on a suspect list, but that doesn't mean Emma intends to do us harm."

"It sure feels that way to me."

"Because you're over-protective, especially when it comes to me. Give the woman a chance. If she's the person I think she is, she'll find the truth."

"Then why do I have this sense of impending doom?"

Ann's lack of a snappy response troubled Carter more than her usual chatter.

❖

Night had settled on the park when Emma pulled up to her cabin and scanned the nearby woods for another prowler. Darker shadows streaked the walkway, and she wobbled across the paving stones trying not to fall. Crickets chirped nearby, and frogs croaked from the lake as she made her way to the door. The chill in the air reminded her of Carter's facial expression when their cars had passed earlier. Ann seemed friendly enough, but Carter hadn't acknowledged her, not even a glance.

She dug through her bag for the key and found it at the bottom tangled up with something else. She yanked hard, and the bag's contents spilled on the ground. Swearing under her breath, she knelt on the path, fumbled for her scattered items, recovered them one by one, and stuffed them back into her bag.

As she knelt on the uneven surface, a chill shot up her spine before she heard the crunching footsteps behind her. From the corner of her eye Emma saw a dark-clad figure moving toward her. She felt for the small mace canister that usually hung on the side of her bag, but it wasn't there. Willing herself not to panic, she clutched the cabin key on the ground with her right hand. She gauged the distance to the porch and her chances of outrunning whoever was behind her and opening the door before he caught her. Emma remained crouched on the path formulating a plan.

She wrapped the bag straps in her fist, took a deep breath, and dashed toward the porch. Her heart pounded wildly as the footsteps behind her drew nearer. She skipped the steps onto the landing and jabbed at the lock with her key. Her hands shook violently. She was trapped. The figure coming toward her blocked her exit to the left, and the table and chairs to her right made a run toward the woods impossible.

"Who are you?" Emma yelled, trying to control her trembling body. "What do you want?"

The intruder strode silently, deliberately onto the porch, his muscular body covered entirely in black. Tiny slits in the center of the ski mask revealed eyes that flashed with anger. He paused momentarily before raising a large tree limb in his gloved hands. Then with a high-pitched, guttural yell he swung at her head. She ducked, and the branch swooshed by, crashing against the doorframe. Emma dropped to the floor and rolled away as the assailant regained his balance. He swung again, and Emma felt a sharp pain in her left arm when he made contact.

Adrenaline and redheaded determination kicked in. Emma's fear turned to anger and defiance. She pretended to coddle her injured arm and clenched her bag tighter in her right fist. The attacker stood over her, and Emma willed herself to wait as he raised the tree limb over his head for another strike. Then she rose and brought her bag from behind in a full roundhouse swing. The upward arch slammed into the side of the rogue's body, sending him into a backward fall off the porch.

Emma rushed to the edge of the landing, bag clutched in her hand, ready for another volley. The masked figure lay on the ground, struggling to get up. As she raised her arm, a stream of light illuminated the woods behind her. A vehicle bounced over the pavers and skidded through gravel up to the porch steps. When she looked back, the assailant was gone.

Donovan slid across the hood of her car onto the porch just like a television cop, and Emma wanted to snarl at the perfect execution. "What the hell is going on? Are you okay?"

Emma trembled as she stared into the woods. "Did you see that? He tried to kill me!" Her legs suddenly felt rubbery as the adrenaline surge passed.

"Take it easy, Ferguson. He's long gone. We need to make sure you're all right."

"Of course I'm all right." Emma's bravado didn't match her quivering insides. "My arm's aching, that's all."

"Let's get you inside. Give me the cabin key."

She allowed Donovan to help her to the door and handed over the key.

"Does trouble follow you around, Ferguson, or have you pissed somebody off?" Donovan closed the door behind them and helped Emma to the sofa. She examined the swelling lump already forming on Emma's arm and then ran her hand gingerly over Emma's other arm, across her back, over her rib cage, and down her legs.

Emma brushed her hands away. "What are you doing?"

"Don't get excited, Ferguson. I'm just checking for fractures or other injuries. Do you hurt anywhere other than your arm?"

She sat motionless, as if the events of the past few minutes had happened to someone else and she'd watched from a distance. But Donovan's question forced her to consider her physical situation, and when she did, pain throbbed in her left arm. "Just there."

"I'll get some ice. You could have a hairline fracture. At the least you'll have a great bruise. Do you have any idea why someone would come after you?"

"I'd like to think it was a case of mistaken identity or just random, but I had a prowler recently, and somebody slashed two of my tires."

"That doesn't sound random. You should file a report with the sheriff, just in case."

"I was willing to write off the first two incidents as teenage pranks, but this was definitely personal. I looked into his eyes and saw pure hatred." She shivered as Donovan placed a makeshift ice pack on her arm. "Can the report wait until tomorrow?"

"Sure, but we have to consider the possibility the attack is connected to this case."

"Why?" Emma had a feeling Donovan could be right but wanted to hear her reasons.

"Maybe someone doesn't want the truth to come out. The construction company that wants to raze the old factory can't be happy about the delay the investigation is causing."

"That's for sure. The same guy has harassed me about it twice," Emma said.

"Really? What does he look like?"

Emma recalled the mediocre man and pictured him dressed in black swinging a tree limb. "Medium height, muscles, shaved head, always sitting at the same table in the diner by the door like he doesn't have anything else to do."

"I'll pay him a visit tomorrow." Donovan took a seat beside her on the sofa. "Do you have any idea where the groundskeepers were tonight?"

"If you're referring to Carter and Ann, forget it. They were leaving the park when I drove in." Damn it, she sounded defensive again.

Donovan held up her hands. "Hey, I'm just covering all the bases. They could've doubled back. What are the chances your assailant was a woman?"

Emma considered the possibility as she replayed the attack in her mind. The dark clothes and night had blended together, blurring any distinguishable features. He hadn't spoken, and his hands and face were completely covered. She'd just assumed it was a man. Her stomach churned when she realized it was possible a woman had attacked her, but she refused to consider that woman might be someone she knew.

"The look on your face tells me the answer to my question is yes."

"I suppose it's possible, Donovan. It's just not possible Carter or Ann would've attacked me." She shifted the ice pack from the numb spot on her arm and then pushed it off entirely. She was annoyed with Donovan for making her consider things she didn't want to see. "Why are you here anyway?"

"I thought I'd come by and update you. Unfortunately, I didn't find anything new today, but I decided to come anyway. And it's a good thing I did. You're welcome, by the way." She flashed one of her dazzling smiles, and Emma almost liked her.

"I had things mostly handled before you showed up." At least she liked to think she had things under control. Any other scenario was unacceptable. "And thank you."

"Probably, but admit it. You were a little glad to see me, weren't you?"

She'd definitely felt better knowing someone else was nearby. "I'd be happier if I knew who was after me and why. I have no interest in joining Theodore Thompson in the ranks of the not-so-dearly departed."

"We'll get on that first thing in the morning, after we've both had a good night's rest. I'll take the sofa, if you don't mind." Donovan stretched and yawned as she reached for the blanket on the back of the sofa.

"You don't actually think you're going to sleep here tonight."

"You bet I do. After what happened, Rick Hardy would have my hide and maybe my job if I left you alone."

"I'll be fine. You don't need to stay. I'll even sign a note to that effect if you're so worried about Rick's wrath." She couldn't imagine spending a night under the same roof with Billie Donovan. She'd been kind and thoughtful, professionally precise and thorough and, during it all, very charming. So, what was it about Donovan that irritated her so much? Was it her past connection to Carter? Ridiculous. Everybody had a past. She just didn't enjoy seeing Carter's in the form of a gorgeous, talented, sexy, and graceful blonde.

"I'm afraid I have to insist," Donovan said. "The attacker might come back. We need to stick together until we figure out who this person is. Trust me, you'll be safe. I'd never take advantage of an invalid. I prefer my women fully functional."

Emma shook her head to dislodge another image of Donovan and Carter together and walked toward the bedroom. The problem was, she couldn't blame Carter for being attracted to Donovan. She had a lot to offer whereas Emma had nothing.

"I hope you'll be very comfortable on the sofa with your oversized ego." When she slammed the bedroom door, she heard Donovan's cocky laugh in the other room.

Chapter Thirteen

Carter patrolled the upper ridge behind Emma's cabin, refusing to actually go down her road, a childish indication of how upset she still was. When she topped the hill, she saw a strange car parked in the driveway. Closer inspection showed the vehicle was only inches from the porch and had skidded up a path of gravel as it slid to a stop. The porch table and chairs were overturned. Had Emma come home and tripped over the furniture, or was something wrong?

She put the Jeep in reverse, but just before accelerating, she saw a petite blonde step from Emma's cabin onto the porch. She stretched and pulled a blanket tight around her otherwise-naked body. Carter stared, trying to convince herself there was a logical explanation but always coming up with the obvious one.

Emma had slept with another woman, and only two days after they'd been together. A feeling bubbled up, bringing anger and pain—not jealousy. She wasn't jealous of *any* woman. This felt more like the sting of duplicity. She tried to argue that it didn't matter, but the energy bouncing around inside her told another story.

Carter's ego urged her to charge the imposter and find out what she was doing at Emma's cabin, but her appearance had already answered that question. Carter wanted to disappear, to be far away from this scene and from the unfamiliar ache throbbing inside her.

As she stared at the stranger so comfortable on Emma's porch, something about her seemed familiar, but her presence here was totally foreign. The woman scanned her surroundings and, when she saw Carter sitting in the Jeep, waved enthusiastically before going back inside. Carter willed herself to move and slowly backed her vehicle onto the main road.

So what if Emma already had another lover? Carter knew better than to care about her in the first place, and she'd been lucky to get out when she did. She didn't need or want Emma Ferguson in her life. Their night together meant nothing to her. As she willed herself to believe the words, Carter knew they were a lie.

❖

Emma sat up in bed, the mouth-watering smell of bacon snapping her fully awake. A dull pain throbbed in her left arm when she stood, reminding her of the attack and her unwelcome houseguest. Donovan, Egomaniacal Agent Extraordinaire, had slept on her sofa and was now apparently in her kitchen. Emma pulled on a pair of sweats and opened the bedroom door.

"Good morning. It's about time you woke up. Did you sleep okay?"

Donovan was entirely too cheerful first thing in the morning and looked as perfectly coiffed as if she'd slept standing up. Emma stared as the toga-clad figure scurried around the kitchen, scrambling eggs, flipping bacon, and pouring coffee like a domestic goddess. And talking, always with the talking.

"Let me guess. You're not a morning person." She handed Emma a cup of coffee. "Maybe this'll help. How's your arm?"

Emma flopped onto the sofa as the first sip of coffee blazed a warm trail down her throat. She prayed the caffeine would be swift and merciful.

"You should've felt very safe last night. I was here, and your park ranger was patrolling the grounds early this morning."

"Carter was here?" Emma's groggy mind struggled into action.

"I was standing on the porch enjoying the view, and she was on the upper terrace."

"You were outside…naked?"

"Of course not. I had this blanket around me."

"You were on the porch like *that*?"

"Yeah. I couldn't very well sleep in my clothes, could I? Is there some park law against standing on the porch wrapped in a blanket?" Donovan grinned as she flipped an egg.

"What did she do? Did you talk to her?" The caffeine was definitely not working fast enough. Emma's mind was churning in low gear as the scenario played in her mind.

"I waved, and she left. We didn't talk. What's the problem?"

Emma imagined what Carter must be thinking, seeing Donovan half naked on her porch first thing in the morning, as if they didn't already have enough issues between them.

"Oh, I get it." Donovan turned toward Emma and made an exclamation mark in the air with the spatula. "You two have had a little encounter of the personal kind. Am I right?"

"Get out." Emma stood and pointed to the door. She didn't want Donovan knowing anything about her relationship with Carter. Emma was already making comparisons between herself and Donovan and coming up short in every category. She didn't need the arrogant agent doing the same.

"What?" Donovan stopped in the middle of the kitchen holding a plate in each hand.

"Get out now."

"But what about breakfast? What about my clothes?"

"Take them with you."

"What's the big deal about Carter West seeing me in a blanket anyway? She's apparently seen both of us in less." Donovan walked toward Emma and stopped, staring into her eyes. "Unless there's something you're not telling me about your relationship."

Emma studied her coffee.

"It's more than a fling for you, isn't it? That's why you're unwilling to consider the possibility that she's involved in this case?"

"Are you dense, Donovan? The woman was *two* when the murder happened."

Donovan placed the food on the coffee table and stood toe-to-toe with Emma. "But she could be covering for someone who *was* involved. Someone like her aunt."

Emma worried about the same thing, but she wasn't about to admit it to a BCI agent, especially not this one. "I asked you to leave. I have nothing else to say on the subject."

"You haven't said anything yet, but it certainly speaks volumes. I'd recommend you stay clear of Carter West and her aunt until this case is resolved. Your credibility could be jeopardized if you don't." Donovan brazenly dropped the blanket and started dressing. "I'll go, but at some point I'm going to put all the pieces together, with or without your help."

"Do you love Carter or hate her, Donovan? I can't figure you out yet." Emma didn't like the look in Donovan's eyes when she talked about Carter. The intensity betrayed her calm, professional voice and demeanor. For the first time since Emma had met Donovan, she looked uncomfortable, trying to button already fastened buttons on her shirt.

"I'm trying to find the truth, which is what you should be doing." She stopped at the door. "And Emma, don't presume to know anything about my relationship with Carter. She's a much more complicated woman than you'll ever know." She started to close the door but stuck her head back in. "And tell the sheriff about last night."

Emma collapsed on the sofa when Donovan was gone, her statement replaying in her mind. *Don't presume to know anything about my relationship with Carter.* The vehemence in her voice made it sound as if their relationship was special. Maybe it was. Maybe that was why she was steering Emma away. Had Carter shared her past with Donovan—the horrific story of her parents' death and her childhood fears for Ann and Cass? Was Billie Donovan the reason Carter wouldn't commit to anyone else? Carter had said she was *mostly* single.

Emma sipped coffee and refused to eat Donovan's exquisitely prepared breakfast, though her stomach rumbled for food. She debated how to shield Carter and Ann if the facts proved they were involved in Thompson's murder and/or cover-up. Could she even get involved at that point? Every aspect of her life revolved around and intertwined with the successful resolution of this case. If she reported an objective and compelling story about the whole affair, she could write her own ticket professionally but potentially lose Carter. If she protected Carter and Ann, she just might have a chance at love but in the process sabotage her career.

Her phone rang and she punched the answer key. "Hello."

"Emma, is that you?" Harriett Smoltz's nasal voice asked.

"Yes, Harriett. How can I help?"

"Are you okay, honey? You sound a little stressed this morning." Like a bloodhound, always sniffing around for gossip-worthy news.

"Somebody tried to crush my head with a tree limb last night."

"Oh my Lord, are you all right? Why would someone want to hurt you?"

"I'm okay. Maybe somebody isn't happy I'm looking into Theodore Thompson's murder and have gotten the BCI involved."

"Did you get a look at the scoundrel who attacked you? Any description at all?" Harriett's capacity for acquiring and disseminating information was a thing of beauty. Donovan would do well to elicit her assistance.

"It was dark. All I know is the guy was very strong."

Harriett let out a long sigh, probably upset with Emma's lack of juicy details. "Maybe I can help. You asked for a list of folks who lived in Stuart then and now. You've met and talked with most of them already, but I have one more to add."

"Whatever you have, Harriett, would be greatly appreciated."

"You should talk to Daniel Tanner, the druggist. He was open that night and might've seen something. Nobody ever questioned him. I hope it helps."

"Thanks, Harriett. I'll keep in touch."

"Be careful, Emma. Folks in this town can be ruthless when pressed."

Emma dressed and slowly cruised by the ranger's office to be sure Carter wasn't inside. She needed an uninterrupted talk with Ann. She wanted answers to questions she had no right to ask, and Ann was her only hope.

When she opened the front door, Ann waved her in with a mock salute. Her outfit for the day was beige camouflage pants, T-shirt, and a black beret.

"Commander West at your service, ma'am. How may I be of assistance?"

"Ann, you're a hoot. I love how you're just right out there, like it or not."

"You know what they say: An ounce of pretension is worth a pound of manure. The outfit is actually for the kids. We've got a group checking in later today. Come sit down and tell me why my niece thinks the world's coming to an end and you're the reason."

"I wish I knew. Seeing a half-naked woman on my porch this morning probably didn't help."

"Oh, my. Do tell. She didn't mention that."

"It wasn't the way it looked. The BCI agent assigned to this case came over to talk. Just so happened, I was being mugged at the time."

"Being what?" Ann ushered her to a recliner, her hand resting on Emma's shoulder. "Darling, are you okay?"

"Just a bruised arm, but the agent thought I wasn't safe so she slept on the sofa. Carter saw her this morning when she was making rounds, and I can only imagine what she thought." Emma rubbed her arm and winced.

"I'm sure her mind jumped to several wrong conclusions and confirmed her lack of trust in womankind all over again."

"To add insult to injury, this story I'm doing sends her over the edge for some reason. I guess she told you about it."

"According to her, you're the Antichrist digging a black hole to suck us all in. Honestly, I don't know how she comes up with this stuff."

"Ann, you have to believe me. I had no idea this disappearance story would have anything to do with you or your family. I swear it. I never meant any harm."

"I believe you, Emma. And I don't really think it's the story that scares Carter so much as it is the possibility of dredging up things she can't remember."

"What do you mean she doesn't remember?" A shaft of pain shot through Emma. She couldn't bear it if she'd unearthed more grief from Carter's past.

"Carter told you about her parents' death when she was two."

Emma nodded, her pulse racing at the memory of her night with Carter after their chat.

"It took her a long time to adjust afterward. Then, just when she was settling down, something else happened, and she withdrew from everybody." Ann paused and covered her face in her hands.

"What happened? Withdrew how?" The questions poured from Emma before she could stop them.

"I'm not sure I should be telling you any of this. If Carter finds out, she'll be madder than a wet setting hen. But if you're going to understand her at all, you need to know."

Emma took Ann's hands and looked her in the eyes. Her unspoken promise was all the encouragement Ann needed.

"This second event sent Carter into a withdrawal so complete she didn't speak for almost a year. She wouldn't communicate with anyone."

"Oh, my God, Ann. How awful for a child."

"We took her to therapists, specialists, and even a few woo-woo doctors, but nothing helped. None of them could tell if it was the accident, losing her parents, an unconscious sense of guilt, or this other thing that caused her withdrawal. She blocked an entire segment of time from her life."

"But you finally got through to her?"

"Cass did. She'd take Carter down to the lake, and they'd play for hours and just be with nature. She never tried to push Carter to talk. Their excursions went on for almost a year, and one day Carter looked up and said Cass's name. Then little by little she came back to us."

Emma wiped her eyes. "That's why she wears the cat's eye around her neck. She told me Cass gave it to her."

"But Carter never remembered everything, and I think that's why she's so afraid of you digging up this Thompson story."

"Why didn't you tell her all of it?"

"I tried a few times when she was younger, but she always resisted. This case and that traumatic time in her life are connected in her subconscious, but she doesn't know the details. Guess I figured the truth would never come out, and we'd be okay."

Emma considered her next question, unsure if she wanted to hear the answer but knowing she had to. "And they are connected. Is there something about Thompson's case that could hurt you or Carter? If there is, Ann, I'll drop this story immediately. You're both too important to me."

"Well, I thin—"

The front door flew open and banged against the wall. Carter stood red-faced in the doorway glaring at them. "Ann, I told you she's just after her precious story."

Emma wasn't a stereotypical redhead who flew hot in a strong wind, but when her reputation and integrity were questioned, she employed whatever means necessary. She was already preparing her response when the fear in Carter's eyes registered. She stifled the angry words poised on the tip of her tongue and walked over to Carter. "I'm really sorry you feel that way. I would never do anything to hurt you or Ann." Her eyes met Carter's. She stroked the side of Carter's face, silently urging her to feel her sincerity, and glimpsed a momentary softening.

Then Carter stepped away from her touch.

"Words are cheap," she said.

"Mine aren't. When I say something, I mean it." Before she walked away, Emma felt the heat radiating between them, but Carter's eyes had turned cold and angry again.

❖

Carter slammed the door behind Emma before facing Ann. "Do you *ever* listen to anything I say?"

"I could ask you the same question. And don't take that tone with me, Carter Amelia West. Come over here and sit down."

"I don't want to sit."

Ann pointed to the recliner Emma had vacated. "I said *sit down*." When Carter lifted the footrest and focused her attention on the fire in the stove, Ann said, "Did it occur to you that you're wrong about Emma?"

"She's a liar."

"About what?"

"I saw…never mind. I just know."

"You saw another woman on her porch this morning, and jumped to conclusions. How does that make her a liar?"

"We were together less than—"

"Pot. Kettle. You're the last person who should judge when it comes to one-nighters. Emma Ferguson is a friend, and in your case she could be more, but you're too stubborn to realize it."

Carter shifted, the room suddenly too warm. "Who was she—the woman on the porch?"

"A BCI agent sent to work the case. She was only there because Emma was assaulted last night outside her cabin and the agent didn't want to leave her unprotected." Ann snorted. "Should've been your job, if you weren't so thick."

"Emma was attacked? Was she hurt?"

"He swung a tree limb at her and bruised her arm pretty bad."

Carter's stomach roiled, and she buried her face in her hands. Ann was right. She should've been there for Emma, not some BCI agent. "Did she say what the agent's name was?"

Ann shook her head as if Carter were missing the point completely.

It had to be Billie Donovan. That's why the woman had seemed familiar this morning.

Ann shook Carter's shoulder. "You should be concerned about our friend, Emma, not some random government woman."

"If Emma was our friend, she'd never have stirred up this whole Thompson mess. I asked her to leave it alone, but she refused."

"We've known from day one why she was here. Her story focus only shifted when she uncovered more information. She didn't know Thompson and Cass were married until day before yesterday, when I told her. And she had no idea that Cass Calloway and Sandra Thompson were the same person."

"She should've dropped it when she connected you and Thompson." Carter tried to sound convincing, but she knew Emma had too much integrity to overlook relevant facts in a story.

"Really, Carter? Emma's an intelligent professional who takes her job very seriously. Would you turn away a needy child to save a friendship?"

"Of course not, but that's different."

"How?"

"Helping a child is always the right thing to do." Carter glanced at Ann, certain she was backing herself into a moral corner, assisted by her wise aunt.

"And telling the truth isn't?"

"Of course it is, but what if you only think you're telling the truth?"

"Emma isn't that kind of person. She'll get her facts straight before she goes public."

Carter raked her fingers through her hair. "And that's another thing. Haven't we had enough publicity—my parents' accident and folks glaring at our family like we were lepers for years? Do you really want our life plastered in the newspapers and magazines? I certainly don't."

Ann edged closer to Carter's chair. "Emma is our best chance for a fair shake on the matter. Trust me on this. The way Fannie Buffkin is stirring up dust, she won't be happy until somebody is arrested for Theodore's death, and she won't care if they're guilty or innocent. The BCI will be pressured to close the case quickly and won't waste a lot of time in this Podunk town. I'll take my chances with Emma any day."

Carter watched the glowing logs in the stove turn to embers, wondering how things had been so unbelievably right with Emma and then turned so horribly wrong. "What did you tell Emma about me?"

"You told her about your parents. I only added that you suffered another traumatic event and didn't talk for a while. That's it."

"You didn't say what."

"Figured that was yours to tell, but you better be quick, or I'll have to tell it all. We never thought this would come back to us, but it has. Honesty might be best now."

"I'll think about it, if I can ever face Emma again." The image of blond, naked Billie Donovan flashed through Carter's mind, and she stormed out of the office. Billie was a very sexual and available woman, the kind of person Emma might be drawn to right now— like she'd been to Carter two days ago. The thought of Emma and Donovan together made Carter feel sick.

CHAPTER FOURTEEN

Emma's thirty-minute drive to Tanner's Drugstore wasn't enough to erase Carter's angry expression from her mind. She struggled with a desire to rush into her arms one minute and completely ignore her the next for her irrational behavior. The only thing likely to distract Emma from the situation with Carter was total absorption in her work. She pulled beside Tanner's Drugstore and vowed to finish this story and get out of Stuart as soon as possible.

"Good morning, ma'am," a deep baritone called from somewhere in the store as Emma entered. A young man with reddish-orange hair, acne, and a scraggly goatee walked toward her.

"Can I help you?" The booming voice emanated from behind a beaming smile.

The old-fashioned drugstore housed a long marble counter and bar stools that reminded Emma of soda shops from her childhood. Fifties-style blenders stood ready to whip up her favorite concoction of chocolate, chocolate, and chocolate. "Good morning. Is the owner here?"

"No, ma'am. Mr. Tanner doesn't usually make it in until mid-afternoon. Something I can do for you? Would you care for a soda?"

"I'll have a double chocolate malt."

"Yes, ma'am. One double chocolate malt coming up."

Emma watched the young man pull the ingredients from the cabinet and pour them into the blender. As the mocha-colored elixir spun around in the pitcher, she refused to consider the number of calories in it, preferring to guiltlessly indulge in a favorite childhood treat.

"You must be the reporter who's doing a story on the town."

"That's right. Emma Ferguson. Where could I find your boss before he comes to work?"

The young man handed Emma the malt and glared at her with wide eyes. "I wouldn't recommend that, no, ma'am."

"Why not? It's important that I talk with him."

"Well…Mr. Tanner's a night person. He doesn't function too well before noon." The man pulled at his already stretched T-shirt as if grappling for the right words. "You'd be more likely to catch him in a talking mood tonight over at Wally's."

"I'm not familiar with Wally's."

"It's a local watering hole…our only bar, outside of town about thirty minutes down Highway 57. You missed it if you came in from Bassett. Don't go alone. Guys can get pretty rough after they've had a few drinks."

"Thank you very much." Emma polished off her malt, paid, and exited the drugstore. Revived by a double blast of caffeine, she reviewed her options. Her next contact wasn't available until tonight, but she couldn't afford to waste half a day if she expected to stay ahead of Donovan. She'd check in with Harriett again.

As she rounded the corner near the library, Emma stopped. Donovan's state-issued car was parked in front of the entrance. She knew she'd have to talk with Donovan sooner or later, but she voted for later. Emma spun around and headed for the Riverside Hotel.

Sylvie Ferguson gave Emma a reserved smile as she entered the lobby. "Ms. Ferguson, I hadn't expected to see you again so soon, but I want to thank you for the referral." Emma cocked her head to the side and Sylvie added, "The BCI agent."

"Of course. You're welcome." Emma smiled, happy to refer the business to such a nice woman and even happier that Donovan wouldn't be staying at the park.

"What can I do for you today?" Sylvie led Emma into the office.

"I was just wondering if anything else had come to mind since our last chat. Did you remember any other details about the night Theodore Thompson disappeared?"

"You mean was killed, don't you? The whole town is buzzing with the news."

"Yes, I'm sure it is. Anything else?"

"No. I've told you everything I know."

"Are there still people in town that lived here then?"

Sylvie closed her eyes and stroked her chin for several seconds before raising her hand and counting off as she went. "There's Tim Black with the funeral home, Daniel Tanner at the drugstore, Fannie Buffkin, Ann and Carter West, and myself. And of course, the twins, Harriett and Hannah Smoltz. They're the youngest, aside from Carter. Everybody else is either dead or moved away."

Emma's excitement vanished until another possibility occurred to her. "You mean there could be others who've relocated?"

"Lots of folks left after the plants closed, but I can't say how many of them were here that long ago or how many are still alive. The only one I know for sure is old Clem Stevens over in Rocky Mount. He was a janitor at the first Thompson plant for years. He pulled up stakes about the time of Thompson's disappearance, but I can't be certain if it was before or after."

Emma silently prayed for two miracles—somebody who knew the truth about Thompson's murder and to find him before Donovan did. "You don't happen to know where in Rocky Mount I might find him, do you, Sylvie?"

"Last I heard he was doing night janitorial work for the new super-store warehouse."

By nightfall Emma was on her way to Wally's pub to find Stuart's druggist. The twenty-eight-mile stretch of roadway loomed in front of her like a dark tunnel into the abyss. She was used to the city with streetlights and lots of traffic, and the contrast made her jittery. Emma questioned the wisdom of making the excursion without telling anyone. What if she had a flat tire, ran off the road, or even had an accident? Would she ever be found?

A dull set of headlights several car lengths behind suddenly appeared in her rearview mirror. Maybe she hadn't given Donovan the slip after all. The momentary relief of having company on the deserted road vanished when the car sped up, cut its headlights, and came within a few feet of her bumper. The car's interior was too dark to get a glimpse of the driver. After a few seconds of tailgating, the vehicle backed off but continued to follow. All she could tell about the car was that it was dark and old.

When the vague neon lights of Wally's bar appeared ahead, she accelerated. The car behind matched her pace and quickly closed the gap. A light tap from the vehicle sent Emma's pulse racing. The car maintained contact with Emma's, pushing it forward. She gripped the steering wheel harder and applied the brakes. Her car skidded to the right. She overcompensated, and the skid morphed into a slow-motion sideways spin. Emma wrestled to keep her vehicle between the ditches on either side of the road as it swerved violently back and forth.

She stood on the brake pedal and cut the wheel sharply to the right again. When the car finally stopped, her right rear wheel was inches from a very steep ditch. Her pulse pounded, and her palms were slick with sweat. She looked around for the other car. It was nowhere in sight. She took several deep breaths and tried to swallow, but her mouth was dry and cottony.

What the hell was going on, and why was someone trying to kill her? If she was getting too close to the truth, she really wished someone would tell her, because she didn't have a clue.

She should've reported last night's assault, as Donovan suggested. The sheriff was likely to regard her claim of four potentially threatening incidents with suspicion. Fortunately, she'd kept notes on each and would produce them when she reported this latest attempt. Emma waited for her nerves to calm before restarting her car and coasting into Wally's lot.

Emma sat in her car, staring at the bar with broken windows and peeling paint. Why had she thought this was a good idea? She got out of the car on trembling legs and did a quick survey of her bumper for damage. Not even a scrap of foreign paint. When she opened the tavern door, the stench of stale beer and cigarette smoke made her nauseous. Men crowded around the small bar and yelled to be heard over the melancholy wail of country music. Everybody stared at her as she elbowed her way up to the service area and ordered a vodka tonic.

A fake redhead with skin textured by sun and cigarettes responded. "We don't have none of them fancy drinks. Just beer." Her raspy voice made Emma swallow in sympathy.

The men around the bar rolled their eyes at each other and grinned. Several blew streams of cigarette smoke in her direction.

She hadn't thought this little excursion through carefully. She was usually better prepared. "I'll have whatever's on draft."

When the barmaid delivered the drink, Emma asked, "Is Daniel Tanner here tonight?"

The woman pointed toward a small booth near the pool tables in the back. "He's here every night, one of my best customers, when he's not smashing up the place. You ain't here to haul him off, are you?"

"No, ma'am. I just want to talk to him."

"Well, you better hurry. He goes downhill the later it gets."

Emma walked toward the hunched-over figure seated in the back booth. She watched as the white-haired, seventyish man stared into his mug of beer, oblivious to her presence. His large frame had probably been muscular in his younger days, but now his bulk simply sagged into a resigned pose.

She cleared her throat. No response. "Excuse me, sir." He still didn't respond. She bent closer and repeated herself. "Excuse me, sir."

The man gave a startled jolt and rose from his seat. His eyes were clear and focused but shot angry sparks in her direction. "Yeah, what do you want?"

The rapid transformation from despondent barfly to irritable aggressor surprised Emma, and she mustered her most authoritative voice. "I'm looking for Daniel Tanner."

"You've found him. Why are you bothering me? Can't a man drink alone any more?"

"Ferguson, my name's Emma Ferguson. I'm a reporter."

"I don't care who you are." Tanner continued to stand, making no offer of hospitality.

"I'm just asking a few questions of folks who were around when Theodore Thompson disappeared."

"So? Got nothing to do with me."

"I understand you were working at the drugstore that night."

"I work every night. Go away."

Emma wasn't going to be dismissed like a pesky kid. "I'll go a lot quicker if you answer my questions. Were you alone at the drugstore?"

Tanner seemed to consider his options for a few seconds before answering. "I couldn't really afford any other help at the time. Things were pretty tight financially, as I recall." He took a long gulp of beer and gazed past Emma into the bar. After his protests to be left alone, he was being more forthcoming than Emma expected.

"Did the police interview you about Thompson's disappearance?"

"No. They didn't really interview anybody. They just went around asking general questions a few weeks after but never made it to me."

"Did you see Thompson at all?"

"No, but that's not unusual. He never came into my store, and it's a good thing too." Tanner's eyes narrowed, and his jaw worked in time to his clenching teeth.

"What do you mean?"

"We didn't care for each other. His family owned almost everything in town, and what they didn't own they tried to control. They had the mayor, city council, and the bank manager in their back pockets. You couldn't spit in this town without the Thompson family's permission."

"So you disagreed on politics or principle?"

As if he'd run out of steam, Daniel Tanner slumped back into the booth and slapped his hands on the table in front of him, motioning for Emma to sit.

"We disagreed on everything, but I wasn't the only one. The whole town hated Theodore Thompson. His grandfather and father were admired men, but Theodore didn't inherit any of their genes, just the money. He thought that bought him respect, but his power was intimidation."

"And he intimidated you?" Emma contained her excitement as another possible suspect rose from the mire of Theodore Thompson's past. Extortion wasn't a large leap from intimidation.

"He *tried* to intimidate everybody. He also tried to buy my store more than once. He wanted it for one of his shady schemes."

"Obviously he didn't succeed."

"Nope. He disappeared before he destroyed the entire town. And I have to tell you, Ms. Ferguson, not many people were sad about that. I certainly wasn't."

"Does anything else about that night stand out in your mind? It might seem small, but it could be helpful." Her enthusiasm waned as Tanner talked.

"I remember it was cold as blue blazes. Not many people were out. That's why I thought this was a little strange." Some of the fire left Tanner's eyes as he seemed to recall something.

"What?" Emma leaned closer, hoping this would be the lead to set her on the trail of a killer. "What seemed strange?"

"I saw Ann West and little Carter walking down Main Street. I thought it was unusual because of the weather and because they live so far out of town. I remember thinking they could both catch their death of cold."

Emma's heart skipped a beat, and she silently prayed that Tanner's next statement would help rather than hurt Ann any further. "And what time was this, Mr. Tanner?"

"Somewhere around ten thirty. I can't be certain, but I know it was about that time. I'd closed early since there weren't any customers, and I was headed out here."

"Which way were they going when you saw them?"

"Toward the factory."

"Why didn't you tell anyone about this before?"

"Nobody ever asked. Besides, I always liked Ann and Carter. That poor child had been through enough in her short life, and neither of them deserved to be mixed up in that hateful man's disappearance. I'm sure they didn't have anything to do with it anyway. How could they?"

Emma wondered the same thing as she exited the bar and surveyed the parking lot, but it would take more than two people's opinions to prove Ann wasn't involved, especially if Donovan got wind of this latest piece of information. She seemed intent on making Ann her prime suspect. Emma shivered as she walked toward her car and thought of the long, dark drive back to the park.

"Anything you'd like to share with me, Ms. Ferguson?"

The voice from behind her startled Emma, and she turned with fists clenched.

"Hold on, slugger." Donovan stepped back and raised her hands in mock surrender. "What's got you so jumpy tonight?"

"Damn it! Why are you sneaking up on me? Why don't you try starting a conversation face to face for a change? Are you following me? Are you here by chance, or do you know what happened?" Emma's jabbering was a sign of raw nerves, but the cause could've been any number of things—the crazy driver, Tanner's statement, or Donovan sneaking around.

"What are you talking about? What else happened?" Donovan actually looked concerned as she moved closer and placed her hand on Emma's shoulder.

"Somebody tried to run me off the road on my way over here."

"Are you serious? Did you call the locals? You probably didn't even report the assault last night, did you?" Without giving Emma a chance to respond, Donovan guided her into her car. "Let's get out of the cold while I put together an alert." Emma relayed the details of the event while Donovan interrupted with questions.

When she finished the story, Donovan stared at her in disbelief. "I was willing to consider the possibility the incident at the cabin might've been random. It would've been a stretch, but now I'm convinced somebody wants you off this case in a big way, and we have no leads at all. You didn't get a look at the vehicle or the driver, so there's nothing for an alert. There's no damage to your car, so I can't get any physical evidence. That settles it. I'm taking you home. We can pick up your vehicle tomorrow. Consider yourself in protective custody."

"I'll consider no such thing. And I'll drive myself home, but thanks for the offer."

"I can't let you do that. I've been interviewing people for two days, and I'm no closer to a suspect. This person could be waiting down the road for you to come back so he can try again."

Hearing the words aloud convinced Emma maybe she should accept some help, but she would dictate the boundaries. "Feel free to follow me home, but I'm driving myself."

"Why do you have to be such a stubborn redhead?"

"It's in the genes."

"Have it your way, but I'm spending the night again, just to be on the safe side."

"No." Her voice sounded weak and unconvincing. The last thing she wanted was to spend the night alone in a cabin in the woods with a killer on the loose. The next to the last thing she wanted was for Billie Donovan to spend the night with her. But her nerves were taking a beating from the threats, so she'd be grateful to have someone close by, even if it was annoyingly perfect Agent Donovan.

By the time they reached the park, Emma was almost calm, except for the prospect of Donovan spending the night again. She'd just ignore her and go to bed. The fear of nearly dying and the ups and downs of Tanner's recollections had been exhausting. The bright spot of tonight was Donovan didn't know about Daniel Tanner's statement, and Emma wasn't going to tell her.

When Emma saw the red convertible parked in front of her cabin, her emotions rose hard and fast, and her skin flushed hot. She considered ramming the sleek, sexy machine but couldn't afford either repair bill. She slammed on her brakes so hard Donovan almost rear-ended her. Emma amended her earlier list. The absolute last thing she wanted tonight was to see her ex.

CHAPTER FIFTEEN

Sheri slouched in a rocker on Emma's porch holding a beer. Emma had admired and at times despised Sheri's cocksure confidence, but this was a new level of brazen after what she'd done. Emma took several deep breaths and pushed the image of infidelity from her mind. She wouldn't give Sheri the pleasure of upsetting her again.

The slim, five-six woman rose unsteadily as Emma approached the porch. She wore her favorite low-slung jeans that hugged her narrow hips and a T-shirt under her signature jean jacket. She still looked almost edible, but Emma had never developed a taste for the fruit. From the corner of her eye, Emma saw a flash as Donovan darted in front of her. She'd completely forgotten about her police escort.

"Stop right there!" Donovan ordered. "Emma, stay behind me."

"What the hell?" Sheri started down the steps, stumbled, and reconsidered when Donovan pointed her weapon at her chest.

"I said stop. Put your hands where I can see them."

Emma stood back, enjoying Sheri's stunned expression.

"Honey, are you going to tell this storm trooper who I am, or do I have to whip her ass?"

Sheri's bravado was a mixture of alcohol and natural cockiness that Emma had seen too many times. She imagined the tiny hairs on Donovan's neck bristling.

"Bring it on, Betty Badass. Do you know this woman, Emma?" Donovan assumed a sideways stance so she could watch Emma and Sheri.

"Of course she knows me, you reckless government-issued suit. Do you really think I'd be chillaxing on her doorstep sipping a beer if I didn't know her? I'm her girlfriend."

Emma's amusement at the macho-charged standoff shattered with Sheri's last statement. "I know her, but she's *not* my girlfriend."

"That's just a matter of perspective." Sheri flashed one of her come-to-bed grins, and her white teeth sparkled in the moonlight.

Donovan back stepped, holstered her weapon, and whispered to Emma, "You're just full of surprises, aren't you, Ferguson? Want me to run her off? She might not be the stalker, but she's trouble. Nobody with that much mouth is totally harmless."

"I'll be fine. You can leave. I'm sure you have better things to do than babysit me and my ex-girlfriend."

"If you say so. I'm not sure you'll be safe, but at least you won't be alone."

As Donovan turned to leave, Emma caught her arm. "Thank you, really."

"No problem. I need to go back to Wally's at some point anyway. I know you weren't there for the company." Donovan gave her one of those cop stares designed to make her spill her guts, but she didn't flinch. "Is there anything you'd like to tell me? Might save me a trip."

"Not really." She didn't *want* to tell Donovan anything about her conversation with Daniel Tanner until she'd had a chance to look into it further.

"Even more reason to return. I think you're hiding something from me, Ferguson, and I intend to find out what. You've got my number if you need help." Donovan nodded toward Sheri as she walked away.

As Emma turned back toward the cabin, Carter's Jeep pulled into the driveway. She stopped alongside Donovan's vehicle, and the two exchanged greetings. Carter got out and stood, too closely,

Emma noted, talking with the BCI agent. Donovan touched Carter's arm as she spoke before locking her car and getting into the Jeep. Maybe Emma had been right, and whatever those two had was still going on. Her insides burned as she watched the two women together. Donovan wasn't Rick Hardy's type at all. She was Carter's, and Emma had known it from the moment they met.

"Hell-o!" Sheri called from the top of the steps. "Remember me?"

"Unfortunately," Emma mumbled as she passed, still looking over her shoulder.

"This place is worse than Grand Central Station. Who the hell was that pistol-packing dyke?"

Emma practiced her most neutral expression while looking down on Sheri from the top of the steps. Sheri's betrayal flashed through her mind in slow motion, but she maintained her composure. "She's none of your business. What are you doing here, Sheri? I thought I made it clear I didn't want to see you again."

"I thought I'd give you a chance to cool off before we talked about what happened."

"You've made it perfectly clear what you want, on more than one occasion. I just wasn't smart enough to get the hint until I saw it with my own eyes. And trust me, seeing is believing."

Sheri stepped up and lightly touched Emma's arm. The gesture reminded her of the kind and attentive Sheri she'd first met. They'd become friends quickly, but as their relationship changed, Emma had never felt an intimate connection with Sheri even when they'd made love. Now she knew why—Sheri wasn't her true love. Emma needed to resolve this situation quickly.

"Can I please come in for a few minutes, Emma? I've driven almost two hours. The least you can do is hear me out."

The smell of alcohol wafted up Emma's nostrils, and she recalled that same foul odor when she and Sheri had sex. Why hadn't she caught on sooner? "You could've had the decency to show up sober."

Emma pushed the door open and reluctantly motioned her inside. As she passed, Sheri purposely brushed her muscular body against Emma, but she felt not even a flicker of arousal. "You have five minutes. I've had a long day and am in no mood for a walk down memory lane."

Sheri scanned the meager cabin furnishings and settled on the sofa. She patted the seat beside her. "Please sit with me. It's easier to talk if you're close."

Against her better judgment, Emma sat down next to Sheri but looked straight ahead.

"I know I messed up, but you have to believe it didn't mean anything."

"Why do I have to believe that, Sheri, because it didn't mean anything the three other times?" Emma tested the rumors.

Sheri's eyes widened and her mouth dropped open, but in a blink she recovered and continued her line. But Emma had seen her momentary shock and disbelief at being found out.

"I'm not sure what you're talking about, Emma. I want us to try again." She took Emma's hand and held it gently between hers before bringing it to her lips. "I've missed you. We've had our problems like everybody else, but we can get past them."

In one swift motion, Sheri pulled Emma to her and kissed her hard. Her tongue parted Emma's lips and stroked the softness inside.

I don't want this. Emma felt no sexual stirrings, but her mind was spinning its own fantasy. Sheri actually wanted her again. The difference was this time Emma *wanted* Sheri to want her, to beg her to come back, and then she'd refuse.

Carter's face flashed through her mind. Carter's hands stroked her body, and Carter's kisses covered her neck. She felt the warm invitation of Carter's arms and their soothing effect. Carter's trust, so fragile, so elusive, snatched her back from the brink of deception.

Emma pushed Sheri away. "Stop. I don't want this."

"Of course you do. I felt it in your kiss for the first time. You're hot."

"For someone else."

Sheri got very still and stared her down. "What did you say?"

"It doesn't matter. You cheated at least four times, and we'd only been together a year."

"I don't know who's feeding you that crap, but it's not true. I—"

"Sheri, stop. If you can't be honest with me, don't say anything." Emma played her bluff, scooting closer to Sheri on the sofa. She stared into the deep-brown eyes and raked her fingers through Sheri's black, close-cropped hair. She hated the deception, but she had to know the truth.

Sheri's eyes shifted down and her head bowed. "Okay. I wasn't exactly faithful, but I was just trying to get your attention. You didn't seem interested in sex, at all. I thought if I made you a little jealous, you might come around. The others didn't mean anything, really."

The simultaneous joy and sorrow of being right struck Emma like the backside of a hand. "That's where you're wrong, Sheri. It meant you didn't care enough to be faithful or honest. It meant you made a fool of me, and I was so desperate for affection that I let you. It meant we didn't belong together—then or now. That's what it meant, and thanks for helping me see it."

This time when Sheri's eyes widened and her mouth fell open, she didn't quickly recover. "But Emma...I really...lo—"

"Don't say you love me. It's an insult to the meaning of the word."

"This is all my fault. I'm so sorry, baby." Sheri actually sounded contrite.

Emma had thought about their relationship since she'd been at the park and realized some things about herself. If she expected honesty, she had to give it as well. "It wasn't all you, Sheri. I have to take my share of responsibility too. I wasn't totally honest either. You're basically a good person, but we're not right for each other. I'm sorry if that hurts. I'm not in love with you, and that's why I wasn't into the sex. I've only recently realized that it matters to me." She rose from the sofa and motioned toward the door. "Now, I'd like you to go, and don't come back."

Emma escorted Sheri out, and they stood on the porch watching moonlight sparkle on the lake. This was supposed to have been a new beginning for them, not the end. The angry response she'd expected from Sheri didn't come. The energy between them was finally free of the push-and-pull of expectation and disappointment.

"I'm sorry, Emma. I think I've known for a while we weren't right. Guess it would've been easier to tell the truth. May I kiss you good-bye? You really are a wonderful woman."

Emma didn't resist when Sheri's arms encircled her and pulled them together. She inhaled as their lips met and waited for some sign that she was making a mistake. Instead she felt only a slight change in temperature when their lips parted. The absence of emotion confirmed she'd never really loved Sheri.

"Okay, guess I'll go. Thanks for listening." Sheri stepped back, lost her footing at the top of the steps, and stumbled forward into Emma's arms again.

Emma's conscience kicked in. "Sheri?"

"Yes." She looked up at Emma with her most innocent expression.

"Are you kidding around, or are you drunk?"

"I think I might actually be drunk. I polished off a six-pack while I was waiting."

Sometimes Emma hated having a conscience. She desperately wanted Sheri to leave so she could think about Carter and the murder, but she couldn't let Sheri drive drunk. She wouldn't treat her worst enemy like that. "You're in no condition to be on the road for two hours. I hate how you've treated me, but I don't want you hurt."

Sheri smiled and hooked her arm through Emma's.

"Don't get any ideas. You're sleeping on the sofa."

The sound of a car engine revving in the distance drew Emma's attention to the terraced hillside behind her cabin.

"Go inside and get ready for bed. You'll find an extra T-shirt on top of my suitcase and a spare toothbrush in the bathroom cabinet. I'll be there in a minute."

Emma watched the dark vehicle with no headlights moving slowly along the path. She backed up against the cabin and peered around the corner. Her pulse pounded and her breathing sounded like a siren. If this was the car that tried to run her off the road earlier, she wanted to get a license plate or at least a better description.

The vehicle passed through a small stand of trees into a clearing and was illuminated by moonlight. Emma held her breath. She should've been relieved when she saw the green Jeep and white circular emblem of the park service, but instead she almost wished for the attacker. Two women were visible inside—Donovan and Carter. Donovan had been clear about her intention to advance her relationship with Carter, and she'd wasted no time making her move.

Had Carter seen her and Sheri kiss? If so, what would she be thinking? She'd already seen Donovan partially dressed on her porch and now this. No wonder Carter didn't trust her. After the Jeep left, Emma stood on the porch watching and listening as the night deepened. Normally the serenity would've comforted her, but tonight it only exaggerated the distance and miscommunication between her and Carter.

❖

"Do you believe me now? I told you that was her girlfriend," Donovan said, a smirk tugging at the corners of her mouth.

Carter shifted uncomfortably as she watched Emma kiss another woman on the porch and go back inside the cabin with her. "And what does that have to do with me?" She tried to sound blasé but felt gutted, even though Emma had said she didn't love Sheri. "She hasn't been honest since the day she got here. I'm just grateful I didn't get involved with her." Her heart wasn't buying Emma's easy dismissal, and she needed to change the subject before the pain permeated her pores like perspiration.

"Are you sure you're okay?" Donovan stroked the back of Carter's neck and moved closer to the gearshift dividing the seats.

"Absolutely. I saw you naked on her front porch yesterday. No biggie."

"You know I wouldn't. I mean, I would, but I didn't. It was strictly business."

Carter's relief had nothing to do with feelings for Donovan and everything to do with the fact Billie hadn't touched Emma. But now, this Sheri person had returned. Why were these women showing up now? Carter wasn't jealous, but her trust issues were going into overdrive. Was this situation some kind of test for Emma...or for her?

"Carter, are you listening?"

"Yeah, yeah." She wanted to talk to Emma, not sit here and wonder what was going on inside her cabin or listen to Billie wax nostalgic about their trysts.

"After our retraining session last year, I asked for a reassignment and was just transferred to the Richmond office. When this case came up, I volunteered. The relocation will make seeing each other easier than driving three hours to Charlottesville."

Did she want to see Billie more often? "Does that mean you're single now?" Carter was interested in Donovan's answer for purely academic reasons because when they'd hooked up the first time, Donovan had concealed the fact she was in a relationship. This time Carter wanted to be sure of the boundaries and of Donovan's motives. She always had an agenda.

"Shortly after I returned from training, we both started seeing other people. Things were getting a little predictable. We still live together, but...I'd leave entirely if you'd—"

"Billie, I told you I wasn't into long term, and I was honest about why. My situation hasn't changed." Was she as callous as Billie sounded? She behaved basically the same, leaving when a relationship became serious, but she'd never cheated on anyone.

"I know. Your aunt. She shouldn't keep us from having some fun now, right?" She ran her hand up Carter's thigh.

"Of course not." Carter moved Donovan's hand and reached for the keys. "Sometime."

"I've thought about you often and wondered if you're involved with anyone. I'm afraid I might be too late."

Carter put on her I-don't-give-a-shit expression. "If you mean Emma Ferguson, you're way off base. She's become fast friends with Ann, but she's digging for information about Thompson's murder. I've warned Ann to stay clear, but she can be so bullheaded sometimes."

"Do you think Emma's trying to make a connection between Ann and this case?"

Carter had been plagued by the same question for days but wasn't ready to admit it to anyone else. "She can't because there's nothing to connect. Ann had absolutely nothing to do with that man's death. She couldn't have." Carter tone was vehement, almost desperate, and she looked at Donovan for reassurance.

"Of course she couldn't. Don't worry, Carter. Emma is heading in the wrong direction on this—straight toward Ann. You know how reporters are, always angling for the next headline. I've never met a trustworthy one. I'll clear the case as soon as possible. Trust me." Donovan placed her hand over Carter's and gave a light squeeze as they patrolled the park.

"I'm glad you're here, Billie." A nagging feeling settled in the back of Carter's mind, but she pushed it aside. Maybe a tumble with Billie was just what she needed to distract her from Emma and this whole mess. She knew how Billie operated, and Carter would manage the situation this time. No harm, no foul.

"I was hoping you would be."

"As long as we both know where we stand." Donovan caressed the top of Carter's shoulder and lightly brushed her breast as she dropped her hand. Carter barely noticed as her thoughts returned to Emma kissing another woman. Carter was supposed to be the one who didn't get involved. Why did she care? They'd shared one night, and that was usually enough for her, but she'd been initially won over by Emma's honesty, endearing clumsiness, and her almost tangible layer of vulnerability. Nothing about Emma fit Carter's normal pattern, and that made her different, special, and unforgettable.

Carter rolled down the window, and the cool air rushed in around her. Could she have sex with Billie again? Their affair had always been easy and enjoyable, no attachments. She looked over at the eager blonde beside her. Carter was willing to try anything to fill the emptiness that bore Emma's name.

Chapter Sixteen

The next morning, while Sheri slept on the sofa, Emma thought about events of the past several days. Who was trying to kill her and why? Was anyone still alive who knew the truth about Theodore Thompson's murder? What was Ann's involvement? What was really keeping Emma and Carter apart? She glanced toward her sleeping ex. Was she so desperate for a relationship that she'd accept crumbs from a person incapable of commitment?

When Sheri woke, they ate a quick toast-and-egg breakfast with a side of stilted conversation. Emma repeatedly checked her watch while Sheri showered, dressed, and finally left. She breathed her first sigh of genuine relief when the red convertible disappeared over the ridge near the ranger station.

It was nearly noon, but she still ached with exhaustion. She'd slept little with Sheri in the other room, on edge as if a stranger had invaded her space. She'd been emotional all morning, near tears one minute and angry the next. She couldn't separate the feelings of being run off the road from Carter's distancing, Donovan's planned seduction of Carter, and Sheri's reappearance. The emotions muddled together and left her lethargic.

She laid her case notes out on the sofa and coffee table and reread each one, praying for a clue that had escaped her notice. The deputy had documented his sparse statements in a most haphazard fashion. If he'd ever been trained in investigations or even report-taking, it wasn't evident in his work. She'd felt just as frustrated about her father's case while plowing through accounts of his mysterious disappearance. The feelings of failure this case resurrected irritated Emma. After several passes, her vision blurred and her eyelids drooped. The writing grew fuzzy, dimmed, and eventually disappeared.

❖

Emma bolted upright on the sofa, and papers flew overhead like swooping gulls. She struggled to open her eyes, grappling among the scattered pages for her ringing cell phone. She shoved a stack of documents aside, and the phone skidded across the floor. Chasing it, she smashed her toe into the corner of the table. "Holy crap." She held her toe with one hand and flipped open the phone with the other. "*Yes*. This is Emma Ferguson."

"Emma, where are you? I thought you'd be here by now. This is your big day."

"My what? Who is this?" Emma fell back on the sofa and glanced at her watch. Five o'clock in the afternoon?

"It's Harriett Smoltz. Are you all right? You sound funny."

"Hi, Harriett. Long story. What's up?"

"You better get over here before somebody else scoops your story. You've worked too hard to have that happen."

Emma's head was spinning from the abrupt awakening, her toe pain, and what seemed to be an urgent message from Harriett. "Slow down. Get where? What's going on?"

"The bleached-blond BCI agent has hauled a suspect in for questioning in the Thompson murder case. There's quite a crowd at the sheriff's office."

Emma ran toward the bedroom, toe pain forgotten. "A suspect? You have to be kidding. Who is it? Do you know?"

"Of course I know." Harriett sounded insulted by the question. "It's Ann West, of all people. Can you imagine?"

Emma's cell phone was still falling when she reached for her clothes and struggled into them. She picked it up on her way out, but Harriett had disconnected.

Emma forced herself to breathe slowly and think as she sped toward town. If Ann was being questioned as a suspect, Donovan had probably discovered more evidence. The possibility of Ann's involvement wasn't so wild, but Emma had spent the last few days ignoring it. She'd desperately wanted to believe she was wrong. She prided herself on being thorough, but had she missed something important?

Donovan had efficiently conducted all the interviews in two days that it had taken Emma several to accomplish. Donovan had followed the facts to a logical inference, while Emma, distracted by her attraction to Carter, had searched for facts leading away from Ann. Her father had stressed the importance of objectivity in journalism. She'd strayed from the concept and would have disappointed him.

As she approached the small wood-framed building that served as the sheriff's office, Emma saw a group of people standing outside pushing and shoving for a chance to peer into the windows. The town center was blocked, so she parked two streets away and ran back. She elbowed her way through the crowd toward the door. As she reached for the handle, she heard raised but inaudible voices from inside. Someone grabbed her shoulder.

"Emma. Over here." Harriett pulled her to the side just away from the surging crowd. "That mob could trample you. I've never seen anything like it." Her amorphous body seemed to vibrate with excitement. "I'm glad you made it. Things have been heating up in there for hours. Sounds like quite a ruckus." Harriett's eyes narrowed, her gray hair shimmered in the sunlight, and her sack dress swished around her in the breeze as she stepped closer to Emma. "So, why didn't you tell me the case was closed?"

Emma ignored the question and moved back to the door. "I don't have time for this, Harriett." When she stepped inside the office, Sheriff Echols, Agent Donovan, Ann, and Carter glared at her with stares that challenged an arctic freeze. The silence deafened her.

"What's going on here?"

Sheriff Echols took a step toward her. "You more than anyone should be able to answer that question. After all, you started this whole fiasco."

Emma looked past Echols to the others. Donovan's expression was almost blank except for a slight crinkling around her eyes that Emma interpreted as smug self-satisfaction. Ann's eyes lacked their usual sparkle, the corners of her mouth turned sharply down, and she was uncharacteristically quiet. Carter refused to make eye contact.

"I don't understand what's happening." Emma searched the group for one sympathetic face. Only Ann gave her an occasional sideways glance. Emma had become the bad guy.

"I'll tell you what's going on." Ann moved closer to Emma, shaking off Carter's attempt to stop her. "This Barbie-doll look-a-like hauled me off the job this morning before the rooster crowed, spouting about some evidence *you* supposedly provided."

Carter tried again to pull Ann back. "Would you please be quiet for once in your life and do as you're told?"

Ann spun out of her reach and pointed at Donovan. "Told by whom, this Angie Dickinson wannabe? I don't think so. We don't even know her. What if she's the one with the hidden agenda? This is my life, and I have a right to speak. So step back, Carter."

"Billie was only doing her job, Ann. You can't blame her."

Emma stared in disbelief as Carter defended Donovan. So, it was Billie now, huh? It hadn't taken Donovan long to turn Carter's head. Emma couldn't believe what she was hearing.

Sheriff Echols waved his arms for everyone to quiet down. "Agent Donovan brought Ann in for questioning, as is her right. No charges have been filed. A lot of other folks in town will probably be put through the same thing before this is over." Echols shot Donovan a look and his brow arched.

He doesn't believe her either. "She doesn't have anything to do with this murder." Emma's shrill words hung in the air and sounded as desperate as she felt.

"I advise you to stop right there, Ferguson," Donovan said. "Don't say anything else. You're a material witness in this case."

"What are you talking about? Get away from me." She pushed Donovan and edged closer to Ann.

"Don't come near my aunt again," Carter said and nudged Ann toward the door.

Emma intercepted them and spoke directly to Ann. "You have to believe me. I had nothing to do with this. I was trying to—" The look in Carter's eyes stopped Emma mid-sentence.

When Carter spoke, her voice was the cold, detached whisper of a stranger. "Did you or did you not tell Billie about Ann and Cass's relationship?"

"It doesn't matter, Carter," Ann said. "Everybody in town knew already."

"It *does* matter. It's a question of trust, not who knew what. Trust. Pure and simple."

Carter's brown-eyed stare was a deep, dark grave, and her callous tone pierced Emma's heart. Ann's brow furrowed, and a pained expression crossed her face as she waited for the answer. Emma sensed no anger beneath Ann's pain, but Carter's face bore the primal rage of something wild protecting her family. Emma's response could seal the betrayal Carter suspected.

"I certainly did not. I might've verified information she already had, but—"

"And did you lead Billie to Daniel Tanner?" Carter hissed through clenched teeth.

Emma shot Donovan her steeliest stare. "Absolutely not."

Donovan pulled Emma away from Carter and Ann. "I told you to shut up. If you're not a witness, you could be charged for obstruction in this investigation."

"I don't care. Let me go." When she turned back toward Ann and Carter, they were both pale. "Carter, please listen to me." She inched closer so Donovan couldn't overhear. "Why are you so ready to believe the worst about me? How can you trust *this* woman? What does she mean to you anyway?"

"I don't trust either of you. Back off and stay away from me and my family."

"Maybe we should at least listen to her, Carter." Ann said. "After all, we've only heard this carcass-climbing bureaucrat's side of things. And Emma said she didn't tell."

Donovan hooked her arm in Carter's and tried to usher her and Ann toward the door. "That wouldn't be a very good idea, Ms. West. I'm trying to help you."

"I don't want to talk to you right now either, Billie," Carter said. "You didn't say anything about questioning my aunt last night. I would've appreciated a little heads-up. Leave us alone."

Donovan focused her megawatt smile on Carter and said, "You realize I was just doing my job."

"I realize you're harassing an innocent woman."

"Carter, please. Can we talk about this privately later?"

"Why? Seems you've already made up your mind."

"Not at all. I'll be interviewing others as well. But you might want to consult a lawyer, just to be on the safe side. I'll come see you as soon as I can, and we'll work out the details." Donovan's hand rested in the small of Carter's back as she escorted her and Ann from the sheriff's office to their vehicle parked across the street.

At least Carter was annoyed with Donovan too. Emma's mood shifted through confusion and disbelief to red-hot anger. Donovan was becoming cozier with Carter and exerting more influence over her. And she'd succeeded in casting the blame for this misdirection of justice on Emma. Agent Donovan seemed to have an ulterior motive, but what?

Emma turned back to Sheriff Echols, who stared at her like he wanted to throw her out of his office. "So, no charges were filed?"

"Why do you care? You've got an ending to your story. Isn't that enough?"

"Please, Sheriff. This is wrong, and you know it."

"No charges yet. Ann was just subjected to hours of questioning, thanks to you."

"I get it, but Ann is *not* the murderer. The suspect is still out there, and I'm convinced he's been trying to scare me off his trail."

"You mean your prowler, slashed tires, assault by tree limb, and hit-and-run reports?"

"Exactly. Ann West could've prowled around my cabin and slashed my tires, but we both know she didn't. And she couldn't heft a huge tree limb above her head, much less swing it with enough force to nearly break my arm. She didn't run me off the road, because she can't even drive." She waited for Echols to process the information.

After a few minutes of stroking his chin, he nodded. "Makes sense, but we'll need more than hunches and circumstantial evidence. Donovan seems to have a hard-on for Ann. At least she's the only one brought in for questioning so far."

"I'm going to find out what's going on. Promise you won't let Super Agent do anything else stupid until you hear from me."

"This investigation is out of my hands. You saw to that, but I certainly don't want Ann dragged through the mud for no reason. Whatever you're going to do, make it snappy."

"I only need twenty-four hours, Sheriff."

Echols stood and offered his hand. "Just bring me something substantial."

Whoever coined the phrase dumb blonde hadn't dealt with Billie Donovan, but Emma refused to be a scapegoat in her twisted plan to frame Ann. As Emma exited the sheriff's office, Donovan was approaching her car in front of the building. Emma grabbed her by the arm and spun her around. They stood so close that Donovan's sickly sweet perfume coated her throat. For the first time, Emma felt a flash of desire to do violence. She clenched her fists, digging fingernails into her palms.

"Well, are you going to hit me? I know you want to. Nothing would give me more pleasure than putting you in a jail cell beside

Ann West." Donovan's voice was controlled perfection aimed directly at Emma's heart.

"I'm not that easily provoked, Donovan. I wouldn't give you the satisfaction. Doesn't this charade seem the least bit unethical to you?"

Donovan brushed her long hair off her shoulders and smiled. "I'm just following leads, doing my job. Admit it. You've had the same suspicious thoughts about Ann. So don't get high and mighty, Ms. Ferguson."

"What do you want? Is it the glory of clearing a cold case, a petty government raise, or another promotion?"

Donovan slid a finger down the side of her face, a smug grin parting her full lips. "Oh no, Ferguson. It's much more important. I want something you can never have now—Carter."

Emma's anger rose quickly. She bit the inside of her gum and tasted the coppery tang of blood. Clenching her fists tighter until she felt pain, Emma focused on Donovan's words, determined to memorize each one.

"You look like you're about to explode. Surely you're not surprised. I told you my intentions regarding Carter the day we met for coffee right over there." She pointed to the Stuart Diner. "You were foolish to underestimate me."

"You'll never have Carter. She's too smart to fall for a scam like this." But Emma's words sounded weak, betraying her lack of conviction.

"She already has, thanks to your little display with Sheri last night. I think the kiss really sealed the deal in my favor. Carter will never trust you again."

Emma's muscles were a coiled spring ready to strike, but her heart ached from the truth of Donovan's cruel words. She'd never known real failure until this moment. Her past missteps had been teachable moments, preparing her for this challenge—and she'd lost the battle.

"My intent was always to clear Ann, not to frame her. You used my information against both of us." Emma hardly recognized her own voice, so low and defeated.

"I just left some bits out. Carter's distrust of you filled in the blanks. I actually defended Ann. I was very convincing."

"You're obsessed. How far are you willing to take this? Will you send an innocent woman to jail? If you do, Carter will never forgive you."

"Trust me. I know how much that old crow means to her. She's the reason Carter hasn't committed to our relationship. If she goes to prison, Carter will finally be free, but it won't come to that. I'll eventually find the real killer or clear Ann on lack of evidence. Either way, Carter and I will be bound. I'll console and counsel her if Ann is charged. If she's exonerated, Carter will be so grateful… you get the idea. Bottom line, I win."

A scene from *The Wizard of Oz* flashed through Emma's mind as she watched Donovan morph from an attractive, blue-eyed blonde into a grotesque, self-serving ogre, complete with warts. "You're a disgrace to the law-enforcement profession."

"And you're a hack reporter who can't find her ass with both hands."

"So you hauled Ann in as a setup?"

Donovan nodded.

"You had to make it appear Ann was in real jeopardy. When the time's right, you'll ride in and play the hero. Carter will be so impressed and, as you predicted, grateful."

Donovan didn't respond but flashed a wide smile as she drove away.

Emma considered calling Rick Harding and reporting Donovan's questionable practices, but what could she really prove? Donovan hadn't violated the law; she'd been doing her job questioning a potential suspect. If Emma called Rick, she'd sound petty and overreactive because of her concern for Ann. She'd handle the situation and report Donovan's bad behavior to Rick later.

❖

"Carter, I don—"

Carter raised her hand to stop Ann's pending tirade and rested her head against the steering wheel of the Jeep. She couldn't wrap her mind around what had happened in the past few hours. She wanted to believe Emma, but Billie's argument had been compelling. Emma was a reporter looking for her next big break, and Billie was a law-enforcement professional searching for the truth. If either of them had a hidden agenda, it had to be Emma. Didn't it?

She thought about Emma kissing another woman last night and the emptiness she'd felt, the sense of loss. When Billie suggested they ramp up their affair, she'd been only mildly interested. But she couldn't base Ann's future on her level of emotional attachment to these women. She needed facts. She raised her head and shifted the Jeep into first gear.

"Carter, what in the Sam Hill is wrong with you? You treated Emma like a leper."

"As opposed to how generously she's treated us lately? I told you not to talk to her anymore, but you wouldn't listen. Now the whole town knows you were dragged into the sheriff's office and interrogated for hours. Plus, she's stirred up your relationship with Cass, and that'll be on everybody's lips again. Why are you sticking up for her after all she's done?"

"Because something about this situation stinks to high heaven. And I don't care what these people think. They've known about Cass and me forever, and if they didn't, they're blinder than widow Crewson's three-legged cat."

Carter started to respond, but Ann said, "I don't believe for one minute that Emma would purposely hurt either of us. How are you so sure she would and Ms. BCI wouldn't?"

"I know Billie Donovan. We met a year ago at in-service training, and we've been seeing each other off and on since. She's a BCI agent, for goodness' sake, and I trust her." She didn't tell Ann that Billie had lied about being in a relationship when they met.

"I see. Because you have the hots for her, that means she's all right? A few days ago you thought Emma was pretty hot too, or have you forgotten? So pardon me if I don't rely on your hormones as the ultimate measure of reliability and trustworthiness."

"It's not about that, Ann. Emma misled us from the beginning about this story—a history piece, my ass." Damn it, why couldn't Emma just leave it alone? Carter wanted to believe in her, or had she been expertly manipulated?

Ann slapped her on the arm. "Don't you listen? Emma didn't know about the connection between me and Thompson or even Cass until *I* told her. If you're angry, it should be with me. Everybody's known about Cass and me since high school because I refused to hide. And Emma said she didn't tell Donovan anything. I believe her. Hasn't that blonde ever told you a lie?"

An intimate lie of omission. Carter shook her head. "I just want to protect you."

"I know you do, Carter, but that's never been your job. People in this town have embraced our relationship the best way they could. I've never been in any danger, contrary to what you might think." She patted Carter on the arm. "Can you let go a little?"

"No. You're in more trouble than ever."

"Emma's not the kind of person to let an injustice slide. She won't give up until she finds Thompson's killer. But that's beside the point as far as I'm concerned because I know I didn't do it. There's really only one mystery, as far as I can see."

The slight shift in Ann's tone alerted Carter that the conversation was about to get personal. She wasn't sure she wanted to engage, but if it took Ann's mind off her legal troubles for a few minutes, she'd play along. "And what's that?"

"Do you still have feelings for Emma, or has that poster child for Botox turned your head completely?"

"It doesn't matter how I feel. She's messed with my family, and I can't forgive that."

Carter hoped Ann couldn't see through her façade, but Ann was too wise and loved Carter too much to let her lie to herself.

"You might be able to peddle that garbage to some stranger, but not to me. If you care about Emma, talk to her, soon. If Ms. BCI has her way, you'll never see Emma again. That blond viper will have your head so twisted, you won't recognize the truth if it jumps on top of you."

"Why don't you like Billie?"

Ann chuckled. "That's easy. She's a fake, and I can smell one a mile away."

"I don't know about talking to Emma. I have so many questions. The most important one is can I trust her?"

"Just go to her. She'll do most of the talking. Your challenge is to listen, really listen with an open mind. When she's finished, let your heart be the judge of whether she's been honest. You'll know."

When Donovan's car turned beside the post office and disappeared, Emma shuffled across the street toward the Stuart Diner. Her stomach churned in protest when she thought about food, but she needed nourishment for the long night ahead. She'd lost the first round with Billie Donovan, but she was more determined than ever to find the killer, clear Ann, and somehow convince Carter that Donovan wasn't the woman for her.

"Hey, Emma, wait up!"

Harriett's voice was a foghorn piercing the quiet street. Emma walked faster, hopeful to avoid another grilling by the nosy librarian.

Harriett sprinted two blocks from the sheriff's office and joined Emma in front of the diner, barely winded from the exertion. Her trademark sack dress swished to a stop around her. Without taking a breath, she launched into questions Emma didn't want to hear or answer.

"How long have you known Ann was the killer? What led you in that direction? Criminals and the people who track them always fascinate me. And all this sordid business about Ann and Cass, too bad really. Cass was married to Theo Thompson. How can a woman be married and then turn to—"

"Harriett, I really can't discuss the case with you, ongoing investigation and all that. I'm just going to get a bite to eat. Do you mind?" Emma's last nerve sizzled and vibrated from all the shrieked questions, and she needed quiet.

"Not at all. As a matter of fact, I'll join you. I haven't eaten since my workout this morning, and all this excitement sure does wonders for the appetite." Without waiting for a response, Harriett steered her into the diner and nudged her into a booth.

Emma took advantage of the brief silence while Harriett perused the menu. She needed to talk to Clem Stevens, and he'd probably be working the late shift tonight. She'd head over to the superstore warehouse in Rocky Mount as soon as she finished dinner. If he couldn't provide any useful information, she had only one other possible resource. Hannah Smoltz, the mysterious historian, who hadn't been seen in days.

Harriett ordered, handed her menu to Loretta, and turned to Emma, her mouth already open for the next question.

Emma cut her off. "So, Harriett, where's Hannah? I really need to talk with her about this case, but she's quite elusive."

The librarian straightened the front of her meticulously ironed dress before meeting Emma's gaze. "She should be at the museum. Have you checked there?"

The nervous twitch in Harriett's right eye activated Emma's reporter mole—a built-in warning device when someone dumped a pile of decaying manure on her head. Harriett's benign remark poked at her, but before she figured out why, Harriett interrupted.

"I guess I was just a little shocked it turned out to be Ann. I would've put my money on Daniel Tanner."

"Why?" At this point, she was willing to entertain all possible theories. Somewhere in this rambling heap of fact and fiction, the truth waited to be uncovered.

"I'm sure you heard about his financial trouble back then."

"Yes, but that doesn't make him a murderer."

"I know, but Theo kept after Tanner to sell his place because he couldn't afford the taxes. They even came to blows over it once on the street. Everybody saw it."

Emma pulled out her notebook and scanned her conversation with Daniel Tanner but found no mention of an altercation with Thompson. "Really?" Maybe Harriett wasn't such a worthless gossip after all. "Anything else?"

Harriett leaned across the table and whispered, "Nothing other than a bad drinking problem. He blacked out and forgot things he'd done for days at a time, so I heard. But as my ma used to say, 'Where there's smoke, there's fire.'"

"I thought the drinking was a recent problem."

"Oh, no. It's been a lifelong cross for the poor man to bear."

Emma finished the beef stew she'd ordered and dug through her bag for her wallet.

"Why don't you let me get this, honey? It would be a pleasure."

"Thank you very much, Harriett, for everything. You've been a big help on this story since we first met. But I do have one more question, if you don't mind."

"Fire away."

"When we talked initially about the history of Stuart, why didn't you mention Theodore Thompson's disappearance? It's been a big story ever since it happened."

The end of Harriett's long nose quivered slightly as she cocked her head to one side and grinned. "I don't have the vaguest notion. Sometimes I get so wrapped up in minutia that I completely overlook the big stuff. I'm really a detail person."

"I guess that's easy to do. Thanks again for dinner."

As Emma started to leave she turned back, her reporter mole in high gear. "And where did you say Hannah went on vacation?"

She shrugged. "It must've been another one of her last-minute decisions."

Crossing the street to her car, Emma recalled page after page of notes she'd taken over the past several days. Hannah's assistant had told Emma her boss was on vacation, and she'd received the news from Harriett. So why had Harriett referred Emma to the museum earlier to talk to her sister? And just now, she alluded to her sister's decision to leave town as last minute. Maybe she needed to clarify the assistant's original statement. Or maybe Harriett was protecting some secret family scandal.

When Harriett exited the diner and steered her pink Mary Kay Cadillac out of town, Emma trailed her at a safe distance.

CHAPTER SEVENTEEN

Carter argued with herself most of the day, working up the courage to talk with Emma, and now she stood outside her empty cabin wishing she hadn't come. She was breaking all of her don't-get-involved rules, and nothing was going right. Note to self: Stick with what works. But how could she apply her old rules to someone who played a different game entirely?

After her talk with Ann, Carter wondered whom she should trust. Maybe a simple conversation could change her belief in Emma's deceit. Was that even the real issue? Maybe she was afraid of the feelings Emma evoked, afraid of caring too deeply, of commitment. Was she such a coward she wouldn't even consider the possibility? Carter checked her watch. Where could Emma be at this hour? Was it an omen for her to leave well enough alone?

The last several days had stripped Carter emotionally. She couldn't concentrate on her work in the park or on her sessions with the kids, which usually reenergized her. When she met Emma, she'd known they would be together, at least temporarily, but their attraction pulled with a force Carter had never experienced. After four days of staying away from her, the chemistry proved too strong and she'd succumbed, but, as usual, life got in the way. *The story* happened, and things blew apart like a category-four hurricane.

Her internal dialogue continued in spite of attempts at distraction. *I care for Emma more than I want to admit. She betrayed you. Did she, or are you just looking for excuses? What if I love her?*

That's not possible. Shocked by the thought, Carter stared up at the sky and yelled, "That can't happen."

"Carter, who are you talking to?"

Carter spun around, expecting Emma, but instead found Billie Donovan. "Nobody. I just felt like having a rant. It clears the mind sometimes."

Donovan took Carter's hand. "You're still worrying about Ann, aren't you?"

She felt guilty that her aunt's situation had momentarily slipped her mind or at least taken a backseat to her feelings for Emma. "Of course I am. I just don't know what to do."

"You don't have to do anything. I told you I'd take care of it. Why are you here anyway? Are you thinking of confronting Emma again?"

"Well, I—"

"Please don't. I'll clear Ann before the little opportunist has a chance to publish a word."

"I want to know exactly what she told you about Ann. All of it, Billie."

"Of course." Donovan slid her arm around Carter's waist and guided her back to the Jeep. "Why don't we go to my hotel and sort through the whole story? I'll pick up my car tomorrow."

Billie seemed insistent that she didn't speak with Emma, but why? "I really should be at home with Ann. She's probably going nuts trying to decide what to do about all this."

"You know as well as I do Ann had a couple of drinks and went straight to bed. She's not the least bit worried. After all, she has us to worry for her."

She allowed Billie to lead her away because she needed to know exactly what Emma had shared about Ann. "I'm still a little upset with you. What you did to Ann wasn't right." Carter looked back over her shoulder. Where was Emma? She'd worry about that later—after she'd heard Billie's side. As a BCI agent, Billie had factual, objective information that left no room for doubt. And right now, Carter needed clarity.

Billie unlocked the door of her hotel room at the Riverside and led Carter to the settee. "Wait here while I fix us a drink. You like vodka and tonic, right?"

"Make it a double. It's been one of those days."

She watched Billie prepare their drinks at the mini-bar, her movements efficient and alluring. The woman was a sexual magnet who attracted partners without trying. Their first week of training, they'd formed an instant rapport and teamed up for exercises. At night in their shared dorm room, Billie had undressed in front of Carter, slowly removing each piece of clothing like she was performing a strip tease, taking obvious pleasure in her discomfort. Then Billie had slipped under the covers in her own bed and masturbated to a very vocal orgasm before falling asleep. Carter had found her display the sexiest thing a woman had ever done in her presence. She shifted in her chair, her crotch wet and aching just thinking about it again.

The next week, while still in separate beds, Billie had provided an explicit verbal play-by-play of her self-pleasuring and encouraged Carter to follow her instructions. She'd felt as if they were caressing each other instead of themselves. Carter had gotten off with the slightest touch, having been driven to the edge by Billie's graphic directions and the crescendo of her moans. The next night, they'd consummated the affair.

In retrospect, all the hands-off foreplay had simply allowed Billie to simulate continued fidelity in her relationship. In the emotional sense, she'd already strayed. When Carter refused to continue the affair until Billie was honest with her partner, Billie protested, but it had been the right thing to do. They'd started up again when Billie became a free agent and Carter drove to Charlottesville for her studies.

"Penny for your thoughts." Billie sat down next to her on the settee and allowed her thigh to press against Carter's as she nervously bounced her leg.

"I was remembering when we met and our—"

"You have to admit, we're good together." Billie clinked her glass against Carter's. "And we could be great, if you give us a chance."

Carter took a sip, and the tart drink rushed down her throat, warming her stomach and spreading heat. This morning's breakfast and the nightmare that ensued had been over fourteen hours ago. She welcomed the immediate buzz and false courage.

"Do you mind if I get comfortable?"

Carter shook her head and finished her drink in one long gulp. If she wanted to gently interrogate Billie, she'd have to slow down on the drink and keep her wits about her.

"And I'll fix you another on my way back. Relax."

When Billie emerged from the bathroom, she was wearing a sheer nightie that barely covered the fullness of her breasts and her black thong. She mixed two more drinks, handed one to Carter, and stretched across the king-size bed. Billie propped herself up on her elbows, and her nearly naked breasts hung eye level in front of Carter on the settee. "Do you ever think about us when we're apart?"

Carter's body throbbed at the memories. "Of course I do."

"Why don't we start fresh right now?" Billie rimmed the top of her glass with her index finger and sucked it in and out of her mouth. "I want you all the time, Carter. We're perfect together." She cupped her sex and moaned a low, painful sound.

Carter watched Billie's hand move slowly up and down between her legs and grew wetter. "You're one sexy women, and I'd be a fool not to take you up on your offer—"

"Then why am I hearing a 'but' at the end of that sentence?"

"I just can't focus on anything but this situation with Ann." That was partly true, but something else held her back. "You said you'd tell me the truth. I need that, Billie."

"I'm so sorry you were subjected to any of this, but I assure you I'll take care of Ann. Now, let me help you relax. You don't have to do anything." Billie placed her drink on the bedside table and knelt in front of Carter.

"Tell me what Emma told you about Ann and Cass, and how she led you to Tanner."

"Please, Carter, let's forget work for a while. I need you, and you're strung so tight you're almost vibrating."

Part of Carter wanted to resist, but the other part needed relief from the stress and uncertainty of the past few days. When Billie spread Carter's knees and moved between them, she didn't object. Billie's breasts rested on Carter's thighs and brought more heat to her burning center. Carter squirmed and pushed forward in the seat. Billie pressed against Carter's chest and slid up until she reached Carter's mouth, then licked her bottom lip before easing inside.

Carter felt dizzy from the drinks and the closeness of Billie's body. She should be thinking about what happened today and how to fix it, but her energy was redirected below her waist. Having sex with Billie wouldn't solve anything, but she'd definitely feel better and maybe even forget about Emma.

"Billie, please." What was she pleading for? The information to prove Emma wasn't a liar, the quick release her body desperately needed, or the intimacy she'd felt with Emma?

"Let me take care of you. Trust me, baby. Everything will be better tomorrow." Billie stood and pulled Carter against her. She cupped Carter's butt and rubbed their pelvises together. "Come here."

Carter's resistance fell away, and she allowed Billie to pull her onto the bed. She really wanted to be taken care of tonight, loved, and made to feel special.

"Do you need a show or are you ready for me?" Billie slowly pushed the thin straps off her shoulders and eased the negligée over her head, leaving only her thong.

The leisurely reveal of silky alabaster skin mesmerized Carter. Billie lay next to her and intertwined their legs, resting her crotch against Carter's thigh. Carter felt the wet sheer fabric of Billie's thong dampen a spot on the leg of her jeans as Billie rocked against her.

"Billie?" Billie's pace quickened, and Carter knew from past experience it wouldn't be long until she was lost in her own need, which would've normally been fine, but not tonight. Carter's emotional needs were stronger than her sexual ones. "Billie?" Next, Billie would need stimulation from Carter, just before she climaxed.

"Shhh." Billie kissed the side of Carter's face and pulled one of Carter's hands between her legs. "Right there. Make me come."

Carter felt detached lying beside Billie's preorgasmic body, giving commentary like an observer. She was physically aroused by Billie's responses but emotionally unengaged. This whole encounter wasn't about her at all. Had any of her previous sexual partners felt as used as she did right now? She didn't want this any more. Carter rolled away.

"No!" Billie reached for Carter. "Please stay."

She'd been about to betray Emma and herself. The thought was a splash of ice water, bringing her back from an alcohol-and-hormone-induced haze. Her heart and body ached with longing so intense she involuntarily shivered.

"What's wrong? I'm hurting here."

"So am I, but for entirely different reasons." She stood and straightened her clothes

Billie's breathing was still quick and raspy as she rose and started toward Carter with the look of a hungry predator.

Carter chose her words carefully. She couldn't afford to alienate Billie until Ann was cleared. "I can't do this. I'm sorry if I misled you."

"I don't understand. You've never turned down sex."

"There's more at stake now." And it wasn't just Ann's situation. Billie had agreed to answer her questions about Emma's part in it but then reneged. Carter had let a curvaceous body and a tug on her waistband distract her. But Billie had helped her realize she had deeper feelings for Emma. Carter owed Billie for that, and she could only have learned it this way—a stark juxtaposition of her former life with what she wanted now.

"Will you at least stay with me tonight?"

"I can't. I'll come by in the morning and take you to get your car."

❖

"Where the hell are you going, Harriett Smoltz?" Emma had followed her for miles outside the town limits of Stuart and into the next county. She killed her headlights, parked next to a stand of Leland cypress, and watched Harriett's bright-pink vehicle turn into the Gentle Breeze Nursing Home. What was she doing here so late at night? Visiting hours probably ended at sunset in a place like this.

Harriett pulled close to the black wrought-iron gates and punched a code into the security pad. She'd obviously been here before. Maybe she volunteered to work evenings so it wouldn't interfere with her day job. Perhaps she was visiting someone who'd taken a sudden turn.

Whatever Harriett's motivation, Emma didn't have time to find out tonight. Rocky Mount and her interview with Clem Stevens were in the opposite direction. She'd called the superstore earlier to check his work schedule but received a sermon on employee privacy from a grumpy man.

While she drove, Emma replayed the scene in the sheriff's office earlier and the pained and disappointed looks she'd received from Ann and Carter. She brushed tears from her eyes when the road blurred. She'd thought she and Carter had a connection, something real. How could Carter give up on her so easily? At least Ann had been willing to listen, but Carter had completely shut down.

What was Donovan's hold on Carter? Was it just sex, or did their affair mean more? How could Carter trust a woman who was such an obvious fraud—her hair color came out of a bottle, her perky boobs were silicone bags, and she used her looks to manipulate men and women. Emma couldn't understand the attraction. She wanted to believe it didn't compare to her connection with Carter, but so far she'd been proved wrong.

The dark road to Rocky Mount loomed ahead, and Emma wished for more traffic along the deserted stretch. She didn't want a repeat of her drive to Wally's. The fear of that night shivered through her. Thinking about her would-be killer wasn't a good desolate-road pastime, so she pressed her foot closer to the carburetor and hummed an upbeat country song.

A boring hour later, Emma pulled up to the superstore, a huge warehouse that looked more like a storage barn than an actual store. The thrill of chasing the big lead pulsed through her when she grabbed her notepad and considered what Clem Stevens might know about the murder. A man wearing blue khaki pants and a lighter blue shirt indicative of the store's staff stood outside the back door smoking. She put on her best bubba-busting smile and imitated a Donovan sashay.

"Clem ain't here." The man stroked his hand through imaginary hair and grinned a toothless smile.

"Guess I talked to you earlier?"

He nodded and blew a long drag of smoke away from her, but the wind brought it back.

"I've driven a long way. Can you at least tell me when he will be here?"

"I ain't supposed to give out that kind of information."

"Yes, I appreciate you could get in trouble, but you have my word, I won't tell. It's very important I speak to him."

"He in some kind of trouble? I don't want to stitch him up. He's a standup guy."

"Not at all. I swear." She dug inside her messenger bag. "I'll pay."

"Put your money away. If you're that desperate, it must be important." He nodded toward the back door, and Emma followed him into a small snack room. He walked to a coffee machine that looked like it had been in operation since coffee was first ground. "Wanna cup?"

She'd been drowsy on the road and still had a long drive back to the park. "Sure. Let me." She dropped coins into the machine, and they rattled and clanked like a pinball game. When she pressed the selection button, she didn't really expect to get anything, but a cup fell, followed by a hot, inky stream of coffee.

"Ain't as bad as it looks. Fake cream and real sugar." He shoved a square ice-cream carton toward her.

"I'm good, thanks." She bought him a cup, and they sat down at the small table in front of a snack dispenser. The room smelled of cigarettes, reheated food, and stale garbage. She couldn't wait to run back outside and take a deep breath, but she needed this man's help. She took a sip of coffee and almost gagged as the strong, cutting flavor coated and stuck to her tongue. When she could speak again, she said, "I'm Emma, by the way."

He nodded but didn't reciprocate. "Truth of the matter is, Clem don't even work here anymore. He left about ten days ago. He didn't leave a forwarding address or phone number. Hell, he didn't even come back to get his paycheck on Friday."

"Do you know why he left?" She'd never run into so many dead ends writing a story. Maybe Carter was right, and she wasn't supposed to tell this one.

"No, ma'am. Talk to Sissy Brown over in maintenance. She and Clem was pretty tight for a while. If anybody knows, it'd be Sissy."

"Thank you so much," Emma said. "Sorry. I didn't get your name."

"Let's leave it at that. If you're asked, you don't know who told you."

"Smart thinking and thanks again."

"Thank you for the coffee." He raised his cup and directed her to the maintenance department.

She followed the two-lefts-and-a-right directions and wandered around in the belly of the massive warehouse until she located a fortyish woman with stringy dishwater hair whose burgundy smock identified her as Sissy. Emma extended her hand and smiled. "I'm Emma Ferguson, and I'm looking for Clem Stevens. It's very important I get in touch with him."

The woman smiled and offered her a seat on the corner of a pallet of liquid detergent. "I'm Sissy, but I can't help you."

"Because you don't know where he is, or because you promised not to tell?"

"Either way, I can't help you. Clem's a good man, so why don't you leave him alone?"

"He's not in trouble, but somebody else's life could depend on my talking to him."

"Did it ever occur to you that his life might depend on you not doing that?" The concern in her eyes made Emma wonder if she and Clem were more than coworkers.

"What's he afraid of? Has he been threatened? Because I know how that feels."

Sissy stood. "We're done here."

"Has Clem ever mentioned the murder of a man in Stuart thirty-seven years ago? Please, Sissy, it's urgent I get in touch with him."

"Like I said, lady, I *cannot* help you."

The optimism Emma had felt earlier settled heavily in her stomach along with the bitter coffee. "Would you at least tell him I came by? Give him my business card, and tell him Ann and Carter West are being railroaded and need his help."

"If I see him, I'll give him the card, but I ain't saying I'll see him."

Emma took Sissy's hand and held it tightly. "I know you'll do what's right. Thank you for your time."

On the drive back to the cabin, Emma tried to stay awake by replaying the facts of the case, but memories of Carter interrupted. She recalled their night together and how vulnerable Carter had been when she'd told Emma about her parents. They'd shared intimacies and been tender in their lovemaking. Carter had even surrendered control, something she now understood didn't usually happen, but which Emma had needed.

Had she become so emotionally invested in Carter after only one night of making love? Or was she drawn to the way Carter had spoken about her life with Ann and Cass? Maybe her attachment began when she saw Carter with the children, so attentive and devoted to their needs. Perhaps Carter's protectiveness of those she cared about and the stable, loving life she and Ann shared had captivated her. She couldn't possibly choose only one. Carter was all those things and so much more, and somewhere along their short, bumpy road, she'd fallen hard.

Emma jerked, startled by her last thought. Had she really fallen for Carter? The voice from Emma's past that always kept her dreams in check boomed with deafening clarity. *You might have fallen for her, but she will never love you. You're not right for someone like Carter West.* Billie Donovan's grinning face mocked her. Carter had sided with Donovan. Emma might not be right for Carter, but she wasn't giving up until Carter said so. Jealous ex-lovers and self-doubts be damned.

When Emma focused on her driving again, she was pulling into the park entrance. She glanced longingly at the office, remembering the great conversations she and Ann had enjoyed there, Carter's stricken face the night she couldn't find Emma on the trail to Lookout Pointe, and Carter's sincerity as she apologized for bogarting her that evening. Emma's throat tightened, and she fought back more tears.

After she found Theodore Thompson's killer, she'd confront Donovan about her lies and loose interpretation of the law, and she'd find the nerve to tell Carter how she felt. When Stuart, Virginia was in her rearview mirror, she'd secure a position as an investigative reporter with a reputable paper. And finally, Emma vowed *never* to listen to that nay-saying voice in her head again…not about work, not about life, and especially not about love.

When she pulled in front of her darkened cabin, Donovan's state car occupied Emma's usual parking space. She called out as she walked to the porch. No response. Where could Donovan be on foot at night in the woods? Emma felt as if someone had jammed a pin in her inflated plans. Her positive attitude popped, and that damn voice announced, *She's with Carter.*

CHAPTER EIGHTEEN

Emma spat the hot water into the sink and lifted the lid of the pot. No coffee. Great. She'd finally abandoned the possibility of sleep around five thirty, drank a pot of coffee, and fixed another. While she spooned coffee into the filter, she listened for the sound of tires or footsteps outside. Where the hell were Carter and Donovan? It was almost ten.

She tapped her fingers on the countertop while the coffee brewed, shoving her cup under the first drip. When she brought the steamy, rich-smelling brew to her lips, she heard a car pull up outside. She raced to the window, coffee sloshing down her T-shirt and burning her chest. "Damn it." She pulled the hot fabric away from her skin and peered through the sheer curtains without moving them.

Carter's Jeep slowly approached the cabin down the long gravel drive. Donovan was in the passenger seat way too close to Carter. They had been together last night. Her stomach churned, and the wet spot on her shirt made her shiver. She wanted to look away, but instead she watched, waiting for the horror-show reveal she really didn't want to see.

Carter and Donovan sat in the vehicle, talking for what seemed an eternity. Donovan tossed her blond hair from side to side as she laughed and then rested her head on Carter's shoulder. Emma suppressed an urge to claw Donovan's eyes out and then considered doing the same to her own. Why hadn't she told Carter about her feelings before now? Why hadn't she trusted her instincts and her heart? The questions tore through her mind while she tormented herself with the scene outside.

Donovan reached over, cupped the back of Carter's neck, and pulled her closer. Just before their lips met, Emma turned away. She'd seen enough. Carter had obviously made her choice, and no matter how much it hurt, Emma would have to accept it.

One car door slammed, then another, and tires crunched on gravel. Maybe she was a masochist, but something pulled her back to the window. Donovan's car disappeared toward the park exit, but the Jeep remained. Carter sat in the driver's seat, hands on the steering wheel, staring toward the cabin. She pounded the wheel with her fist, opened the door, and stepped out. Emma held her breath, willing Carter nearer. She took a few steps toward the cabin, stopped, and then ran back to the Jeep. Gravel peppered against the side of the cabin as she sped away.

What now? She couldn't go back to a passionless, disconnected life—always remembering and longing for what she'd felt with Carter. Emma sank into the sofa and played several scenarios of what Carter might've said if she'd come inside, but none of them ended with "I love you."

Her last chance to turn things around was to clear Ann and expose Donovan as a fraud. Time was running out to locate a viable suspect to replace Ann on the top of Donovan's list. Timothy Black and his assistant had worked at the funeral home until after two in the morning, clearing them of suspicion. Daniel Tanner certainly had motive, and Harriett said the two men had fought publicly. She'd dig a little deeper in that direction, and if nothing else, it would take her mind off Carter for a while.

After her first luxurious soak in the claw-foot tub, she dressed and was in the tax department office downtown two hours later. A clerk escorted Emma to the computer room and demonstrated how to use the outdated equipment. She drummed her fingers on the side of the antique as the cursor on the screen flashed. She imagined tiny minions inside the archaic machine running back and forth, climbing miniscule ladders, and dragging huge tomes of fifty-year-old tax records on Daniel Tanner. She laughed aloud but covered her mouth when the clerk eyeballed her.

When the screen filled with data, she clicked through each page until she found the information she needed. The results were much better than she'd expected: months of delinquent notices, lien advertisements, and foreclosure papers on Tanner's drugstore property. A special notation on two pages indicated Theodore Wayne Thompson had made an offer to assume Tanner's loan and the tax debt. She made a copy and highlighted the pertinent data. This information might not solve the case, but it could take the spotlight off Ann long enough for Emma to find the killer. Adrenaline surged as she ran across the street toward the sheriff's office.

Sheriff Echols met her at the door. "You look like a little kid with a new toy. What's up, Ferguson?"

"We have another suspect to consider."

"Come in, and let's take a look. I sure hope you're right."

Emma spread the tax records across the desk and tried to wait patiently, drinking more coffee and pacing.

Echols read the papers and checked something on his computer. He finally scratched his chin and pushed his chair back from the desk. "This isn't going to work."

"Everybody knows Thompson wanted to buy Tanner's store and even tried to force the bank into early foreclosure."

"But what I'm telling you is—"

"Anybody could've had a gun back then, and just about everybody did. I admit that part would be hard to prove, but he certainly had the opportunity. By his own admission he closed the store early that night." Emma leaned over Echols's desk, desperate to make her point.

"Yeah, he did, but—"

"*And* folks witnessed the two of them in a fist fight on Main Street about Thompson trying to buy him out."

"There's still paperwork on file to back that up, but, Ferguson—"

"*Plus* Tanner's reputation as a drinker started about the same time, and he hasn't slowed down much, maybe a man with something to hide."

"You're right again, but—"

Emma threw her hands in the air. "But what, Sheriff? It doesn't sound like you want to consider this at all."

"I've been listening. You wouldn't let me get a word in edgewise. If you had, I'd have told you Daniel Tanner couldn't be a suspect."

"But this," she pointed to the papers on his desk, "raises enough doubt to take a look."

"But Tanner was in jail that night."

"Sheriff, I really don't—" Echols's words registered, and Emma stared at him. Her rush of adrenaline evaporated, and she slumped into a chair. "He was in jail?"

"Contrary to what Ms. Donovan thinks, I'm not some hayseed playing at being a sheriff. I checked on everybody who could've been a suspect. The records clearly show Tanner was in jail that night for affray, disorderly conduct, and destruction of property."

"How is that possible, Sheriff? He admitted he was at the store until after ten o'clock."

"I've got a copy of the original report. He told the deputy he started drinking before he left the store because Thompson called, taunting him about his financial situation again. He closed just before ten thirty and went to Wally's. He was almost crocked when he got there.

"He started a fight with the first guy who looked at him crossways. They tore up the place pretty good, and the owner pressed charges. He was in lockup before eleven o'clock and left around noon the next day. Thompson was seen on the street after eleven. I'm sorry to blow your theory apart."

"None of that was in the statements."

"The deputy didn't see the need to document it. An error on his part," the sheriff said.

"I can't believe it. I thought we had something." Emma dropped her head into her hands.

The phone rang and the sheriff answered, making notes as he listened. A few minutes later he hung up and pulled his coat off the back of his chair. "I'm sorry as I can be about this, but I've got to go over to the curb market. One of the local kids stole a bunch of cigarettes and beer. Will you be all right?"

She nodded. "Mind if I sit here a few minutes until I figure out what to do next?"

"Make yourself at home. There's even some relatively fresh coffee in the back." He grabbed his hat from the coatrack and closed the door softly.

Emma's head pounded. She felt like a cub reporter on her first story. She should've checked the jail records to tie up loose ends. What a rookie mistake. "Sorry, Dad."

The shrill ring of her cell phone pierced her aching head, and she searched her bag for aspirin. "This is Emma Ferguson." She downed four pills with lukewarm coffee and waited for the caller to speak. Her disappointment was so thick she had to muster even the tiniest bit of enthusiasm. "Hello. Is anyone there?"

"Ms. Ferguson?" a soft female voice asked.

"Yes, how can I help you?" Emma prayed the caller would get to the point as soon as possible. Her head was a bowling pin with the ball barreling her way.

"Ms. Ferguson, this is Sissy Brown from the superstore. Remember me?"

Emma's energy returned and she forgot all about her headache. "Of course I remember you, Sissy."

"Clem, that is, Mr. Stevens, wanted me to tell you that he'd meet you tonight."

Emma's body tingled, on high alert once again. "That would be great. When and where?"

"He said to come by the Food Lion warehouse in Stuart around eleven tonight. He's got a job doing evening maintenance. Won't be nobody there but him. He'll leave the back door unlocked. Just holler out when you come in."

"Sissy, I really appreciate this. You have no idea—"

"There's one more thing, Ms. Ferguson. Clem said to bring the sheriff. He don't feel safe otherwise. Besides, he only wants to tell this story once."

"Of course, and thanks again, Sissy."

Emma disconnected and wrote a message for the sheriff with the particulars about the interview. She folded it over, scribbled *Urgent* on the outside, and left it in the center of his desk. She argued with herself for several minutes before leaving a message on Donovan's voice mail about the meeting. She wanted Donovan to be there with the sheriff to hear what Clem said so she couldn't possibly distort it later.

❖

When Emma's car pulled into the park entrance, Carter jerked her hand out of the way just before the office door closed on it. Emma accelerated and then slammed on brakes so hard the old car stalled and rolled limply into the parking lot and stopped in front of them. How did Emma manage klutzy while driving a car? She wanted to talk to Emma, and she didn't. She followed Ann toward the Jeep. If she didn't make up her mind soon, she'd lose the opportunity. Emma made the decision for her.

"Ann. Carter. If you have a few minutes, I'd like to discuss something with you." Emma lurched toward them, her gait one of uncertainty or impending flight. She wound a strand of her long red hair around a finger and pulled at tangles.

Carter stared at Ann, willing her to speak, but Ann was apparently leaving the decision to her. The awkward silence stretched, and the longer it continued, the more Emma's face paled. "Yeah. I think that would be a good idea."

Once Carter had broken the ice, Ann jumped in. "You're darned right we need to talk, but not in the parking lot. We'll follow you to the cabin so we can have some privacy."

In the Jeep, Ann placed her hand on Carter's arm before she cranked the car. "You know I love you more than my life, don't you?"

The words landed with a sick certainty in Carter's gut. "Yeah. What's wrong?"

"You're in for a shock tonight, but just remember everything I've done in my life, I've done for you."

Carter felt like the Jeep was closing in on her. She pulled for breath. "What are you saying, Ann? Should we leave? Go somewhere else? I'll take care of whatever it is." She'd lost everyone she loved once when she was helpless to do anything about it, but she wasn't going to let it happen again. She'd protect Ann no matter what the cost.

Ann leaned over and kissed her cheek. "I know you would, child, but we have to stay and face this together. It's long overdue."

"If you don't tell me what's going on, I can't protect you, not even from Emma."

"That's not necessary. Let's go."

The short distance to Emma's cabin felt like a long, slow drive to a future she wasn't ready to face. Carter and Ann had kept a secret for years, but Carter had never known what it was. When she'd asked Ann about Cass's appearance in their lives, she'd been told it was divine intervention. She'd always known there was more to the story but never broached it again. Was she ready to hear it now, or would it destroy everyone and everything she loved?

When they entered Emma's cabin, Carter smelled fresh brewing coffee with a hint of Emma's distinctive fragrance in the background. She glanced at the sofa, and flashes of her night making love with Emma returned. She considered running, but she would've left something vital behind. And tonight Ann needed her support and possibly her protection.

"Either of you care for something to drink?" Emma asked. "I have fresh coffee and a little brandy. It's not as good as yours, Ann, but it'll do in a pinch."

Carter shook her head.

Ann said, "I'll take a shot of that brandy. Think I'll need it."

Emma poured a healthy dose for Ann and handed it to her. "Okay, guess I'll get star—"

Ann held up her hand and knocked back half of the brandy in one swallow. "I hope you don't mind, but I have a few things to say first. Get comfortable. It's going to be a long evening."

Carter tried to intervene. "Ann, don't you think you should let Emma—"

"Absolutely not. What I have to say affects both of you and has already caused more trouble that it should've for a lot of people."

Carter and Emma approached the sofa they'd made love on a few days ago from opposite ends and sat as far apart as possible. Emma looked as scared as Carter felt.

Ann pulled one of the kitchen chairs over in front of the coffee table. "First, I want to tell Emma the rest of mine and Cass's story."

Carter shook her head. "Please, Ann."

"Carter, it's time." Ann's voice had a hard, cold edge she'd never heard. "You need to hear this as much as Emma does." Her tone softened and became almost a whisper. "I'd never do anything to hurt you. Please, just listen. I've held this inside too long."

Carter felt like Ann was about to dissect their lives and open old wounds for the world to see. She wrapped her arms around her middle to stay the sick feeling.

"Now, if I remember, the last installment of the story ended when I found out Cass was pregnant by that scumbag Theodore Thompson."

Emma nodded.

"We didn't see each other for a while, as you can imagine. I was pretty devastated. One night out of the blue she called and asked to see me. She wanted to meet at the furniture factory because she was closing up after the cleaning crew left. She said Thompson was probably with one of his other women."

Ann rocked as she talked, her gaze focused on the ceiling as if seeing her story unfold like a movie. "I bundled little Carter up and drove into town. I parked the truck in the alley beside Tanner's drugstore, and we walked to the factory, keeping to the shadows. The streets were mostly deserted because it was colder than a witch's tit in a brass bra."

Carter suppressed a grin and shook her head at Emma. The little smile that curved Emma's lips did more to reassure Carter than anything in the past several days.

"You two stop making goo-goo eyes at each other and listen. Here's where it gets interesting. Cass got there around ten forty-five, and we walked through the plant to make sure nobody else was there. We ended up by the discard chip pile, and she told me the best news I'd heard in years. She'd decided to leave Thompson and live with me, convention be damned."

Emma shivered beside her. "Cass finally came to her senses. What happened next?"

Ann smiled, and her eyes sparked like a fire had reignited inside her. "I kissed her within an inch of her life, that's what. I was completely lost in that kiss and will remember it in slow motion as long as I live."

"That's the most beautiful thing I've ever heard." Emma sighed and gave Carter her hungry look that had made Carter want to kiss her the first time.

Carter felt tears welling in her eyes. "You never told me this before."

"I never told you, darling, because of what happened next. We were so happy at that moment neither of us saw or heard it coming."

"Saw or heard what?" Emma moved closer to the edge of her seat, reached for Carter's hand, and then quickly withdrew.

"Theodore burst out of the shadows, running toward us like a mad bull. He'd followed Cass from their house. His face was bright red, and he was yelling and cussing, calling us vile names. He head butted Cass in the stomach at a full run and knocked her for a loop."

"Oh my God," Carter and Emma said in unison.

Carter clenched her fists and felt the blood rush to her face. "That son-of-a-bitch. What happened then?"

"Well—"

"Maybe you shouldn't answer that," Emma said.

A few seconds later, Emma's warning registered, and Carter glanced at her. "Emma has a good point. I can see the headlines now: FEMALE LOVER KILLS HUSBAND IN JEALOUS RAGE."

"Be quiet, both of you. The truth is coming out, and I'd rather you hear it from me before I tell the cops." Ann took another swig of brandy. "You can imagine when he hit Cass, I was all over him. I could smell the booze then. He kept swinging and missing, and I kept landing punches. Carter was scared, crying in a corner, and Cass crawled over and shielded her. Thompson and I took a couple more swings before I landed a good one right on his nose. It opened up like a gusher."

"You go, Ann. Give it to him." Emma was on her feet cheering like she was at a boxing match. Then she froze. "Oh, shit."

"Yeah," Carter said. "She just admitted assaulting a murder victim. The good news is Thompson was still alive at this point." She pulled Emma back down on the sofa, praying she would keep an open mind.

"And then what?" Emma asked.

"I collected my little family and left. The last time I saw Thompson, he was wallowing on the floor next to the chip pile holding a handkerchief to his bloody snout. And just so there's no confusion, I didn't have a weapon of any kind, and he was very much alive when we left."

"Is that the last time you saw him?" Emma's tone was flat, making the question sound like a police inquiry.

"Yes. I helped Cass off the floor and scooped Carter up in my arms. She was still crying when we walked down Main Street to the car. We hadn't gotten very far when Cass started having abdominal pains. I tried to call an ambulance on the pay phone, but it was out of order."

"Oh, no." Emma wiped tears from her cheeks. "Is that what happened to the baby?"

"We got to the hospital just as Cass started bleeding. She lost the baby a few hours later. The doctor kept her for observation. Carter wouldn't let go of her hand, so we slept on a rollaway right beside her."

Carter's chest was tight. She coughed for a clear breath, and her cheeks burned from tears. She grabbed a tissue from the coffee table and dabbed her eyes. The tears kept coming. Ann had fought for their family and might have to do so again. Carter would do the same to save her. Whatever it took.

Emma scooted closer and pulled Carter to her side. She rocked back and forth as Carter cried. "You're all right. Ann is going to be okay too. I'll make sure of it."

Ann squeezed onto the sofa with them and put her arm around Carter's shoulder. "There's no need to cry, my sweet girl. I didn't do anything terribly wrong, and the three of us had a great life, didn't we?"

Carter nodded.

"This was the second trauma and the reason Carter didn't speak for months." Emma's question sounded more like a statement.

"Is that right?" Carter asked.

"Yes, darling, it is." Ann rubbed her back and tried to calm her.

"And this is what you've been keeping from me all these years? Oh, Ann, I'm so sorry. I knew something bad had happened, but I couldn't figure out what."

"You probably thought I killed the bastard. That's why you've stayed so close through the years, never going after your dreams or falling in love, even when I told you I was fine."

"I never believed you killed him." Carter held Ann's gaze. "Really. Never."

"You've always thought I gave a flying rat's ass what the people in this town thought of me—then or now. You wanted to protect me from the story, from the police, and from Emma."

"Why didn't you tell me before?"

"It was ancient history. You didn't remember what happened, and the story died down over the years."

"Can you ever forgive me?" Carter rested her head on Ann's shoulder.

"There's nothing to forgive, child. I was protecting you, and you thought you were doing the same for me. That's what families do."

She and Ann held each other and cried, purging years of secrets and pain and comforting each other in the process. They'd devoted much of their lives to shielding each other from a harm that didn't exist.

After they stopped crying, Ann gave Carter a final hug and rose from her sofa. "That completes my portion of this evening's entertainment. I'll give my statement to the sheriff and Ms. BCI tomorrow. You're welcome to come along if you want a repeat of the story."

"Of course I'll come with you," Carter said.

Emma wiped her eyes again and cleared her throat. "Before you leave, Ann, I'd like to apologize to you and Carter for the problems I've caused with this article. I never meant to hurt anyone, especially you. I'm meeting with someone tonight who might know the truth about how Thompson died. He's been reluctant to come forward until now."

"It's just a big misunderstanding. Billie's going to take care of everything." Carter's voice lacked the conviction she'd hoped to relay, and Ann rolled her eyes.

"Well, that's certainly my cue to leave," Ann said. "The two of you have some talking to do. And just for the record, Emma, I don't believe one measly word that comes out of that fake Dolly Parton's mouth. I know you'll get to the bottom of this."

"Thanks for the vote of confidence, Ann."

Carter hugged Ann. "I love you. Wait for me at the office. I'll pick you up shortly."

"Take your time. You have things to say." Ann kissed her cheek and closed the door behind her.

When Carter turned around, Emma was sitting rigid on the sofa like a soldier waiting for orders. Carter wanted to go to her but couldn't without touching and reassuring her. She'd need all her concentration and courage to get through this conversation. "Can we talk?" Carter twisted her cat's-eye necklace, hoping Cass would send some divine intervention.

"That's probably a good idea. We need a strategy to protect Ann."

Carter was momentarily taken aback. She'd been thinking of a more personal topic, but how would Emma know that? "The truth is our strategy. Ann won't have it any other way. Actually, I meant a talk about…us."

"Carter, I'm in love with you. You don't have to say anything because I saw you and Donovan this morning. I know you spent the night with her. The only thing left for me here is to find the murderer."

Emma's voice was strained, trembling at the end, and Carter started toward her but stopped. *She's in love with me?* She stared at the old wooden floor. Why had she even considered getting more involved with Billie? How could she make Emma understand she'd been trying to help Ann? "I'd like to explain."

"You went home with her last night?" The words sounded forced.

"Yes. I mean, no. I went to her hotel but—" The room closed in on her as she struggled for an answer, and Emma drifted farther away.

"And you had…sex…with her." Emma almost spat the words between choking sounds.

It should be so easy to just say no, but she'd considered having sex with Billie. Carter wanted to explain how her feelings had shifted. Carter's necklace was knotted at her throat and she kept turning. Her words and her tongue were as twisted as the chain of her necklace.

"Where's that Carter West honesty?" Emma tried to laugh but coughed instead. "Did you have sex with her? Please say it, so I can move on like I did with Sheri. I can't do this again."

"But I don't want you to move on." Carter's world was turning on end. Ann's confession and now Emma's admission had stirred too much emotion at once. She retreated to her quiet, safe place. Her words wouldn't come. She needed time to think, process what she wanted to say. She always choked at emotional conversations on the fly, but Emma wasn't in the mood to give her more time. "I can explain."

"I'll survive without a play-by-play of sex with Donovan. I get the picture." Emma fumbled with her watch.

"But, Emma...I...like...you. I mean...I—" Carter's next words were frozen on her lips by Emma's icy blue stare.

"I see."

"No, you don't." Carter's chest tightened, and for a second she felt light-headed. Emma loved her. *Tell her you love her too. Do it now.*

Emma glanced at her watch again, jumped from the sofa, and ran toward the door. "It's almost eleven, and I have to meet someone." She grabbed her messenger bag and looked back at Carter one final time. "I hope you'll be happy with Donovan. You deserve it. But please be careful with her. She's not what she seems."

"But..." Carter started after her, but Emma slammed the door. "Wait..."

CHAPTER NINETEEN

"You idiot!" Emma ran from the cabin to her car, trying to outrun the events of this night. She'd blurted her feelings to Carter, only to have her evade the question about having sex with Donovan. Her words had exploded like something foul and putrid, destroying their one beautiful night together. Game over.

How could she have been so wrong? She'd known from the beginning that Carter was a player, but she'd thought their attraction was strong enough to hold her, at least until they fell in love. She should've known better, based on her track record.

She'd gone into their affair backward, disregarded her internal warnings because of chemistry. She'd felt a connection with Carter she'd never experienced before, a joining of kindred spirits and an unparalleled passion. With each recrimination, the pain in her chest circulated faster. She pressed her palm against the pressure and cried out. Her stomach churned, and she swallowed the bitter taste bubbling up. *How do people recover from feelings this powerful?*

Emma rolled down the windows, and the inside temperature dropped quickly. She welcomed the cold damp air to soothe her raw emotions. Her skin prickled and her hair whipped into an uncontrollable mass. As she raced toward Stuart, teeth chattering, she forced her thoughts away from losing Carter and back to the Thompson murder.

Her instincts about Ann had been right, but now she needed to prove Ann's innocence beyond any doubt. Donovan wasn't interested in letting Ann off the hook. Her freedom didn't fit with

Donovan's plan for Carter. But in Emma's opinion, Billie Donovan didn't fit into Carter and Ann's life, whether Emma was in it or not. As Emma had watched Carter and Ann support and comfort each other tonight, she realized they'd always be a part of her understanding of family and love, even if she never saw them again once her assignment ended.

She pulled up to the back door of the warehouse where Clem Stevens worked and parked beside an old pickup truck. Sheriff Echols wasn't here yet, but she didn't intend to wait. If this was her only chance to help Ann, she didn't want to blow it by being late. She brushed and patted her tangled hair but gave up on taming it. She silenced the phone's ringer, opened the voice-memo app, and slid it into her coat pocket.

She entered the door, leaving it unlocked for the sheriff and Donovan. The huge room housed loading pallets stacked almost to the roof, their contents obscured by green plastic wrap. Overhead fluorescent lighting flickered sporadically, alternating dim light with eerie shadows. She followed a narrow path through the slanted walls and called out. Her words seemed to fall around her, absorbed by the overstuffed room.

She wandered farther into the storehouse, wishing with every step she'd waited for the sheriff. What if this was a trap set by the murderer? What if Donovan had arranged it so Emma would be killed, and she could have Carter? But she already had Carter.

"Mr. Stevens?" Emma called as she walked. "Mr. Stevens, are you here?"

"What's the matter, Ferguson? Your source didn't show?"

The voice behind Emma sent a spark of fear through her. She whirled around to Donovan, who stood with hands on her hips, looking too perfect in all black.

"I really wish you'd stop sneaking up on me."

Donovan's self-satisfied grin irritated Emma even more today, since she'd spent the night with Carter. She fought the urge to rip the tailored ninja suit off her shapely body. "I didn't see your car out back."

"I parked in front. So, where's your informant?"

"Don't worry. He'll show up, and when he does, I'll finally get the facts I need to clear Ann from your bogus suspicion."

"Have you forgotten you gave me the information implicating Ann in the first place, Emma dear?"

"I'm not sure who told you about Ann and Cass, but it certainly wasn't me."

"But we're the only ones who know that. As far as Ann and Carter are concerned, you're the bad guy, not me."

"I don't think that'll last. It's just a matter of time before the truth comes out. You can't fool Carter for long."

Donovan laughed out loud and slid a hand over her breasts and down her torso. "I wouldn't count on that. After last night, Carter's all mine. You should've been there, Ferguson. Want me to tell you what happened?"

Emma's stomach roiled. She burned with anger, but her heart bled with each hurtful word. Donovan had gouged her wound and broken it open again. She was paralyzed by her feelings, unable to move or respond. She prayed to disappear, but instead a faint voice pulled her back to her purpose.

"Ms. Ferguson, is that you?"

Flashing Donovan an I-told-you-so look, Emma turned and called out, "Mr. Stevens, I'm here. Where are you?"

"Follow the yellow overhead lights. I'm up in the office."

"Who is this Stevens person anyway?" Donovan asked.

"Be quiet for once and listen. Maybe you'll learn something." Emma heard a noise from behind a stack of bundled paper towels and hoped it was Sheriff Echols finally joining them.

She and Donovan followed the overhead lights into a clearing, where the office was constructed on a raised platform in the center of the space. The half-glass, half-aluminum sides made it resemble a hovering spacecraft grounded only at two corners by heavy metal steps. The landing provided an excellent perch for supervisors to keep an eye on employees.

Emma climbed the stairs and entered the front of the office as an elderly black man entered from the back. He had salt-and-pepper hair, wore creased khaki pants and a white shirt, and stood tall as he walked. Emma's immediate impression of Clem Stevens was of a proud man who would make a great witness.

"Are you Ms. Ferguson?" he asked.

"Yes, sir. Thank you for agreeing to meet me, Mr. Stevens." Emma offered her hand and was impressed with his firm handshake and direct eye contact.

"Call me Clem." He pointed behind her. "This doesn't look like the sheriff."

"He's on his way. This is Agent Donovan with Virginia BCI. She's working the case."

Clem shook his head. "I only want to tell this story once."

"He should be along any minute." Emma pulled her phone out of her pocket, tapped a couple of times, and placed it on the table between them. "We can get started, if you don't mind. I'll catch him up when he gets here."

Clem seemed to consider his options. "I guess that'd be all right."

Donovan stepped between Clem and Emma. "This concerns an ongoing murder investigation, and since I'm the only law-enforcement officer present, I'll conduct the interview."

Emma elbowed Donovan out of the way. She wasn't about to railroad this man like she'd done Ann. Before Emma could tell her so, Clem waved her off.

"No disrespect intended, but since Ms. Ferguson went to the trouble to find me. I'll address my comments to her. Of course you're free to listen."

Donovan's cheeks reddened and she flashed Emma a killer stare, but didn't respond.

Emma grinned and slid the phone closer to Clem as they took seats around the small circular table. She chose a chair facing the front entrance and overlooking the main floor below so she could attract the sheriff's attention when he arrived. She was about to ask her first question when a red light above the room's two doors flashed and an alarm sounded.

Donovan stood and looked around the warehouse floor. "What's that?"

"You sure are jumpy," Clem said. "Lets me know somebody came in the back door. Hopefully it's the sheriff."

"Clem, I'm ready when you are," Emma said. "Do you want me to ask questions, or would you rather tell your story first?"

"It would be easier for me to talk, and then you can ask questions."

"Okay. For the record, Clem Stevens will be telling me, Emma Ferguson, and BCI Agent Billie Donovan what he knows about the night Theodore Wayne Thompson died."

"I know more than I want to." Clem rested his arms on the table and laced his fingers together. "I was working later than usual that night. Mr. Thompson liked me out of the building before ten thirty so they could close up, but I didn't make it. I was in the third-floor office mopping when I heard an awful commotion from somewhere downstairs. There wasn't supposed to be anybody else in the building, so I started down to see what was going on.

"I was on the second-floor landing when I saw somebody dressed in dark clothes slip behind one of the staining vats. My first instinct was to run after him, but then I heard a yell from over by the chip pile. When I got closer, I saw Mr. Thompson screaming at Miss Ann West and creating a big ruckus. Mrs. Thompson and little Carter were huddled together in a corner. They were both pale as ghosts, and I could tell the child was scared to death."

"Could you hear what was being said, Clem?" Emma wanted details.

"Not really. I wanted to step in, but I didn't have to."

"And why not?" Donovan's superior tone elicited only a sideways glance from Clem.

"Because Miss Ann jumped on that man like a June bug on stink. Thompson bobbed and weaved like a drunkard, kept swinging and missing, and Miss Ann kept connecting. She landed a solid one right on the end of his nose, and he went down like a sack of flour."

Donovan slapped her hand on the table. "When did she shoot him? For God's sake, man, get on with it. I don't have all night."

This time Clem turned toward Donovan, and his calm eyes settled on her. "You're the one who ran Miss Ann in, aren't you? If you'd listen, you might learn something about your job and about people in general."

Emma laughed out loud and nodded for Clem to continue. Donovan's face turned redder.

"I moved closer in case Thompson got up, but he didn't right away. Mrs. Thompson was still on the floor, holding her stomach and shielding the baby. Miss Ann ran over, helped them both up, and they left."

"But Ann came back, right?" Donovan's voice spiked at the end.

"No, ma'am, she didn't. I decided to let Thompson suffer a little before I helped him. He was a nasty man, no respect for people or how hard they worked. After a few minutes, he got up, still wiping his nose with a handkerchief, and started toward the exit. Before he got far, somebody else showed up."

Emma scooted her chair closer to Clem. "Somebody else *was* there. Go on."

"It was the same person I'd seen earlier dressed in dark clothes by the vats. This time I was close enough to see he had a hood over his head and to hear what was being said. When they started talking, I realized he was really a she. The woman tried to help with Thompson's bleeding nose, but he pushed her away. She begged him to leave his wife so they could be together."

"Well, don't keep us in suspense. Who the hell was she?"

Donovan's lack of patience and tact didn't surprise Emma, but it was becoming a nuisance. "Will you at least try to act like a professional? Let the man finish."

"Thanks, Ms. Ferguson. Next, Thompson laughed in this woman's face. She stopped begging and got mad. She pounded on his chest with her fists, but he kept laughing. He told her he'd never leave his wife for her. She'd just been an easy lay. She clung to him, but he pushed her away again and slapped her hard across the face. That's when the hood fell off, and I was finally able to see who it was."

"And…" Emma encouraged Clem without being pushy. She looked out across the wide expanse of boxes and wondered where the sheriff was. He really needed to hear this. If he'd come in several minutes before, he should've reached them by now.

"It was one of the Smoltz sisters."

Donovan was on her feet. "What do you mean, *one* of the Smoltz sisters? Which one?"

"I didn't know then, and I don't know now. They're twins, and I never could tell them apart. That falls under the category of your job, doesn't it?"

Emma recalled the last nine days of information she'd accumulated. She'd never even seen Hannah Smoltz, but she'd spent a considerable amount of time with Harriett, who hadn't done anything to raise Emma's suspicions. Maybe Hannah was the killer and had skipped town when Emma started looking into the murder again, and Harriett was covering for her. Emma had hoped Clem could positively identify the killer.

She returned her attention to Clem. "What happened after the slap?"

"She pulled a gun out of her coat pocket and pointed it at Thompson. I heard a loud pop and saw him fall."

"And you did nothing?" Donovan rose from the table and paced.

"Lady, the woman had a gun, and I wasn't about to confront her unarmed. I just kept watching. I knew one day I'd have to tell what I'd seen, and I wanted to get it right."

"You're doing a great job, Clem. Go on," Emma said, patting his arm.

"I couldn't believe what happened next. She stripped him down, buried his body in the chip pile, and tossed his clothes in the incinerator. That was cold."

Donovan leaned over Clem's shoulder and whispered. "I'll tell you what's cold, Mr. Stevens—not helping this man, leaving him to die, and then not telling anybody for thirty-seven years. Do you realize you can be charged with obstructing justice?"

"I couldn't have done a thing for that man. He was a goner when he hit the floor. She shot him right between the eyes. And as for your threat, do whatever you have to about that. I'd much rather take my chances with a jury now than back then. Nobody was going to believe a poor black janitor over a white woman. Besides, I would've come forward sooner if somebody was unjustly charged."

Emma shooed Donovan away from Clem and offered her hand. "And you proved that by telling your story now. Ann West can be cleared because of your statement."

"Thank you, ma'am. I'm glad I could help. Ann and Carter are good people."

"And if Agent Donovan follows through with her threat, I'll serve as a character witness on your behalf." Emma slid her phone toward the edge of the table and started to pick it up. When she did, the door behind her burst open, startling her. She dropped the phone, and it skidded under the table.

Donovan reached for her gun.

CHAPTER TWENTY

The figure reflected in the glass in front of Emma was dressed entirely in black, held a dark-colored gun, and motioned toward Donovan. "I wouldn't do that. Keep your hands where I can see them."

The screeching voice sent shivers down Emma's spine, but this woman didn't look like Harriett Smoltz. Maybe this was her missing twin, Hannah.

"You know, the old man's got a point. Nobody would've believed him then, and they won't believe him now, because they're not going to hear his story. Donovan, drop your weapon and cell phone on the floor, and kick them over here."

"You're making a big mistake." Donovan's voice sounded almost defiant. "It's a felony to assault a law-enforcement officer with a weapon. You're already in enough trouble."

Emma turned enough to look into the intruder's eyes, and then she knew. "Donovan, I'd like you to meet the murderer of Theodore Wayne Thompson, Harriett Smoltz." The woman's shoulders jerked slightly. She'd called it right. "Of course, she'd have you believe it was her sister, Hannah, Daniel Tanner, or even Ann West. Isn't that right, Harriett?"

"You're just too smart for your own good, Emma. Things were going fine until you showed up. Folks had nearly forgotten about Theodore and the blight he left on this town."

"But, Harriett, you had nothing but nice things to say about your lover before."

"Shut up." Harriett waved the gun in Emma's direction. "He was a lowlife who used me for his amusement."

Donovan asked. "What do you plan to do now? You can't kill all of us."

"I did it before and got away with it for thirty-seven years. Your bodies won't be found for days out here in the middle of nowhere, and by then I'll be long gone." She pulled a set of handcuffs from behind her back, slid them across the table, and motioned to Donovan and Clem. "Cuff yourselves to the chairs and each other. Be thorough. It's important to be thorough. Don't you agree, Emma? Intertwine your hands through the chair arms. I don't want you trying to escape during the best part."

Emma would be next. This Harriett Smoltz bore no resemblance to the mild, helpful librarian she'd spoken with so many times recently. The black outfit clung to a toned body that had been hidden beneath her customary baggy garb. Her eyes flashed anger and hatred, and the corners of her mouth clamped tight with the determination of the deranged.

When Harriett was satisfied that Donovan and Clem were restrained, she poked Emma in the back with the barrel of her gun. "Now, the moment I've waited for. You've been a tough one to stop. You wouldn't take a simple warning, or even three, and leave town. We need to go for a walk. I'll be back for the rest of you later."

Emma had to delay her and pray the sheriff showed up soon. "How did you find me?"

"When I saw you rush into the sheriff's office earlier, I knew you'd uncovered something important. He wasn't around, so I read the note you left. Fortunately, you didn't know anything about me, so I saw no harm in leaving it for him. My business here will be finished before he arrives, and he'll still be in the dark. Now move."

As Emma turned to go with Harriett, a door creaked from the direction of the stairway behind her. Finally, the sheriff had arrived, and just in time. She held her breath, but Harriett had heard the noise as well.

Harriett grabbed her around the neck from behind and spun her toward the office door, placing the pistol barrel against her temple. "Show yourself, or I'll kill them all." Seconds stretched into endless minutes with no response. "Last warning. Come in now!"

Out of the corner of her eye, Emma saw Donovan struggling with her restraints. Would she risk her life to save Emma or Clem? She seriously doubted it. She was on her own.

"I'm going to count to three, and then somebody dies. One..." Harriett backed them farther away from the door. "Two..."

The door slowly opened, and Carter stood in the doorway, her gun trained on Harriett. "Drop the weapon and move away from Emma."

Instead, Harriett shoved the gun barrel harder against Emma's temple. "Drop yours."

Emma's knees shook as the expression on Carter's face registered. She was afraid, but not for herself. Carter's eyes found hers and in that moment relayed things she'd been unable to say before. Emma decided then she couldn't die yet.

Carter held firm, and Emma struggled to find a way to help her, to distract Harriett. But Harriet's muscular arm squeezed her neck so tight, Emma could hardly breathe. She tried to move, but the cold barrel at her temple deterred her.

"I think you better drop that gun, Ranger, unless you want me to kill your friend right here in front of you. Put it down, and get over there with the others." Harriett barked the words and jerked Emma's neck farther back.

Emma gasped and stretched on her tiptoes to relieve the pressure.

"Okay, okay. Just don't hurt her." Carter placed her weapon on the table, her eyes begging Emma to forgive her.

When Carter reached the other two captives, Donovan grabbed her with her free hand and pulled her closer. "I knew you'd come."

"That's disgusting." Harriett spun Emma around toward Donovan and Carter. "How do you like your ranger lover now? It took the two of you four days before you were all over each other. She followed the agent to her hotel bed in a matter of hours."

Emma tried to turn and confront Harriett but was firmly restrained. "How could you possibly know that? Unless you've been stalking me."

"At last the light dawns. The first day you came to the library I knew you were going to be trouble. So, I kept you under surveillance. I saw you two groping and sweating all over each other. You proved whoring isn't exclusive to the male of the species." Harriett's body stiffened and grew warmer as she talked.

This could be Emma's only chance. Her insides shook, but she took a deep breath. "You'd know about whoring, wouldn't you, Harriett? You were sleeping with the biggest womanizer in town and didn't even know it."

"Shut up, you perverted slut!" Harriett squeezed her arm tighter around Emma's neck, and her vision blurred.

"You thought you were special." Emma struggled to speak above a whisper.

"I said shut up, or I'll snap your neck with my bare hands."

"He obviously didn't think you were as good as his lesbian wife, because he wouldn't leave her for you." Emma's attempt to laugh came out as a squeak.

"I'm going to choke the life out of you. Lying bitch!" Harriett loosened her grip slightly and lowered the gun barrel as she repositioned herself.

Emma took another gasping breath and jammed her right elbow backward into Harriett's chest. An explosion ripped through the small room as the gun hit the floor. Somebody howled in pain, and she prayed it wasn't Carter.

Harriett stumbled back but maintained a grip on Emma's shoulder with her left hand. Emma stomped Harriett's right foot and swung her left arm up and out to break her hold. Before her captor recovered, Emma turned and shoved the heel of her hand into Harriett's nose, crunching it into her face.

"Bitch." Harriett screamed and grabbed her nose as blood oozed between her fingers. "You broke my nose." She fell against the wall and slid to the floor.

When Emma stepped back, Carter was standing beside her with her gun pointed at Harriett. Carter pulled out her handcuffs, and together they restrained Harriett and set her at the table.

"Remind me not to get on your bad side." Carter was teasing her. "Are you okay?"

"I think I'm fine." She rubbed her neck and took a deep breath. "What are you doing here? Not that I'm unhappy to see you."

"Sheriff Echols, but we can talk about that later. Where did you learn those moves?"

"Writing a story on self-defense. I never thought they'd come in handy." The adrenaline dissipated, and Emma grabbed the table for support. She was safe. Carter was safe. She wanted to rush into Carter's arms, but her legs wouldn't move.

"Hell—o." Donovan waved from under the table. "Would somebody mind uncuffing us? And if anyone cares, I've been hit."

Emma and Carter walked over to the pair under the table. Clem was staring at his cuff-mate with disdain, while she pointed to her butt. Planted in the center of her left cheek was a tiny hole in the tailored ninja suit surrounded by a small amount of blood.

Emma snickered. "Yep. It's a perfect bull's-eye."

Clem offered his arm so Carter could unlock the cuffs. "She couldn't have been hit anywhere else. When the fighting started, she dove under the table so fast she almost ripped my shoulder out of the socket."

"I was protecting the life of an innocent civilian and a prime witness." Donovan's voice regained some of its arrogance as she slid from beneath the table. "Somebody call an ambulance. I've been injured in the line of duty."

Emma retrieved her phone from under the table and clicked off the recorder. As she started to dial 911, the door lights and alarms sounded.

Sheriff Echols led a group of deputies and EMTs up the stairs and into the room. "Is everybody all right?"

"Everybody is certainly *not* all right," Donovan said, pointing to her backside.

"You okay, Emma?"

"I'm good. What took you so long, Sheriff? You missed all the fun."

He motioned for his deputies to take Harriett away. "I see that. Sorry. I got sidetracked. I'll fill you in tomorrow when everybody comes to the station for statements. Nine o'clock?"

Emma nodded. "I've got Clem's statement and Harriett's admissions on my phone."

"Got to love technology." Echols shook Carter's hand on the way out. "Thanks for getting here so quickly. My guys will finish up. Why don't the rest of you head home?"

When the room cleared, Donovan hobbled over to Carter, ignoring Emma completely. She hooked her arm through Carter's and said, "I told the EMT guys you'd take me to the hospital? Is that okay, hon?"

Carter looked down and shook her head in disbelief. "No, as a matter of fact it's not okay. And just for the record, I'm not now, nor have I ever been, your hon. After what you did to Ann and the way you played me, we don't have anything else to talk about. Better hurry or you'll miss your ride with the EMTs."

Donovan's eyes grew wide. "Carter, I didn—"

"Don't bother denying it. I heard everything."

Emma glanced up at Carter. "That was you I heard behind the boxes earlier?"

"Yep. Sorry for the delay. I got a call from the sheriff. Guess Harriett slipped by me in this maze of a place."

Donovan squinted and her mouth hardened into a thin line. "Fine, go with your little storyteller. You'll never have sex like we had."

"I certainly hope not." Carter took Emma's hand and led her from the warehouse. When she opened the outside door, she pulled

Emma close. "When you left the cabin earlier, I wasn't sure you'd ever speak to me again."

"I told you I loved you, but you said you'd spent the night with Donovan. And that you *liked* me."

"I said everything wrong, Emma, but the words wouldn't come. I almost lost you in there. Can we try again?"

Emma stroked the side of Carter's face, her brown eyes so sorrowful and pleading. "I'd like that very much, but after this case is finished. You and Ann need to be at the sheriff's office in the morning. She deserves to hear the whole story too."

"I thought I'd never get to tell you that I lo—"

"Shhh." Emma placed her fingers over Carter's lips. She wanted to hear those words more than she wanted to breathe, but not like this. "Be careful what you say. I won't be your consolation prize." Emma wanted to believe they had a future, but her heart still ached. Carter had spent the night with Donovan, and Emma didn't understand why. "I'll see you tomorrow."

Emma turned toward her car, but Carter caught her arm and pulled her back. "You could never be a consolation prize." Carter traced Emma's lips with the tip of her tongue. "I need you."

Emma's breath hitched, her body instantly afire. She opened for Carter to explore her lips, her mouth, and her soul. She moaned and pressed harder against Carter, pleading for more. Carter kissed and held her until every inch of Emma's body was fully aroused, and then she pulled away.

Carter stared into her eyes, gasping for breath. "Please don't give up on me, on us."

She reluctantly released Carter and stepped back. "Give me a reason not to."

"I will. The last thing I want to do is let you go home alone," Carter admitted.

"I need to think, but I'll see you in the morning." When she walked away from Carter, she immediately missed her. She wanted to hold Carter and never let go, but what did Carter want? Was she ready for a commitment?

As Emma settled into bed, her near-fatal encounter with a killer finally sank in. When she considered what could've happened, her whole body shook. But even in the face of seemingly insurmountable obstacles and danger, she'd risen to the challenges. She'd finally help Fannie Buffkin find closure, clear Ann, bring a killer to justice, and write a story any investigative journalist would be proud to claim.

Most important, she'd trusted her instincts and taken a chance on love. Her last memory before falling asleep was Carter's smiling face.

I love you, but what happens now?

Chapter Twenty-one

The next morning, Emma sat in front of the sheriff's office at exactly nine o'clock. She was anxious and jittery, about the case and seeing Carter. What happened today would determine the direction of her life both professionally and personally. Was she ready?

She scanned the crowded parking lot for Carter's Jeep, didn't see it, and went inside. The small office was packed with deputies and townspeople, shoulder to shoulder. Everybody was talking about the case and straining for a glimpse of Harriett Smoltz behind bars. When Emma closed the door behind her, the focus of interest shifted, and everyone surged toward her with a barrage of questions.

"How did you find Clem Stevens?"

"When did you figure out the killer was really Harriett Smoltz?"

"How did you overpower her when she had a gun?"

"Where is Agent Donovan? Why isn't she here?"

As Emma glanced from one questioner to the next, Sheriff Echols reached through the crowd and pulled her aside. He waved his hands and yelled, "Everybody out. This is official police business, not a sideshow. Everything will come out soon enough. Move along."

A couple of deputies escorted folks outside and stood guard in front of the door. The room became suddenly very quiet.

"Are you okay today?" Sheriff Echols placed a hand on her shoulder and guided her to a chair. "The shock of a deadly situation hits you after the fact, not when you're forced to take action. I guess you figured that out last night when you got home."

Emma nodded and accepted the cup of coffee he offered. "I have to admit I was beyond scared." But the danger was past and now she needed answers. "Have you interviewed Harriett yet?" Only one of the questions she wanted to ask, but she'd start there.

"I talked to her last night and confronted her with the recording you made. She admitted everything, filled in all the blanks."

Before Emma could ask any more questions, Ann and Carter walked in. Ann wore a pair of blue jeans, white shirt, and blue-jean jacket with pink trim and pink cowboy hat and boots, festive for the occasion, Emma surmised.

Emma rushed over and was sandwiched between them in a group hug.

"I knew you'd do it, Emma. I had faith." Ann kissed her on both cheeks. "Carter told me all about it last night. We didn't sleep a wink. Girl, you're a pistol. You showed that BCI agent a thing or two." She looked around the office. "Where is the Charlie's Devil anyway?"

"She left town early this morning. Didn't even thank us for our help," Echols said. "But I made a call to her supervisor about some of her questionable tactics. She'll have some explaining to do back in Richmond." He set an industrial-sized coffee pot on a side table, took a seat, and motioned for the others to join him in chairs he'd placed around his desk. "I was about to fill Emma in on the details."

Carter filled Styrofoam cups with coffee for her and Ann before joining them. "What happened to you last night, Sheriff?"

"I rerouted to the Gentle Breeze Nursing Home on an emergency call—a reported kidnapping. That's what I was just getting ready to tell Emma."

"How did Carter know where we were?" Emma had wondered all night how Carter got involved in the warehouse incident.

"I called and asked her to swing by and listen to Clem's statement. My deputies were away on a training course, and she's the only other sworn officer close by. I had no idea I was sending her into a firefight." The sheriff shook his head. "Sorry, Carter."

"And what does a kidnapping have to do with this case?" Ann wanted to know.

"You won't believe it when I tell you," Echols said.

"Then get on with it, man." Ann rolled her hand at him. "Daylight's burning."

"The reporting party at the nursing home was Hannah Smoltz. She told me she'd been drugged and involuntarily committed to keep her quiet."

"That's a scenario I hadn't considered," Emma said.

"She knows the whole story about the Thompson murder," the sheriff said.

"How did she find out? Did Harriett admit it, or was she in on it?" Carter scooted her chair closer to the desk.

"She put it together after the fact. The night of the murder, Harriett was the switchboard operator and connected the call from Cass to Ann arranging their meeting at the factory. Harriett left work early and went there as well. She planned to confront Cass, tell her about the affair with Thompson and force her to give him a divorce, but she was too late. Cass and Ann had gone.

"The rest of the story happened just like Clem said. After Harriett killed Thompson, she went back to the phone company, but Hannah had already arrived for her shift. Harriett told Hannah she'd gotten sick and walked to the drugstore for medicine. She asked Hannah to lie for her so she wouldn't lose her job for leaving the phone lines uncovered for thirty minutes."

"That accounts for Mr. Livengood not being able to get through to the funeral home," Emma said. Timothy Black's statement made perfect sense now.

"And I couldn't get through to the ambulance on the pay phone. They might've been able to save the baby." Ann's eyes flashed with rekindled grief. "My Cass could've died too."

Sheriff Echols nodded.

Emma's cell phone rang, disrupting the flow of the story. She glanced at the unidentified number, pushed the mute button, and added, "That also means Sylvie Martinez really did see Harriett going toward the factory. It wasn't Hannah going to work at all."

"Right again." Sheriff Echols refilled everyone's coffee cups. "Hannah suspected Harriett was involved in the murder and confronted her. When Harriett admitted it, she blackmailed Hannah and told her if she came forward, Harriett would swear she was an accomplice. Hannah went into a depression, and Harriett seized the opportunity to have her committed for three months. After that episode, Hannah was pretty much doomed to do whatever Harriett said. She was counting on no one believing the ramblings of a mental patient."

"So, Hannah hasn't been on vacation," Emma stated.

"Nope. When you came to town and started digging up this story again, Hannah begged Harriett to come forward. Harriett drugged her instead and eventually had her confined to the nursing home. Harriett went by every morning and evening and gave Hannah drugs to make her appear psychotic. We're having her blood tested to determine what Harriett used."

Carter shook her head. "How did Hannah become lucid enough to figure this out?"

"The nursing-home staff was getting suspicious. Hannah seemed more coherent first thing in the morning and late in the day, always before her sister visited. They felt confident none of their staff was involved, and Harriett was the only other person who had contact with Hannah. They posted a nurse in the room with her when Harriett came to visit so she couldn't administer the drugs. On the second day, Hannah woke up, ready to tell her story."

Ann tossed her empty cup in the trash. "I knew something was off with Harriett Smoltz. She was always too nosy for my liking."

Emma's cell phone rang again and she answered. "Yes, I'm Emma Ferguson." She waited for the caller to state their business. "I'd like to talk to you about it, but I'll have to call you back. I'm in the middle of something."

Emma hung up and turned back to the sheriff. "Sorry. Did Harriett tell you who helped her with the stalking, slashed tires, the attack at the cabin, and running me off the road?"

"She took full responsibility for everything. She's also the one who told Agent Donovan about Ann and Cass's relationship. She's been watching Emma since she came to town, staying close to keep tabs on her investigation. She slashed your tires and went after you with a tree limb. I have to tell you, that one surprised me."

"Yeah. I thought the attacker was a man." Carter shook her head. "I was even watching that construction guy who'd rented the cabin next to Emma."

"You were?"

Carter placed her hand on Emma's shoulder and gave it a light squeeze. "I wasn't about to let anything happen to you...whether we were...talking or not."

"Thank you." Emma turned back to the sheriff. "The woman I fought last night definitely could've been the person who attacked me, but she didn't seem like the same Harriett Smoltz I'd been talking to at the library."

"Harriett admitted she attacked you at the cabin. She's been working out in her basement for the past five years, twice a day. Nobody could tell because she wore those awful sack dresses. She knew this day would come."

"What about running Emma off the road?" Ann asked. "That wasn't Harriett's pink Cadillac."

"She used Hannah's old heap that's usually in Harriett's garage. I've got a search warrant for her property. We might find some trace evidence from Emma's car."

The cell phone in Emma's bag rang again, and she muted it without looking. "Where were we? Oh yeah, I have one more question, Sheriff. Was the gun she had last night the same one she used to kill Thompson? Not that we could ever prove it."

"She said it's the same weapon, an old Ruger .22 semi-automatic blue-steel her grandfather gave her years ago. But you're right. We'll never be able to prove that's the murder weapon because neither a shell casing nor a slug was ever recovered." The sheriff closed the file on his desk. "I think that wraps it up. I can't think of anything else to tell you, except thanks for your help, Emma and Carter. And my apologies to you, Ann." He stood and offered his hand.

Emma started to thank him when her cell phone rang again. "Sorry, better get this."

Carter and Ann said their good-byes to the sheriff and started toward the door.

"I can come by right now if that's okay with you." Emma closed the phone and shook hands with Sheriff Echols. "I really appreciate all you've done. You'll get an honorable mention in my story."

"That's not necessary. All in a day's work for a small-town sheriff."

When Emma joined Ann and Carter outside, Ann grabbed her arms and spun her around on the sidewalk. "Let's go to the cabin and celebrate. My treat. Girl, this is big. I'm not even sure I've got enough liquor to do it justice."

"There's nothing I'd rather do, but I have a stop to make before the celebration begins. Can I catch up with you later?"

"Sure you can," Carter said. "Is that what all the phone calls were about?"

"Sort of, but not exactly. I'll explain when I see you. And don't forget we have a conversation to finish."

The comment brought a big smile to Carter's face. "Oh, I won't forget."

Emma made the short trip across Main Street to the property overlooking downtown with a lightness of step she hadn't experienced in years. She'd persevered on a case that at times had seemed hopeless. Her father would've been proud, and she was about to make an elderly woman both happy and sad with the news.

Emma raised her hand toward the brass knocker, but the door opened and Fannie Buffkin enveloped her in a hug.

"Come in, Emma. I've been waiting for this day for thirty-seven years." Fannie led her toward the sitting room.

The home and its occupant had obviously received a bit of attention. Emma inhaled the sweet fragrance of fresh-cut flowers instead of mothballs. The old wing chair and sofa covers had been cleaned, and the window curtains stood open to allow light to fill the rooms.

Fannie Buffkin's bun-coiffed hair shone as if it had been freshly washed and brushed. Lightweight rimless glasses replaced the old Coke-bottle variety she'd previously worn. She was dressed in a yellow-flowered frock, not an evening gown, fur wrap, and gloves.

Emma's surprise must've been evident because Fannie laughed out loud. "I've spruced up a bit."

"Very becoming."

"When you left last time, I had a premonition you'd get to the bottom of my brother's disappearance, and it gave me hope. Neither my husband nor my brother would've wanted me to stop living because they're gone. I even started going out to bingo occasionally."

A spark had returned to Fannie's eyes, and Emma smiled, grateful to have helped.

"But that's not why you're here, is it?"

"I wanted to tell you about the case."

Fannie held up her hand. "I've heard about Harriett and why she killed Theodore. Dreadful what jealousy does to people."

"I'm sorry you found out through the grapevine. I should've been the one to tell you."

"Don't worry about it, Emma. You can't keep salacious news quiet in a town this size. Three people called me before Sheriff Echols locked the cell door behind Harriett."

"Are you all right? It must've been a shock."

"I've suspected for years that he was dead, and now that you've solved the mystery, I can rest easy. Thank you for keeping your promise. You were at considerable risk at times. Now I know why Harriett Smoltz has been so nice to me all these years. And I finally know what kind of man my brother really was. As I told you before, he wasn't always respectful to me, but I thought it ended there. Another hard truth to swallow. But you got to the bottom of it because you're a very talented reporter, Emma Ferguson, and I want to do something to show my appreciation."

"That's not necessary, Fannie. I'm just happy I could help."

"You should be proud of your work. I'm sure your father would be. I hope you don't mind, but I took the liberty of calling a few newspapers and magazines and giving them a teaser about your story. You'll probably be getting a call or two."

"So, I have you to thank for blowing up my phone this morning?"

"I thought it couldn't hurt." Fannie winked from behind her new glasses.

"You have no idea, Fannie. It's probably the best thing that's happened to my career in years. I don't know how to repay you."

"You already have…but maybe one more thing."

"Yes?"

"I'd like you to write a series of stories about this whole sordid affair. Would you?"

The request was unexpected, especially now. "You *want* me to write the truth about your brother's life and how he died?"

Fannie nodded.

"You realize I'll tell the *whole* story, not just the parts that make him look good."

"There are no parts that make him look good. I owe it to those he mistreated, myself included, to acknowledge the kind of man he really was. If anything, history should be as accurate as possible. We've got a lot of correcting to do."

Emma took Fannie's hands. "Then I'd be honored to tell the story."

"Let's have coffee and chat. You can shake my family tree and see what else falls out. Then we'll talk money."

Emma pulled the notepad out of her bag and clicked her pen. "Deal."

❖

The cool autumn air nipped at Emma's cheeks with a hint of coming winter as she strode down Main Street toward her car. She checked her voice mail and saved the numerous calls from publications offering her up-front money for her story. She'd have time to call them back tomorrow. Her priority now was getting to the park, to Carter. She hadn't realized how much time she'd spent with Fannie sipping coffee and gathering background.

Her thoughts turned to her conversation with Carter. What did she need or want to say? She'd already said the three most important words—I love you. Everything else was filler. Maybe it was time to just listen, with her heart.

When she pulled up to the office, the closed sign was already out. She felt a knot of disappointment in the pit of her stomach. Why hadn't she called to let them know she was on her way? She pulled down to her cabin and dialed Carter's cell. Gripping the steering wheel with one hand, she listened to Carter's cell phone ring, willing her to answer. She couldn't spend another night without knowing where they stood.

"Hello?" Carter's professional voice answered.

"Carter, it's Emma. I'm sorry I'm so late. Have I missed the celebration?"

"You should go home, Emma. Ann sends her best and her thanks."

The knots in Emma's stomach migrated upward and constricted her airway. She swallowed repeatedly and tried to speak while holding back tears. She'd been certain Carter would wait for her, no matter how late. She couldn't possibly have imagined the chemistry between them at the warehouse, the fire in Carter's eyes this morning, or her own feelings.

"Emma…are you there?"

"Yeah. Okay. I'll see you."

Chapter Twenty-two

Emma's heart was breaking, and she couldn't see through her tears to get the key in the cabin door. When the lock finally clicked, she stumbled through the entry and almost landed on the floor, but strong arms caught her.

"Welcome home." Carter brought her upright against her. "Are you surprised?"

Emma wiped her eyes with the back of her hand. "Uh-huh."

A fire shimmered and crackled in the fireplace, and candles cast a romantic glow throughout the small space. Two champagne flutes and a chilling bottle rested on the coffee table. And Carter's eyes were almost as hot as the heat radiating from the fire.

"Emma? Was this a bad idea? I shouldn't have teased you, but I wanted to surprise you. Forgive me?"

The tears Emma tried so hard to control broke free again and slid down her cheeks. She grabbed Carter and pulled her close. "This was an excellent idea. I couldn't be happier."

Carter breathed a huge sigh. "Good. Ann helped but wouldn't wait around. She said we needed time alone." She poured the champagne and handed Emma a glass. "I'd like to make a toast to great reporters with integrity and humanity, like you, Emma Ferguson, and to all the wonderful stories you have yet to tell." They clinked glasses.

Emma sipped the bubbly liquid, and it exploded into fizzing foam in her mouth and tickled all the way down. She attributed the immediate euphoria to a big dose of Carter West and her amazing surprise. *She really does care.* For a moment, neither spoke as their eyes connected with a soul-piercing stare only lovers know.

Carter placed their glasses on the coffee table, took Emma's hand, and led her to the sofa.

"Are you sure you're okay?"

"Absolutely. You?"

"Really nervous, because I have things to say, but I'm good with it."

"Take your time. We have plenty." Emma stroked the side of Carter's face and watched her eyes darken with desire.

"You'll need to hold off on that for a few minutes, or I won't be able to concentrate."

Emma took Carter's hand where it rested on her lap and laced their fingers together. "Better?"

"Much." Carter straightened and pulled a huge breath from down deep. "Here goes. Since what happened at the factory all those years ago, I've had trouble expressing my feelings. But I've never wanted anything to be as perfect as what I'm about to say. Every time I've rehearsed this, I never make it to the end without breaking down. Please don't let go of my hand."

"I've got you, Carter."

"I've made a lot of mistakes with you, the first being treating you like all the other women I've known. I'm not sure how to make it right, but I want to. I'm so sorry."

"You've made a great start. Keep talking." A light film of perspiration covered Carter's forehead as she fingered her necklace. Emma wanted to rescue her, to tell her the words weren't necessary, but Emma needed to know certain things, and she sensed Carter needed to say them.

"I was wrong about you, and I should've been more trusting. You opened up the first time we slept together, sexually and emotionally." Carter swallowed hard. "That took a lot of courage and, frankly, scared me a little, but you touched my heart. You took a big leap of faith. I'm not sure what I did to deserve you, but I'm thankful you took that chance.

"Then you risked your job and your life to clear Ann, which took another kind of courage. I'm sorry for not trusting you, and I'm grateful for everything you've done for me and Ann."

"You're welcome." When Carter took a gulp of champagne and licked her lips, Emma almost came apart. She looked so vulnerable and afraid, but Emma had to be patient. "You're doing great."

"Since the day you got here you've been doing your job. I, on the other hand, tried to stonewall you at every turn."

"You thought I was a threat to Ann." Carter's eyes held a softness Emma had never seen, and she adored the protectiveness Carter felt for her aunt. It was one of the many things she loved about this woman.

"I should've been trying to help you clear Ann instead of throwing up roadblocks, but I was feeling things for you I didn't understand. I was too busy protecting myself to be myself. So, when Billie told me about you and Sheri…"

"What about me and Sheri?" Donovan didn't know anything about them. She'd only seen them together once—the pieces fell into place.

"The night I saw you kissing her, Billie told me Sheri was your girlfriend and the two of you were getting back together. That hurt so much I could barely breathe."

"She told you *what*?" Emma felt her face flush as she tried to contain her anger. "But I'd already told you it was over and that I didn't love Sheri."

"I know, but seeing the two of you kissing sent me over the edge. I played right into Billie's hands. I'm not making excuses, just trying to explain."

"Just so we're clear, Sheri is my *ex*-girlfriend, and we definitely are *not* getting back together. That kiss was her last desperate effort to change my mind. And Donovan knew damn well what was going on."

"She lied."

Emma nodded. "Duh."

Carter's face registered only mild surprise. "But why?"

"She did it for you."

"For *me*. How do you figure?" Carter's face paled as the truth finally dawned. "You mean…"

"Yes, darling, to *have* you. I was an obstacle, and she needed to get me out of the picture. She applied the same twisted logic to get rid of Ann, as you heard her admit at the warehouse. It was all about having you to herself. She'd become obsessed with you." Emma stared into the fire, unsure she wanted to ask the next question, certain she had to.

"What is it, Emma? Don't hold back now."

"Did you have sex with her that night?"

Carter looked at the floor and her shoulders dropped. "Billie promised to tell me how she got the information on Ann. I wanted to know for sure if you'd lied to us. That's why I went with her. And…" She couldn't meet Emma's eyes.

"And what, darling? Tell me." Emma's heart was pounding.

"And part of me wanted to have sex with her—at first, but I changed my mind."

Emma couldn't afford to guess about something so important. "Why? I'm dying here."

"Because of how I feel about you. I could never be satisfied with just sex again, not after what we shared."

Emma finally exhaled the tension locked in her body as she watched Carter twist her necklace. She hadn't had sex with Donovan. Emma felt vindicated and extremely happy. But Carter obviously had more to say. She looked tense and was fidgeting. Carter's gaze returned to Emma, and its intensity made her body burn.

"There's one more thing." Carter scooted nearer on the sofa and brought her face so close that Emma could feel the heat of her breath. "The thing is…I've become…I mean…I'm in love with you, Emma Ferguson. I think I have been since the moment we met." She searched Emma's face and swallowed hard. "I've never said that to another woman."

Emma had waited to hear Carter say those words, knew they'd come, and even imagined how she'd feel hearing them for the first time, but she failed to anticipate their impact. She was speechless. Her pulse pounded in her ears. Her mouth was dry, and the light musk of Carter's perfume made her dizzy. Carter's breath across her face made her shiver and ache to be touched.

"Emma, say something, please. You're killing me."

"I…I'm so happy. I love you so much." She hugged Carter and felt the hot press of their bodies. "Thank you. I love you. I love you so much," she whispered over and over.

Carter made a strangled noise, and Emma pulled back, then kissed the tears from Carter's face. "What's wrong, darling? You're okay. I've got you."

"I'll never get tired of listening to you say you love me. I've heard the words before but never trusted they were intended for me, never trusted they were real. But now, deep down where the truth registers, I know they are. These are tears of joy."

Carter ran her fingers through Emma's hair, brought a handful to her nose, and inhaled deeply. "You smell so delicious."

Emma's mouth watered as she watched Carter's lips, wet and open, move gradually toward her own. Her body tingled. Unable to bear the slow torture, she entwined her fingers in Carter's curly brown hair and pulled her in.

Carter's tongue teased across Emma's lips like a soft breeze, stirring up thirst. An involuntary moan sounded deep in her throat but was muffled as Carter's mouth found hers again and again.

"I love you so much." Carter pulled Emma tighter and moved against her. "I've waited all my life for you."

Pleasure-pain shot from Emma's breasts through her body in one swift electric charge. Her nipples hardened and throbbed with the tenderness of wanting. "And I've waited all my life to feel like this. I never knew how powerful sex could be with someone you love. Take me, Carter."

Carter rose from the sofa and led Emma through the candlelit path to the bedroom. Their shadows flickered and danced along the walls as they moved, leaving a trail of clothing behind. When they reached the bed, Emma appreciated the full beauty of Carter's nude body.

"You are so gorgeous."

Emma stared at Carter's tanned skin, feasted her eyes on the slight swell of her breasts and their deep mocha centers. She followed Carter's waist to the curve of her hips and down her long muscular legs. Emma stepped closer and lightly brushed her fingers through the neatly trimmed tuft of hair between Carter's legs. "Mine."

Carter cried out and grabbed Emma's hand to stop her. "If you do that again, I'll—"

"You'll what?"

"I'll come in your hand like a teenaged-boy on his first date. And that would not be okay. She guided Emma down onto the bed and joined her. "I want this night to last a very long time."

Emma remembered the texture of Carter's hands before they touched her—the softness of her fingertips that produced ripples of pleasure and the small callused pads near her palm that reached into Emma's depths. "Touch me."

Carter's long, skillful fingers danced up and down Emma's body, barely contacting the surface, but her skin tingled uncontrollably. Carter's actions, like her words, were slow and methodical with nothing wasted. She flicked Emma's nipples with her tongue, using the lightest pressure, and heat rose between her legs. Carter sucked a nipple just into her mouth and teased it with her teeth.

"You are so good at that, but I need to feel you, everywhere."

Emma shivered and pulled Carter down on top of her. She craved full-body contact, but even their skin would be too much of a barrier. As they merged, Emma felt her softer, fuller figure accommodate Carter's firmer body, and she moaned with the perfection of their joining. They rolled against each other, heat and moisture increasing with every movement.

Carter moved with long, deliberate strokes while she kissed and tormented Emma's breasts and neck.

"Oh, yes," Emma cried as she clawed Carter's back. She arched and thrust her pelvis upward but met air. "Please don't stop. I love feeling you against me." She grabbed Carter's butt and tried to reconnect, but Carter grinned and held back.

"You'll like what I do next too. Relax." Carter was already too aroused to last long, but she needed to be touching Emma intimately when she came. She pressed Emma's legs farther apart, lowered herself on her thigh, and rubbed her stiff clit while she massaged Emma's with her fingers.

"Oh, Carter."

"You are so unbelievably sexy. I've never been this turned on." The truth of her statement made Carter's clit twitch with anticipation. She slid along Emma's knee to her thigh before she felt a mini-spasm of warning. Carter raised her butt in the air to break contact and moaned like a wounded animal. She didn't recognize the sound as any she'd ever made before.

"You don't have to stop, Carter." Emma breathed into her neck.

"I do." She clutched between her legs and pinched her clit to stave off the pending orgasm. She wanted to take Emma with her when she came, and she hadn't had nearly enough of her yet.

Emma captured Carter's hand and guided it to her center. "I want your fingers inside me." She opened her thighs wider. "Please, Carter."

Emma's direct expression of her need seared through Carter, and a trickle of arousal slid down the inside of her leg. She rose on all fours and kissed Emma so deeply when they parted, they both gasped for air. Then she lowered herself between Emma's legs, rubbed her pubic mound against the cool sheets, and scooted her shoulders under Emma's thighs.

"Would it be cruel if I just looked at you for a while. You are so beautiful, and I've waited so long to be here. I don't want to rush."

"Carter…"

"Just for a second then." Carter loved Emma's vulnerability, how open she was to anything Carter wanted and how needy of her touch. She enjoyed watching Emma squirm, knowing she'd caused her discomfort and only she could ease it. She breathed deeply and inhaled the mixture her musky fragrance mingled with Emma's lighter, flowery scent.

Emma writhed under her. "Carter, please touch me. This is torture."

But Carter could tell it was torture Emma craved. Her pleading face smiled down at her. Carter's soul already held the imprint of this woman's love. Now she wanted her body to be branded as well.

While maintaining eye contact with Emma, Carter stuck her index finger into her mouth, wrapped her lips around it, and slowly withdrew it, making sure it was wet. "Are you ready?" she asked, teasing, and Emma raised her hips.

"So very ready."

Carter captured Emma's taut clit between her fingers. The pulsing flesh and Emma's deep-throated moan almost made Carter come. "Do you like this, baby?"

"Uh-huh." Emma breathed and matched Carter's rhythm.

Carter felt her own control slipping and caught her lip between her teeth. She slid her fingers down Emma's pulsating shaft and stroked the base with the rhythm of lovemaking. She was ready to see Emma come undone under her.

"I need to come, Carter. A little harder…right *there*!"

Carter manipulated Emma's body like they'd been lovers for years. And for the first time, she wasn't afraid to show her own physical and emotional needs. Her body and soul hungered for love, and Emma knew how to feed her.

"That's so good…now go inside me. I'm ready." Emma guided Carter's hand.

Emma's instructions excited Carter as much as the responses they produced. Her nipples brushed the covers, and she grew wetter. She couldn't allow even the slightest contact with the wet sheet beneath her, not yet. She looked up into Emma's blue eyes, hooded with need, and brought her own fingers again to her mouth. "You taste so good."

Emma buried her fingers in Carter's hair and forced her head down.

When Carter brushed the outside of Emma's opening, she lunged forward. Carter sucked Emma's clit and simultaneously slid two fingers inside of her. Emma tightened around her immediately. Carter established a rhythm, and Emma clung to her, begging for more. Carter wanted to crawl inside and fill Emma physically the way Emma had filled her emotionally. She pumped harder, and Emma met her stroke for stroke. Emma's legs stiffened over Carter's shoulders. She was so close.

"Another finger." Emma panted. "Fill me."

Carter purposely withdrew completely before complying.

"No!" Emma pressed her legs tighter around Carter's shoulders to hold her in place.

When Carter entered her again, she wasn't so gentle, but Emma met her insistent strokes, her ass never touching the bed.

"Faster…that's so good."

Carter's rhythm increased, and her tongue matched the tempo on Emma's clit. "Ohhhhh, yes, Carter."

Carter watched as Emma's climax built. Her skin flushed and her body stiffened. She sat almost completely up, trembling, then collapsed. She gasped for air and clenched her fists in Carter's hair, released and then clutched the sheets convulsively. "Come for me now, Emma."

"Deeper, darling, deeper," Emma begged. "I'm coming." She squeezed and pinched her nipples, and Carter felt her release. Emma grabbed a pillow, and a raspy moan tore from deep in her throat. "Aaahhhh…oh, my God, Carter! So good!"

Carter breathed in sporadic pants as she fingered and sucked every ripple of orgasm from Emma. She withdrew her fingers, wrapped her arms around Emma's thighs, and buried her face deeper, tonguing every ounce of arousal from her. When Emma slowed beneath her, Carter wasn't ready to stop. Her body was close to exploding. She wanted to hold Emma, to feel her body cool in her arms, but she needed release. Her body jerked involuntarily.

"Come here, Carter." Emma urged Carter up beside her. "Tell me what you want."

"I can wait until you're—"

"I don't want to wait one more second to satisfy you." Emma slid her hand down Carter's torso and nestled her fingers between Carter's legs. "Is this okay, or do you need my mouth?"

"That's…good." Carter's breath hitched. One touch of Emma's hand and she was about to pop. She didn't want to come so quickly, but she ached from holding back.

Emma scissored Carter's clit between her fingers and stroked. "Do you want me inside?"

"Ahhhh…no. Just like that. Won't take lo—"

Emma's last pull was long and firm, and Carter buried her face in Emma's shoulder. The first prickles of orgasm started low, and her legs went numb. When all sensation exploded under Emma's touch, Carter clung to her. "*Please* don't stop. Ooohhh, yes!" Tears streamed down her face as she came again and again. Emma rolled them over and covered Carter with her body until she stopped shaking.

When Carter opened her eyes, Emma was staring down at her, her forehead crinkled. "What's wrong, Emma? You look like you're about to cry." She tucked a strand of Emma's hair behind her ear.

"Was that all right? I've never been very good at this whole sex thing." She looked everywhere but into Carter's eyes.

"I love you, Emma Ferguson, and I've never been as satisfied as quickly by anyone in my life. You're absolutely perfect for me, in every way."

"Are you sure? I couldn't bear it if I found out later that—?"

"Whoever told you that crap was obviously not the right person for you." Carter kissed Emma and snuggled her head against her shoulder.

"Finally." Emma laughed. "I'm finally perfect at something. I love you. I've never made love to anyone like that before. I felt completely free to do and be whatever I wanted."

"Like trusting it's all right to just be yourself?"

"Exactly. And what about you, Ranger West?"

"I've learned one very important thing being with you, Emma." Carter kissed her again and pulled a sheet over their cooling bodies. "How love feels. That's been missing from my past relationships."

"I always thought my relationships didn't last because I wasn't perfect enough, didn't work hard enough, or stay long enough."

Carter stroked Emma's hair and hugged her closer. "And I realize I've never committed to anyone because I was afraid I'd never feel what I feel for you. I'm so glad I was wrong."

"What does that mean exactly?" Emma rose on an elbow and stared at Carter.

"It means, my adorable lover, I'm ready to give long-term a try."

"Really?"

The surprise in Emma's eyes was almost humorous. "Yes, but it seems the woman I love is leaving soon."

"Who said anything about leaving?"

"I thought since the story was finished, you'd be going home." Carter's heart ached as she said the words. She wanted Emma's home to be here with her and Ann. Maybe she was expecting too much too soon. Just because she was ready to make a commitment didn't mean Emma was.

"Well, I don't really have a home anymore. I left the apartment with Sheri, and my work has come to me. I'm staying to finish the Thompson murder story and then do a few features for the Richmond paper. They've offered me a job."

"Is that what you want?"

Emma nodded.

Carter smiled, suddenly as mentally light as her body felt. "You'll need a place to stay." She kissed Emma's nose, her cheeks, and ended with what she hoped was an invitation to more lovemaking.

Emma moaned and pulled her closer. "I thought I'd rent the cabin indefinitely."

Carter flipped her over and looked down at her, trying to keep a straight face. "I'm afraid that won't work. It's rented again, starting tomorrow. However, I know a place that could put you up as long as you want. It would make Ann very happy. And I make it a point to always keep my aunt happy."

"You mean…live with you and Ann?"

"If you didn't like it, you wouldn't have to stay. I know it wouldn't be the same as having a place to yourself or even just the two of us."

Emma put her fingers over Carter's lips. "Ann is a wonderful woman, and I'd be honored to have her in my life."

"We have three bedrooms. You'd have your own private space. We wouldn't have to necessarily share a—"

"And would it make you happy, this cohabitation?" Emma leaned forward and kissed Carter lightly.

"It would make me beyond happy." Carter tried to pull Emma into another heated kiss, but she pulled back.

"Under one condition, Ranger."

Carter nibbled Emma's ear and down the side of her neck, unable to get enough of her taste and scent. "Name it. Anything."

"You have to promise to finish your doctorate and start doing what you love. I've seen you with children, and it's definitely your calling."

Carter stopped and met Emma's gaze. "The only thing that would make me happier than helping children is having you by my side while I'm doing it. I promise."

"In that case, I'd love to stay with you and Ann, for a while, until we see how *we're* going to work out…if it's okay with Ann."

"She wouldn't have it any other way. And we're going to work out beautifully." Carter pinned Emma's arms above her head and grinned. "What about my conditions?"

"I'll consider all legitimate requests, Ranger."

"You have to promise to do that thing you did to me the first time we had sex—at least once a month from now until eternity."

Emma's face lit up as she tumbled Carter over beneath her. "You mean you actually *want* me to lead?"

"If you think you can handle it, but I have to warn you. I won't come as easily this time." Carter spread her arms and legs across the bed, opening herself fully to Emma.

"Oh, I can handle it, darling. The question is, can you?"

About the Author

A thirty-year veteran of a midsized police department, VK was a police officer by necessity (it paid the bills) and a writer by desire (it didn't). Her career spanned numerous positions including beat officer, homicide detective, vice/narcotics lieutenant and assistant chief of police. Now retired, she devotes her time to writing, traveling, home decorating, and volunteer work.

VK can be contacted at vk@vkpowellauthor.com

Website: http://www.vkpowellauthor.com/

Books Available from Bold Strokes Books

18 Months by Samantha Boyette. Alissa Reeves has only had two girlfriends and they've both gone missing. Now it's up to her to find out why. (978-1-62639-804-7)

Arrested Hearts by Holly Stratimore. A reckless cop with a secret death wish and a health nut who is afraid to die might be a perfect combination for love. (978-1-62639-809-2)

Capturing Jessica by Jane Hardee. Hyperrealist sculptor Michael tries desperately to conceal the love she holds for best friend, Jess, unaware Jess's feelings for her are changing. (978-1-62639-836-8)

Counting to Zero by AJ Quinn. NSA agent Emma Thorpe and computer hacker Paxton James must learn to trust each other as they work to stop a threat clock that's rapidly counting down to zero. (978-1-62639-783-5)

Courageous Love by KC Richardson. Two women fight a devastating disease, and their own demons, while trying to fall in love. (978-1-62639-797-2)

Pathogen by Jessica L. Webb. Can Dr. Kate Morrison navigate a deadly virus and the threat of bioterrorism, as well as her new relationship with Sergeant Andy Wyles and her own troubled past? (978-1-62639-833-7)

Rainbow Gap by Lee Lynch. Jaudon Vickers and Berry Garland, polar opposites, dream and love in this tale of lesbian lives set in Central Florida against the tapestry of societal change and the Vietnam War. (978-1-62639-799-6)

Steel and Promise by Alexa Black. Lady Nivrai's cruel desires and modified body make most of the galaxy fear her, but courtesan Cailyn Derys soon discovers the real monsters are the ones without the claws. (978-1-62639-805-4)

Swelter by D. Jackson Leigh. Teal Giovanni's mistake shines an unwanted spotlight on a small Texas ranch where August Reese is secluded until she can testify against a powerful drug kingpin. (978-1-62639-795-8)

Without Justice by Carsen Taite. Cade Kelly and Emily Sinclair must battle each other in the pursuit of justice, but can they fight their undeniable attraction outside the walls of the courtroom? (978-1-62639-560-2)

21 Questions by Mason Dixon. To find love, start by asking the right questions. (978-1-62639-724-8)

A Palette for Love by Charlotte Greene. When newly minted Ph.D. Chloé Devereaux returns to New Orleans, she doesn't expect her new job, and her powerful employer—Amelia Winters—to be so appealing. (978-1-62639-758-3)

By the Dark of Her Eyes by Cameron MacElvee. When Brenna Taylor inherits a decrepit property haunted by tormented ghosts, Alejandra Santana must not only restore Brenna's house and property but also save her soul. (978-1-62639-834-4)

Cash Braddock by Ashley Bartlett. Cash Braddock just wants to hang with her cat, fall in love, and deal drugs. What's the problem with that? (978-1-62639-706-4)

Gravity by Juliann Rich. How can Ellie Engebretsen, Olympic ski jumping hopeful with her eye on the gold, soar through the air when all she feels like doing is falling hard for Kate Moreau, her greatest competitor and the girl of her dreams? (978-1-62639-483-4)

Lone Ranger by VK Powell. Reporter Emma Ferguson stirs up a thirty-year-old mystery that threatens Park Ranger Carter West's family and jeopardizes any hope for a relationship between the two women. (978-1-62639-767-5)

Love on Call by Radclyffe. Ex-Army medic Glenn Archer and recent LA transplant Mariana Mateo fight their mutual desire in the face of past losses as they work together in the Rivers Community Hospital ER. (978-1-62639-843-6)

Never Enough by Robyn Nyx. Can two women put aside their pasts to find love before it's too late? (978-1-62639-629-6)

Two Souls by Kathleen Knowles. Can love blossom in the wake of tragedy? (978-1-62639-641-8)

Camp Rewind by Meghan O'Brien. A summer camp for grown-ups becomes the site of an unlikely romance between a shy, introverted divorcee and one of the Internet's most infamous cultural critics—who attends undercover. (978-1-62639-793-4)

Cross Purposes by Gina L. Dartt. In pursuit of a lost Acadian treasure, three women must not only work out the clues, but also the complicated tangle of emotion and attraction developing between them. (978-1-62639-713-2)

Imperfect Truth by C.A. Popovich. Can an imperfect truth stand in the way of love? (978-1-62639-787-3)

Life in Death by M. Ullrich. Sometimes the devastating end is your only chance for a new beginning. (978-1-62639-773-6)

Love on Liberty by MJ Williamz. Hearts collide when politics clash. (978-1-62639-639-5)

Serious Potential by Maggie Cummings. Pro golfer Tracy Allen plans to forget her ex during a visit to Bay West, a lesbian condo community in NYC, but when she meets Dr. Jennifer Betsy, she gets more than she bargained for. (978-1-62639-633-3)

Taste by Kris Bryant. Accomplished chef Taryn has walked away from her promising career in the city's top restaurant to devote her life to her five-year-old daughter and is content until Ki Blake comes along. (978-1-62639-718-7)

The Second Wave by Jean Copeland. Can star-crossed lovers have a second chance after decades apart, or does the love of a lifetime only happen once? (978-1-62639-830-6)

Valley of Fire by Missouri Vaun. Taken captive in a desert outpost after their small aircraft is hijacked, Ava and her captivating passenger discover things about each other and themselves that will change them both forever. (978-1-62639-496-4)

Basic Training of the Heart by Jaycie Morrison. In 1944, socialite Elizabeth Carlton joins the Women's Army Corps to escape family expectations and love's disappointments. Can Sergeant Gale Rains get her through Basic Training with their hearts intact? (978-1-62639-818-4)

Before by KE Payne. When Tally falls in love with her band's new recruit, she has a tough decision to make. What does she want more—Alex or the band? (978-1-62639-677-7)

Believing in Blue by Maggie Morton. Growing up gay in a small town has been hard, but it can't compare to the next challenge Wren—with her new, sky-blue wings—faces: saving two entire worlds. (978-1-62639-691-3)

Coils by Barbara Ann Wright. A modern young woman follows her aunt into the Greek Underworld and makes a pact with Medusa to win her freedom by killing a hero of legend. (978-1-62639-598-5)

Courting the Countess by Jenny Frame. When relationship-phobic Lady Henrietta Knight starts to care about housekeeper Annie Brannigan and her daughter, can she overcome her fears and promise Annie the forever that she demands? (978-1-62639-785-9)

For Money or Love by Heather Blackmore. Jessica Spaulding must choose between ignoring the truth to keep everything she has, and doing the right thing only to lose it all—including the woman she loves. (978-1-62639-756-9)

Hooked by Jaime Maddox. With the help of sexy Detective Mac Calabrese, Dr. Jessica Benson is working hard to overcome her past, but it may not be enough to stop a murderer. (978-1-62639-689-0)

Lands End by Jackie D. Public relations superstar Amy Kline is dealing with a media nightmare, and the last thing she expects is for restaurateur Lena Michaels to change everything, but she will. (978-1-62639-739-2)

Lysistrata Cove by Dena Hankins. Jack and Eve navigate the maelstrom of their darkest desires and find love by transgressing gender, dominance, submission, and the law on the crystal blue Caribbean Sea. (978-1-62639-821-4)

Twisted Screams by Sheri Lewis Wohl. Reluctant psychic Lorna Dutton doesn't want to forgive, but if she doesn't do just that an innocent woman will die. (978-1-62639-647-0)